# SCALES OF JUSTICE

## TIONCHAR TALES, BOOK ONE

## BRETT HUMPHREY

"The sea, once it casts its spell, holds one in its net of wonder." — *Jacques Cousteau*

*To those who love to read, we can change the world if we choose to positively affect people we come into contact with each day.*

ACKNOWLEDGMENTS

I wouldn't have made it this far in my life and my new endeavor as an author without the following influences:

My amazing family—Jennifer, Kenny, Sarah, Josh, Chelsea, Sofie and Avery. You help make me a better husband, father and Papa. You are supportive of me and these stories I write.

Sister Cyndi and Brother Erich—you know why.

Amazing Beta Readers: Amanda, Brian, Cyndi, Denise, Dianne, Donny, Josh, Kim, Mark and Sarah.

Every fan who bought my earlier books: Awakening, Return, Reunite, Rebellion and Fierce Protector. Your feedback on how much you enjoy my stories keeps me writing.

And finally, my editor and friend, Joe Scholes, who has helped me become a better storyteller and continues to push me to get better.

A heartfelt *thank you* to everyone. Your support, inspiration and participation have all contributed to my happiness and success.

Brett Humphrey — June 2021

ABOUT THE AUTHOR

Brett Humphrey is the author of the Dragonborn Series, the Therian Shapeshifter Academy Series and the Tionchar Tales Series which are all set in the Dragonborn Universe.

He has worked with children and families for over thirty years and has taught in the United States and countries worldwide. His reading passion started when he was a young child, and he is still an avid reader of both fiction and non-fiction. As an author, his greatest desire is to create books parents will want to read to their children, hopefully using different voices for the characters.

Brett lives in Arizona with his patient and supportive wife, who encourages him to sit down and write the stories that live in his head.

## PROLOGUE

*November 20, 1511*
        *Flor do Mar Sailing Vessel*
*Indian Ocean*
*250 Nautical Miles Southeast of Tasmania*

"Captain—Joam is dead," Thomé, the first mate, made the sign of the cross over his chest as he yelled to be heard above the raging storm, "and the galley fires were extinguished. There will be neither hot food nor drink until the storm subsides."

Afonso de Albuquerque was not a happy man. Rain lashed his rigid body from all directions, and he was buffeted by the high winds that were driving his ship forward. The storm came upon them suddenly three days earlier off the coast of Sumatra. He knew the waters around here were dangerous, but the spells he cast around the ship should have protected them

1

from the weather. As he looked at his exhausted crew, valiantly striving to save the ship and its precious cargo, he had to admit the spells had kept them alive so far. The *Flor do Mar* wasn't the most reliable ship but had been the best chance he had to bring his riches to his hidden home.

"Merda," he muttered then yelled to Thomé, "take the wheel," and stormed off before his first mate could reply.

All his plans were falling apart and if he didn't do what he must, he would perish along with the rest of the souls on this ship before he could enjoy the benefits of the riches in the hold. He staggered to his cabin, the ship pitching so hard in the raging sea that he slammed into the walls of the narrow passageway hard enough to cause him to stumble. Before he shut the door to his cabin, he heard the words every seafarer dreaded, *we're taking on water.*

He quickly stripped out of his oilskins and stood wide-legged in the middle of the room. He muttered *lux splendida* while adding his will into the words and glowing bluish-white lights sprang into life along the ceiling and the four corners of the cabin. He walked to his berth and opened the cupboard above and pulled out two identical charms carved from the beam above his bed. The charms were covered in carved sigils and each one had been filled with pure silver.

He continued to mutter incantations as he pulled his knife from the sheath at his belt and drew the sharp blade across his left palm. He placed the charms on the floor at his feet and turned counterclockwise while allowing the blood to pour from his hand in a circle. Before he could complete the circle there was a sudden crash. The ship pitched hard to port, throwing him violently into a bulkhead, breaking his left arm.

"No, no, no," Afonso cried as he replaced the charms within the partially completed circle and knelt next to them as he supported his left hand with his right so he could close the circle with his blood. There was a flash of light as the circle closed and the sound of the storm and shouting of the crew was cut off as Afonso knelt in the artificial calm. He cried out in pain as he squeezed the broken bone with his right hand and ground out the word *"Sanos"* and channeled his will through the spell to heal his arm.

He panicked as he felt himself tipping over the edge of consciousness and cruelly gouged his knife wound to keep him awake. He placed his bloody left hand on the charms and held his right hand towards the men who made up his crew. He paused for a moment, wondering if the sacrifice would be enough but shook his head because he didn't have any other option. His right hand glowed red as he recited the words to the incantation he had created for this eventuality.

The terrified screams of the four hundred men in his crew broke through the silence in his cabin. Afonso cried out in pain as the life-force from each soul on the ship passed from his outstretched hand, through his body and into the charms on the floor. The smell of burning flesh filled his nostrils as the magic melted the silver in the sigils and mingled with his flesh and blood. The ship continued to be tossed violently but he was secure in his magic bubble. Afonso felt it when the last man died and the power coursing through his body abruptly stopped.

His hands were shaking so badly from the power exchange that it took him three tries to unclasp the gold necklace from around his neck and thread it through the hole on one of the charms. It was only when he had the charm around his neck that he broke the spell circle and staggered to his feet. He was still affected by the tossing of the ship, but not as dramatically as when he entered the cabin.

Afonso held the other glowing charm against the beam above his bed and said, "*Tabefacio*," and smiled grimly as the talisman melted into the wood and the ship shuddered with a pulse of power. He shook his head in disgust as he gazed at the chests full of treasure taken from the Sultan of Malacca, knowing he would have to leave it all behind, along with the holds full of gold, silver and precious gems. Before leaving however, he slipped as many jewels as he could carry in a heavy pack on his back. He snapped his fingers as he left the cabin, and all the lights were extinguished except the brightly glowing silver sigils in the charm above the bed.

# CHAPTER 1

*P*resent

*July 8*

*Indian Ocean*

*250 Nautical Miles Southeast of Tasmania*

A tentacle hit my chest and slammed me into the side of a wooden ship hard enough that I crashed through the side and into the hold. Not unusually, my sense of humor conjured a comical cartoon image of a perfectly shaped, Cyndi-sized cutout in the hull of the vessel, complete with pointed mermaid tail and trident.

*Hey*, I mentally shouted, although I was unable to hide my giggle at the cartoon image in my head while I righted myself and tried to get back into the fight.

*Sorry about that, Cyndi.* Brian called, as the tentacle withdrew.

*Are you okay?* Jason asked and stuck his head through the opening.

*No worries,* I answered with a smile, *I got hurt worse the last time I fell down the stairs at the house.*

*You mean last week, before we started this adventure?* Brian called with humor in his mental sending.

*I'm not talking to you, you big oaf. But I am trying to figure out how much calamari I could make out of a kraken,* I said as I swam towards the opening on the side of the ship, slowing down only long enough to give Jason a kiss and grab the trident I had dropped when I slammed into the wooden vessel.

*C'mon Cyndi, I already said I was sorry,* Brian laughed, *besides, I think I've got this beastie wrapped now—oops, no I don't.*

Jason grabbed my hand, and we swam away from the ship and back to where Brian was trying to keep the nekahi from swimming away. It was amazing to see two legendary creatures struggling with each other, but as a mermaid I suppose something like that shouldn't surprise me. I laughed at the sight of a massive kraken wrestling with a fifty-foot sea serpent. Even though Brian was four times the size of the nekahi, he was trying to keep from hurting the animal while the serpent didn't have that same consideration for him.

The nekahi had greenish-brown kelp-colored scales on the upper half of its sinuous body but the scales on its underside were a pale blue. It was smooth like a serpent, but it did have a feathery dorsal fin running along the length of its back. Its huge, emerald eyes were on either side of a diamond-shaped head and its huge mouth, full of triangular teeth, could open wide enough to hold an adult dolphin. It was a beautiful, majestic and terrifying creature.

Even though we were almost four hundred feet below the surface, the sunlight filtering through the water from above was enough for me to see the vibrant colors around me. With my enhanced senses I could see farther on land than a human but my sight underwater was exceptional. Not only could I see clearly for miles when sunlight streaked from above, I could see in the deepest dark of the ocean in shades of white, black and gray. It was just another perk of my mermaid physiology.

We had been hunting the sea serpent for about a week after Brian had seen a story on the news about pieces of humpback whales washing up on Steels Beach in Tasmania. The whale carcasses showed massive bites and many sites were claiming this had to be the work of a megalodon shark. This was close enough to the truth so Brian, Jason and I set out to investigate. We were convinced this was a sea creature from Theria that had made its way to Earth through a dimensional portal.

A few months ago, I learned that my younger brother, who I thought died over a hundred and fifty years before, was alive and had been pranking the people of Loch Ness with his natural form. Nestor was a plesiosaur shapeshifter and was the basis for the Loch Ness Monster myths throughout human history. He would use a forgotten dimensional portal to travel between Earth and Theria whenever he felt like it. Unfortunately, he would leave the portal open for long periods of time while he was on Earth, which gave creatures from Theria the opportunity to migrate here where they caused serious damage to the marine ecosystem.

Before King Alister returned to Theria, he asked me to keep watch for any unusual activity on Earth which could signal the appearance of one of these creatures. Since I'd made Earth my home, and spent a lot of time in the ocean, I readily agreed. He wanted these creatures returned to Theria, if possible, but if not, we were tasked with destroying them before they inadvertently revealed our secrets. We know humans aren't ready to learn about the existence of alternate dimensions or that creatures of myth and legend are based on shapeshifters who used to travel to Earth and interact more frequently with humans in the past.

As I studied the battle between the kraken and nekahi, I idly spun the trident in my hand hoping I didn't have to use it to kill the creature. I thought it was kind of cute, in a scourge-of-the-sea kind of way.

*I've got an idea,* Jason said and darted toward the head of the sea serpent, narrowly escaping its snapping jaws. Even though Jason was a fraction of the animal's size, his sudden movement distracted the nekahi enough that Brian could make his move. He surged forward and wrapped his massive purple tentacles around the body of the nekahi, encasing the creature in a writhing cocoon.

*A little help*, he grunted.

*What else do you want us to do?* Jason asked, *I just swam towards its head to give you a chance to wrap it up. Besides, it seems like you've got things under control, again.*

*Yeah, didn't you say you weren't sure you even needed our help since it was only a nekahi and you could eat one of these for breakfast?* I mentally laughed.

*Okay, I admit I was a bit cocky, but it's been centuries since I've encountered one of these things, I forgot how slippery they could be—*he stopped talking so he could yowl in pain—*and how sharp their teeth are.*

Brian shifted a tentacle away from the mouth of the struggling serpent and wrapped it around the muzzle of the sea creature to keep it from biting him again. I handed my trident to Jason then swam to the head of the writhing animal and looked it in the eye.

*Hey now, it's okay. We're not going to hurt you, we just want to get you back home,* I mentally cooed; the same way I would talk to a spooked horse. *I'm going to try singing to it so prepare yourselves,* I sent and began once Brian and Jason let me know they were ready.

There have been stories of mermaids on Earth for thousands of years and in many of the legends mermaids used their voices to send sailors to their deaths. While I must admit my voice isn't much when I'm on land, I haven't heard of anyone dying from my singing, yet. However, when I'm in my mermaid form, I can use my song to influence any living thing, human or animal.

I sang to the nekahi about its home on Theria, how it was far away from where it wanted to be and how we were friends who wanted to take it home again. As I sang about the warm waters around Cetacea, the country where I'm from, I added a sense of longing to the music and hoped the animal was being affected.

*Whatever you're doing seems to be working,* Brian sent, *it's not struggling as much.*

Making sure to keep away from a mouth that could swallow me whole, I continued to sing as I reached out and scratched a patch of scales near the feather-like fins on top of the nekahi's head. As I did, the creature let out a single deep, bass note I could feel to my core and seemed to relax.

*Jason,* I sent as I continued to scratch the creature's head, *come up here so she can get used to you, too.*

Jason leaned my trident against the hull of the ship and swam up the other side of its head and began petting the nekahi.

*How do you know it's a girl?* Brian asked.

*I'm not sure, I just have a feeling,* I answered.

*She seems to like this,* Jason said as the serpent let out another of those deep groans.

*I'm going to loosen my hold a bit to see how she reacts,* Brian interrupted after a few minutes.

I continued to sing, and we kept our hands on the nekahi's

head as we waited for her to start fighting us again; when she didn't I felt we were in the clear.

*It's not that I'm ungrateful that she seems calmer now, but how are we going to get her back through the portal?* Brian asked.

*I'm working on that;* I answered and began to sing about swimming home and hunting in familiar waters. After about fifteen minutes the nekahi began to struggle against Brian's hold again but this time I was convinced she would be willing to follow us to the portal and I explained my plan to Jason and Brian.

Brian kept two of his tentacles wrapped around the nekahi; one like a leash and the other like a muzzle on its mouth and began to lead the sea serpent in the direction of the portal. Jason and I kept petting and scratching, but we also applied pressure to get the animal moving the way we wanted it to go.

*What about your trident?* Jason asked.

*We'll come back for it,* I sent. *I want to explore the ship anyway so it will give us a good reason to keep the visit with my mom short.*

Brian made a noise that sounded suspiciously like a snort, even though it's hard to differentiate the noises a two-hundred-foot squid-like creature makes, but I agreed with him nonetheless.

*Yeah, that probably won't make a difference, but a girl can hope,* I sighed and kept singing as we swam towards the portal to Theria.

*L*undsail 9, 10,258

*Planet Theria*

*Kingdom of Cetacea*

*Palace Communications Room*

"That was the longest two-hundred miles of my life. While it would normally take me less than an hour to swim the distance, it took us a full day to get the creature back home. With all due respect, the next time you ask me to help capture an escaped nekahi I'm going to say something that will get me banished. So, I'm apologizing ahead of time," I said to King Alister as I finished my report on how we managed to get the nekahi through the portal and back to Theria.

"Surely you must be exaggerating the difficulties," Josef said. The large communication screen was split in two with King Alister's image on the right and Josef's on the left. Josef was the CEO of Rex Industries and the head of the Tionchar organization on Earth.

I narrowed my eyes at the screen and took a deep breath before I answered. Not only was Josef my boss, but he was also my friend. I had only recently joined the secret organization and I really liked being part of a group that tried to make Earth a better place. There were Tionchar operatives on each of the known planets across the dimensions. While each of the planets looked geographically similar, there were vast differences of magical, technological and scientific development between each. The High Kings and Queens of Theria created the secret organization to guide planets from behind the scenes to assist in peaceful growth.

"Imagine a fifty-foot toddler, hopped up on so much sugar it has syrup rather than blood running through its veins, then give it a mouth full of rows of knife-like teeth, and the worst case of ADHD you've ever seen. Are you doing that?" I asked and the two men on screen nodded. "Double that and you might be able to get an idea of what it was like."

I sat back and sipped my tea and felt the healing elixir sooth my ravaged throat. Even with my accelerated healing as a shifter, I was still sore from having to sing so long. Every time I tried to take a break, the nekahi would start to struggle and I had to start singing again.

"The way I hear it, you cried when the nekahi was released back into the wild," Alister teased.

"She was so cute," I sighed.

"And some of the palace guards had to intervene when it looked like the animal was going to come back and attack the ones who had worked so hard to keep it safe," Josef added with a grin.

"I never said Cora was perfect, I just said she was cute," I shrugged.

"Anyway—well done. You and your team have done another amazing job. That brings the total number of Therian creatures you've either rehomed or destroyed to seventeen. Let's hope Cora is the last of them. I look forward to seeing you in person next week. Sire, if you don't need me on this call, I've got a few things to take care of," Josef said to Alister.

Alister smiled, "Not at all, I've just a few things of a personal nature I want to cover with Cyndi. See you next week."

Josef nodded and signed off. Before Alister could speak, his chair was pulled back and his fiancée, Aileene, sat in his lap and got comfortable.

"There's a chair next to me you know," Alister grinned at the feisty red-headed woman on his lap.

"I know, but I like this seat better," Aileene said and kissed him on the cheek.

"My Queen," I said.

"Not officially, at least not for another," Aileene pursed her lips and looked up to the left, "thirty-six days, twenty-three hours, forty-two minutes and give or take thirty seconds—not that I'm counting or anything."

"If you ladies will excuse me," Alister chuckled and started to stand.

"Oh, no you don't, mister, I'm comfortable and think it will be better if you stay right where you are," Aileene smirked.

"Fine," Alister huffed but since he was smiling fondly at his future wife, I knew he really didn't mind.

I laughed, "So, how are the wedding plans coming?"

Aileene beamed while Alister grimaced and muttered, "I had no idea royal weddings were so complicated."

Aileene kissed him lightly. "I suppose that's one of the drawbacks of you growing up on Earth, you really didn't have any idea what you were getting into by becoming the High King."

"I don't mind the High King part, it's all the pomp and circumstance I could do without," Alister grumped.

"C'mon, it's not that bad," Aileene teased.

"I really couldn't care less about the ceremony," Alister said as he rested his chin on Aileene's shoulder. "As long as I get married to you that's all I care about. The ceremony is only a day after all, our marriage will last a lifetime."

It took me two tries to get their attention again after Aileene showed her appreciation to Alister for his romantic comment; at least they had the grace to look embarrassed as they turned their attention back to the screen.

"Enough about us," Aileene laughed, "how are your wedding plans?"

A joyful smile animated my face as I shared our plans. I couldn't believe Jason and I were getting married in just over three months and I was anticipating spending the rest of my life with my true mate.

"I'm looking forward to a small ceremony on the cliff overlooking the beach below my house on Earth. I'm planning on buying the other houses on either side of mine so the private beach will truly be private; that will also give the two of you your own space when you come to visit. You are still coming to officiate the ceremony, aren't you Sire?"

"I wouldn't miss it for the world," he smiled.

"How's Jason adjusting to life as a merman?" Aileene asked.

"He's doing really well. It took him a month to get used to keeping his arms at his sides and only use his tail to swim, but he's got the hang of it now. He's still a lot slower than I am but I don't mind swimming at his pace. It's a small price to pay for someone who was willing to give up being a sasquatch to be with me."

"My dad has never regretted his decision to use his final shift to become a fire drake to be with my mom." Alister smiled.

"I never thought I'd find someone who loved me enough to change species for me," I said in awe.

"Jason would rather give up being a sasquatch than to live without you by his side. Besides, I bet he doesn't think being able to transform into a merman is much of a hardship since you get to swim together," Alister said as he waggled his eyebrows.

"Alister," Aileene laughed as she hit his shoulder, "you're incorrigible."

"What?" he smirked.

"On that note, I think I'll let you two go. I'll see you next month at your wedding and coronation."

"I didn't offend you, did I?" Alister asked sincerely.

"Not at all. You should know by now I don't embarrass easily. Besides, I've got to get off the call so I can get ready for an unpleasant task."

"Do you need to check on Cora?" Aileene asked.

"No, I've got to get ready for dinner with my mother," I sighed and waved goodbye to my friends.

"Thank you, Amphi," I said to the guard as he opened the door to my mother's private dining room. He was in his human form, but still retained scales on his arms and chest as a form of armor. The iridescent green shimmered as he moved and reflected the muted light in the hallway. The doors were intricately carved with scenes of underwater life and I always marveled at the artistry involved.

I stepped closer to the door and ran my hand down my father's face. The artist captured his personality perfectly. How I missed his smile, the one that always implied he was up to something. I looked at the representation of my mother and smiled ruefully; I couldn't remember the last time I saw her smile the way she was depicted in the carving.

"Where's Tang? You usually guard this door together," I said as I glanced to the empty spot to the right of the doorway.

Amphi's face fell as he answered, "He was among those who gave their lives defending the palace."

The Kingdom of Cetacea had been attacked almost a year

before by rebels who were trying to kill King Alister while he was on a mission to reunite the seven kingdoms of Theria under his banner as High King. We were attacked without provocation or warning above and below the waters. While we successfully defeated the attackers, there were terrible losses to my people because some of the rebels were fitted with explosive devices and blew themselves up to cause maximum death and destruction. Nothing like that had ever occurred in Cetacea before and we were still mourning their losses.

"I'm sorry, Amphi. I was so caught up in my own thoughts, I had forgotten Tang was one of our honored fallen," I whispered as a tear slipped down my face.

Amphi opened his arms and I stepped into his embrace. "No worries, Princess; I know this won't be an easy dinner for you," he smiled kindly. "I've been instructed to make sure you don't leave before your mother gives her permission," he whispered then stepped back to his post.

I laughed as he had intended and wiped my face with the sleeve of the velvet dress my mother had sent for me to wear. While I loved the way the amethyst-colored dress looked on me, I didn't appreciate how my mother tried to control my life whenever I set foot in the palace. That's one of the reasons I didn't come home very often. I wiggled my toes in the mermaid pattern Chuck Taylor sneakers I had on my feet and reveled in my little rebellion. Since the dress went all the way to the floor, no one could see my shoes. I refused to wear the heels my mother had left with the dress not only because I didn't want her to think I couldn't take care of myself, but also because I was clumsy enough without adding the additional danger of high heels.

"How's the family?" I asked.

"Quite well, Princess. Marlin is married and has given me the cutest grandkids."

"Do you have any pictures?" I asked.

Amphi looked around furtively then reached beneath his tunic. He wore the green and purple livery of a palace guard. The crest of the Kingdom of Cetacea, a green mermaid on a purple background, was displayed prominently on his chest. He pulled out a small tablet and leaned his trident against the wall so he could show me pictures of his grandkids. I was oohing and aahing over the shots of the children in both their human and mere forms until we were interrupted.

"Before you ask to see pictures from his vacations for the past decade come in here, I'm tired of waiting," Mother's irritated voice called from within the dining room.

I shot a cheeky grin at Amphi and mouthed, 'sorry' before I walked inside, and he shut the door behind me. This private dining room was where we'd eaten our family meals when I was growing up at the palace. The twenty-foot wall opposite the door was made of living coral and there was a ten-foot-wide bay window in the center of the wall which looked out into the ocean beyond. I used to love sitting in this room, long after our meals ended, and watching the sea life swimming outside the walls of the palace. The rest of the room was the deep purple color of the coral and felt more homey than the formal dining room in another part of the palace.

My mother was seated at the head of the oval table with room for eight, her face rigid in displeasure that I'd kept her waiting. However, since that was the look she usually favored me with when we got together, I chose to ignore her.

"Hello, Mother," I said and kissed her on her cheek.

She pointed to the chair on her right and as I sat, I noticed there was a place setting directly across from me.

"Is Nestor joining us?" I asked.

"Your brother is otherwise engaged," Mother said primly.

"Then you relented, and Jason will be joining us?" I asked hopefully.

"No," Mother shook her head. "I said we had family matters to discuss, and he would not be allowed to join us."

"Then I admit, I'm confused," I said and smiled my thanks at the young woman who poured my drink. She must be new to the palace staff since I didn't recognize her.

Before my mother could answer there was a sharp knock at the door and a man walked in.

"Forgive my tardiness, Lady Zhaleh, I was finishing those arrangements you asked me to make."

Mother beamed at the merman, offered her hand and giggled coquettishly as he kissed the back of it with a flourish. He took his place across from me and although he smiled at me, he glanced in annoyance at the kitchen servant as she stepped forward to fill his glass. When she was finished, he dismissed her with a snap of his fingers and shooed her away with a hand gesture.

"Don't worry about it, Tetraodon, my daughter just arrived so you're right on time," Mother said, ignoring the byplay.

"Princess Cynthia, you are looking radiant as always," he said in his deep voice.

"Hello T," I said as I looked at the pain in my flukes sitting across the table from me staring at me with his piercing amber eyes. He was three inches over six feet when standing and had broad shoulders. I knew he had well-toned muscles under his loose shirt because he preferred to walk around shirtless as much as possible. His shoulder-length midnight-blue hair was gathered in a drawstring at the nape of his neck and his lips were curved in a smirk as he looked me up and down.

Tetraodon and I grew up together in the palace, his father was an advisor to mine and our mothers were friends. When we were children, our mothers would talk about how we should be married one day and had plotted our lives out for us. When I left the palace after my father had been killed in an accident, I thought my mother had given up these plans; apparently, I was wrong.

"I thought it would be a good idea for us to sit for a meal and discuss your future together," my mother began as she signaled the wait staff to serve the first course. As my attendant served me, I mentally asked for her name. She showed surprise but quickly covered her reaction and answered me in the same way.

"Thank you, Anemone," I said as I took the first piece of calamari from the dish she set before me. She smiled sweetly and backed away.

Rather than respond to my mother's statement about our future together, I continued to eat quickly. Even though I knew this dinner would be ruined by the conversation we were sure to have, I hadn't eaten a meal prepared by Chef Louis in years and didn't want to miss out.

The next course was eel and seaweed soup seasoned with just a hint of spice and quite delicious. I remained silent as my mother and Tetraodon continued to discuss what life would look like once the two of us were married. They discussed how many children we would have over the fish course and of course Tetraodon expressed his hope the first child would be male so a son of his could take the throne once the two of us decided to abdicate. I was tempted to jump in at this point to goad him into expressing his belief in the superiority of men over women but decided I would much rather enjoy the food set before me.

I had a coughing fit during the salad course after Tetraodon suggested I allow him to rule in my stead during what he called my 'childbearing years' since it was a well-known fact that pregnancy affected the cognitive abilities of women and I might not be fit to rule. My mother finally took exception to this and they had a lively debate over the accuracy of his statement. When he noticed my mother was getting irritated with his position, he quickly backed down and laughed it off as though it were a big joke. I still stayed silent.

The cheese and nut course was especially entertaining as they began to plan the wedding and Tetraodon gave his opinions on the type of dress I should wear and listed the women he had already picked for my bridal party. My mother kept looking at me to see if I would respond to his plans, but I just smiled as I enjoyed the course before dessert. If I had to put up with this insanity throughout the entire meal, there was no way I'd be leaving before dessert.

I laughed in delight when Anemone set the piece of Tiramisu before me. Chef Luis made my favorite dessert from Earth while my mother and Tetraodon were served a Cetacean specialty. Tetraodon frowned at my outburst and began a lengthy discussion about how things would be different when he ruled and dishes from Earth wouldn't be allowed at his table. He didn't seem to notice that my mother wasn't engaging in the conversation any longer because he loved hearing the sound of his voice so much, he didn't pay attention to anything else.

Once the coffee had been served, Tetraodon allowed that coffee would be an exception to his Therian-only food rule, I decided I'd had enough.

"Mother, thank you for a highly entertaining meal. I didn't realize you had such a capacity for comedy, but you and Tetraodon have surpassed my expectations."

"What do you mean?" Tetraodon asked with a confused

look, which he presented first to Mother and then to me. I met his stare until I knew I had his full attention, then primly wiped my mouth and placed my napkin before me.

"I mean you are a joke," I stated flatly.

"Now look here—" he began to bluster.

"Stop," I interrupted him and narrowed my eyes at him. "I don't know who you think you are, but you have absolutely no say over my life and what I do or don't do."

"But your mother—"

"Has no say over my life either," I stated firmly. "I suggest you leave before you embarrass yourself any further, but you should know one thing before you go. I do not want to marry you, will never marry you and actually feel sorry for the poor mermaid you eventually do marry unless you change your antiquated views of women. You aren't superior to me because you are a man, and my father certainly didn't treat my mother as less because she was a woman. He treated her as an equal or better which is why she was given the throne after he was killed, rather than it going to a male relative.

"If the High King were in the room, listening to your drivel, you can be sure either he would adjust your thinking for you or he would let Queen Aileene do it for him. I can't imagine what my mother promised you, but I am getting married to a man who loves me, and you don't factor into my life at all." I finished and took another sip of my coffee.

Tetraodon stood and threw his napkin on the table with such force he knocked over his wine glass, spilling the contents. "I've heard rumors that you were going to marry someone who isn't a natural born merman, but I couldn't believe that was possible since you were promised to me. You're tainted and I can only believe the years you've spent on Earth have somehow twisted your mind. I wouldn't marry you if you begged me to." He nodded curtly to my mother and stalked out of the room, slamming the door as he left.

"Cynthia," my mother began but I stopped her with an icy stare.

"How dare you," I seethed. "You invited me to dinner under false pretense telling me we had important family matters to discuss. I should have known this was just another one of your pathetic attempts to manipulate me into doing what you want."

"But it is important to this family that you marry well. I only want what's best for you and I believed that Tetraodon would be a good match. I can see that he isn't the person I thought he was, so we'll just need to try again," she finished lamely as I glared at her.

"You don't want what's best for me, you only want what you think is best for you. I don't want or need your help to find someone to marry. I have already found my true mate in Jason and he makes me happy."

"You can't mean that. What could he possibly give you that one of the mermen in my kingdom cannot?" she asked in dismay.

I sighed wearily and looked at my mother for who she

really was. She had spent so many years consumed with herself that she was incapable of seeing me for anything but the failure she thought I was. I hoped we could repair the damage to our relationship but realized that was never going to happen because she was unwilling to meet me halfway; she wasn't even willing to take a step in my direction.

"You know, Mother, I have made excuses for you my whole life. When I was younger, I would excuse your criticism because I knew I would be the heir one day and you wanted me to be the best ruler I could be. After Dad died and we assumed Nestor was dead as well, I excused your coldness towards me because you were grieving and didn't know how to deal with the only member of your family who still survived. Even last year when you had me brought to the palace after almost eighty years of being away, I hoped you would be happy to know I was alive and had made the most out of a difficult situation while I'd been trapped on Earth. But once again you had to tell me where I was deficient and what I needed to do to become the ruler you wanted me to be.

"But what you did today is beyond belief and I can no longer excuse your behavior. You asked what Jason could possibly give me that no one else can? It's unconditional love. He loves me so much he was willing to give up everything for me. He gave up his sasquatch heritage to be with me even though I offered to give up being a mermaid for him."

"But you love the water and the freedom of being a mermaid," she gasped with a shocked expression on her face.

"You're right, but I love Jason even more. Maybe you had unconditional love for Dad, but I don't really know if that's possible for you. I give up. You'll never be the mother I wanted and needed you to be, but I'm done holding that against you. You've shown me today that you don't really care about anyone but yourself and I feel sorry for you."

I turned to leave but stopped at the door and spoke over my shoulder. "Goodbye, Mother. You are invited to our wedding and I hope you make the effort to be there. But if you choose not to, that will be your loss."

I'd never have the relationship with my mother that I wanted to have, but I had someone who chose me, and I was looking forward to creating a new life with him. I closed the door behind me and left without looking back. Amphi stepped in my way, his arms outstretched, and I fell into his embrace.

He kissed me on the cheek and whispered in my ear, "I'd be proud if you were my daughter."

I leaned back and looked at him, his image wavering with unshed tears filling my eyes.

*Thank you,* I sent, not trusting my voice at that moment.

He nodded and released me, and I continued down the corridor, my head held high. All I wanted to do was get out of this dress, gather our gear and head back to Earth. Muttering to myself I stomped towards my suite. The more I thought about the last two hours the angrier I became. As I neared my suite in the family section of the palace, I was replaying the final confrontation with my mother on a continuous loop in my head.

Unfortunately, I wasn't paying attention and ran into a wall of flesh and bounced off. Before my butt could hit the ground I was enveloped from behind in a loving embrace and set back on my feet.

"I'd ask how your meeting went with your mom, but I can tell by the look on your face it went exactly like every private conversation you've had with her for the past hundred years," Brian laughed as he grinned down at me. He was my oldest friend and had been a huge support when I was growing up in the palace. In his human form he was six-foot-five and a solid wall of muscle. Working as an Elvis impersonator on Earth, his black hair was always carefully styled in the classic pompadour with bushy sideburns that went halfway down his dimpled cheeks.

Jason moved to my side and I leaned my head on his shoulder as he kept his left arm around my waist. Jason was a couple of inches shorter than Brian but was just as muscular. His dirty-blond hair just brushed his shoulders and his blue eyes regarded me with concern. He reminded me of the actor who played Thor in the movies, except Jason was much better looking.

"Are you okay?" he asked, softly.

I turned toward him and reached my hand up to touch his face. He bent down and placed a soft kiss on my lips, and I couldn't help smiling as he did so.

"I am now," I whispered and kissed him again.

"Well, this is awkward," Brian teased, and Jason and I broke apart laughing.

Jason pulled me to his side again and we began walking. "We already grabbed our stuff; we're ready to go," Jason said as we walked hand-in-hand down the corridor. We chatted and laughed about our encounter with the nekahi, and I filled them in on dinner with my mother. I stopped when they told me Chef Louis had sent them the same food prepared for me..

"You mean to tell me I could have eaten the meal with you instead of my mother and that piece of flotsam?" I grumped.

Brian gently patted me on the shoulder, "You needed to give your mom one more chance. You know you would've felt guilty if you hadn't."

I nodded in response to his comment and we stepped through the doorway to the grotto that would lead us to the ocean. The room was circular and there were pink, blue and green tinted stalactites hanging from the ceiling. There was a pool of blue-green water in the middle of the room and white sand leading up to the water's edge. There were sentries stationed around the room guarding against any possible enemy intrusion through the pool or the tunnel which led out to the open ocean. There were also soldiers stationed on the ocean side of the tunnel to prevent entrance that way. We had discovered the hard way that this was a vulnerable part of the palace when enemies gained entrance through this peaceful pool.

Jason, Brian and I made our way to an alcove where our bags were waiting. We didn't really have too much with us since we'd been traveling for so long underwater as we searched for the nekahi, but I would have to carry what we did have. Fortunately, I had a wonderful bit of magic around my neck that Alister had given me to make my life easier, which until recently, only members of his Inner Circle received.

The thought medallion allowed the wearer to project thought-speak farther than normal but also to shift into their natural form without having to undress first. While shifters aren't concerned about nudity the way humans are, it was convenient to shift back to human and be fully clothed.

The addition of the pocket dimension is what really made the difference to the magical gift. Somehow, Alister had affixed a storage area in another dimension to the necklace which I could access whenever I needed. I learned the hard way that it wasn't a good idea to open this pocket dimension underwater, but I could open it on land without problem. I accessed the dimension, added our bags, my shoes and the clothes Jason and Brian were wearing. Since the bags were stored in another dimension, they didn't add any weight to the necklace. We rarely shifted with our clothes on because we typically shifted into our mere forms after we're in the water; none of us wanted to shift into soaking wet clothes when we arrived where we were going.

"Hey Cyndi, I left you something on the rock," Brian called over his shoulder as he entered the pool. He wouldn't shift into his kraken form until he was through the tunnel and in the open ocean since he was so large.

"Ha-ha, very funny," I laughed as I held up a bikini top made from shells. "You know this would get ripped off my chest the moment we start swimming at normal speed, jerk."

Brian and Jason laughed as I added the bikini top to the pocket dimension. I started to leave the dress hanging on a hook but I loved the way I looked and felt in the dress. I didn't want to associate the dress with the horrible memory of the dinner I just left and decided I'd ask Jason to take me out when we got home, while I wore the dress, creating a beautiful memory for the two of us. Smiling to myself, I carefully packed the dress then walked to the water to join the other two.

Brian disappeared under the water first then Jason transformed into his merman form. His arms and chest grew to accommodate his larger size as he was now over ten feet tip to tail. He turned towards the tunnel opening and dove underwater, his red and purple scales glittering off his tail as he waved it at me to follow.

Laughing, I waded into the water but turned to take one last look at the place I'd called my home when I was younger. Sighing for the loss of what could have been, I let go of the past and dove underwater to follow Jason, excited about the future we would create together.

# CHAPTER 2

*July 10*

*Indian Ocean*

*Tasmania*

Jason's arms wrapped around me as we greeted the rising sun ready to face a new day together. The cloudless sky was bathed with oranges, reds and purples where the splendid golden light chased the darkness from the sky. The sunrise matched my mood and between Jason's arms, his love and the lightening sky, I felt the darkness from yesterday fleeing my mind. I laughed at the sound of a snore and looked to see Brian still lying on the sand where we'd spent the night on this secluded beach in Tasmania. We were up early because we wanted to get back in the water before anyone saw us.

"Do you want to talk about it?" Jason asked as he nuzzled aside my hair and kissed me behind the right ear.

"Mmmm, only if you stop doing that—in ten to fifteen minutes," I breathed.

Jason laughed as he gave me one last squeeze and moved in front of me so I could see his face.

"Hey," I protested, "did you miss the part where I really wanted you to continue?"

Jason smiled, his eyes dancing with mischief, "I know I'm irresistible, but you've only got three months left to wait then you can have all of me. Besides, I really think you should talk about your conversation with your mom; you haven't said anything about it since we left Cetacea."

After we dove into the pool in the grotto yesterday, we left the palace and made our way through the ocean in Theria to the location of the dimensional portal. I half expected my mother to send a contingent of guards to stop us from leaving so she could have the last word, but I didn't hear anything. Once we got to the portal we were met by Muir, the Captain of the Palace Guard and my mother's consort.

*Lady Cynthia,* he sent in thought-speak.

*Captain Muir, what are you doing here?*

*Your mother asked me to oversee the portal after you came through yesterday then close it again once you went back to Earth.*

*Wait a moment,* I held up my hand, *my mother told you I would be heading back to Earth?*

*Of course, she knew you wouldn't be staying in Cetacea, especially after King Alister informed her that you were on a mission for him and needed to be based on Earth to accomplish your task.*

*When did she speak with King Alister?*

*Last week, shortly after we received word there was a Therian creature loose on Earth.*

I shook my head and stared at Muir. Even though I didn't ever think anyone could replace my dad, I'm glad he and my mother found each other. *If she knew I was going back to Earth, why did she plan that charade with Tetraodon?*

He shrugged; *I cannot say. Even though I love your mother, she is a very complicated and difficult woman. I'm sure she has her reasons, but most of the time I cannot figure out what they are.* He smiled fondly, *that's one of the reasons I'm drawn to her.*

Once again, I was baffled by my mother's behavior and her purposely driving a wedge between us.

*This must be your fiancé,* Muir sent as he held out his hand for Jason to shake.

*It's a pleasure to meet you,* Jason sent as I was still unable to put my thoughts into words.

*I'm not sure how you managed it, but Cyndi is speechless for once,* Brian remarked, his laughter clear in his sending.

After a few minutes of conversation, we made our way to the portal so Muir could open it for us. I knew once we passed through, we would find ourselves in the ruins of Atlantis. There were many stories of the legendary lost continent on Earth but none of them hinted that Atlantis was once the location of the best Therian research facilities and scientists studying extra-dimensional travel.

Unfortunately, everything was destroyed thousands of years ago when there was an accident with a dimensional rift and the continent on Earth broke apart and sank beneath the waves. The Therian scientists facilitated that destruction because it was the only way to keep the rift from expanding to each dimension and destroying all worlds.

Much later, King Phillip, Alister's father, limited travel between dimensions and only allowed members of Tionchar to make those journeys. Power to open and close gates was granted to the High King or High Queen and the Atlantean portal was forgotten, except by members of my family and until last year was a closely guarded secret. Once my mother informed King Alister about this portal between Cetacea and Earth he granted permission for the ruler of Cetacea to utilize the portal as she saw fit. Brian and Jason preceded me through the portal, but Muir put a hand on my arm before I swam through. When I looked at him quizzically, he smiled and pulled me into a hug.

*Your mother and I will be at your wedding, even if I must drag her there myself. She really is proud of you, even if she never tells you so.*

It's difficult to tell if someone is crying underwater but I think Muir could tell since he wiped his thumb across my cheeks.

*Why won't she tell me these things herself?* I sent, sorrow evident in my mental communication.

*I don't know, but I want you to know I'm proud of you and would be honored to call you my daughter.*

I hugged him again and waved goodbye as I swam backward through the portal. Of course, I misjudged the direction and hit my back on the side of the portal first, then bounced through. I could hear Muir's mental laughter as I felt myself transported to another dimension.

"Do you want to talk about it," Jason asked again, breaking me out of my reverie.

"Not really. I'm tired of giving my mother power over me. I love her, and she drives me crazy." I turned and hugged Jason, laying my head on his chest. When his arms came around me, I sighed in contentment.

"I've never understood why she pushes me away so much. Yesterday was another example of her sabotaging our relationship for no good reason. She knew I would never choose that pompous barnacle over you, but she staged that entire dinner anyway. I've made my peace with this. I've come to realize that I'll never have the mother I deserve so I'll need to learn how to get along with the mother I have."

Jason kissed my forehead and leaned back to look at me. "Whatever happens with your mother, I'm just glad I get to spend the rest of my life with you. What do you say we head home?"

"I'd like that, but I need to stop by the shipwreck we found yesterday so I can pick up my trident. It'll give us some time to explore the wreck."

"As long as I get a chance to get something to eat, I'm willing to do some exploring on our way home," Brian said as he walked over to where Jason and I were standing. He grinned as he wiped sand off his bare chest and belly.

"Is that The Creature from the Black Lagoon on your trunks?" I asked.

"Yep," Brian replied and pointed to one of his tattoos, "just like this one here. You know I'm a huge fan of the classic monster movies."

"Where did you find those anyway?" I laughed.

Brian shrugged, "you should ask Jason, he bought them for me, at the same time he bought you the shell bikini."

"You," I narrowed my eyes and started stalking towards Jason.

"Now honey, it was only a joke," Jason laughed as he held up his hands and backed towards the water.

"I'll give you a head start," Brian said and picked me off the ground.

Jason turned and ran into the surf, transforming as he dove under a wave.

Brian let me go and we laughed together as we raced towards the water.

*I don't really understand how this ship is still intact after so many centuries under water.* I sent as Jason and I explored the hold of the shipwreck we'd found the other day. While it was obvious the vessel had suffered damage before sinking, it was still structurally sound. Except for the hole in the hull I'd created when my body crashed through during the fight with the nekahi, it was intact.

The deck of the ship was littered with rigging still connected to the foremast which was lying the length of the wreck. The main mast was missing but the mizzenmast was still intact. It was eerie to see the ship lying at the bottom of the ocean as though it had just been sunk. The ropes, which should have rotted long ago, were still strong and the pulleys moved easily when Jason tugged on one end. There weren't any bodies on deck, but the detritus left behind showed the craft faced a violent end.

The on-deck cannons were intact and were still polished, which was another mystery. The name of the vessel was written in large, gilded letters on the stern, and I looked forward to getting to a computer so I could look up the history of the *Flor do Mar*. After we finished scouring the deck, Jason and I decided to keep exploring the rest of the ship while Brian was eating his meal. We swam through the hole in the side of the ship into a treasure trove.

There were hundreds of chests in the hold, many of which had broken open and were spilling their valuable cargo across the hold space. There were also bars of silver and gold stacked floor to ceiling within locked steel cages and barrels filled with loose precious gems.

*I've never seen so much wealth in one place before,* Jason sent, *what are the laws concerning shipwrecks?*

*I don't really worry too much about salvage laws, since there are millions of shipwrecks on the bottom of the ocean and only a small percentage of those will ever be found. That's not including the thousands of cargo containers that fall off cargo ships into the oceans each year. Besides, there seems to be some sort of magic keeping the ship in such perfect condition and we don't want that to fall into human hands. We'll take some of the gold and silver coins, bars and some of the gems with us. After all, that's how I've amassed my fortune over the years.*

We quickly realized the way below decks was blocked and we couldn't remove enough debris to get around the obstruction, so we swam back out the hole in the side and made our way to the upper deck. We could see great damage to the half deck, and it looked like the main mast crushed that portion of the ship when it snapped off, probably due to one of the violent storms common to the waters in this area. If the mast destroyed the ship's wheel at that point, there hadn't been any hope of steering and that was likely what led to its sinking.

We were able to use our hands and claws to clear enough

rubble to swim down the main staircase and finally make our way to the captain's cabin. The door was shut but we were able to use our strength to force it open and swam into another mystery. While we could see perfectly well underwater, we could only see in whites, blacks and greys inside the ship because the sunlight from the surface was cut off. However, the instant we entered the cabin, I could see in vivid color again because there was light spilling from one of the beams above the captain's berth.

The cabin was a mess, probably because the contents were thrown around violently during the storm that led to the sinking of this vessel. Chests containing gold, silver and jewels were burst open but the wood of the chests themselves was remarkably well-preserved.

*Jason, we're going to take as much of this treasure as we can but we must get it to the surface before I can add it to the pocket dimension on my necklace.*

*You're not going to try opening it underwater again?* Jason laughed in my mind.

*Once is enough, thank you very much,* I sent as I stuck my tongue out at him. He laughed harder. I opened the pocket dimension while underwater last year so I could extract my trident and although I didn't notice anything at the time, hundreds of gallons of water poured in my mother's throne room when I opened the pocket dimension later to store the trident. It took a lot of work to get the rest of the water out of the magical storage area in the necklace.

*What do you think this is?* Jason asked as he looked at the glowing object on the wall.

*My guess is it's some kind of protection or preservation charm. It didn't keep the ship from sinking, but it has preserved it for at least four hundred years.*

*Four hundred years?*

*I'm guessing, but this type of ship is called a carrack and they went out of favor with the trading companies in the seventeenth century.* I murmured as I examined the charm.

It was glowing so brightly it was difficult to make out the details but I did notice there were large symbols etched at the four cardinal points of a compass and smaller symbols between each of the larger ones. This close to the object, I could feel waves of energy pulsing from the charm and spreading throughout the ship.

*Let's leave it here for now,* I sent to Jason, *and gather some of this treasure and leave it on the sea floor before we explore the rest of the ship.*

We chatted mentally as we filled ten mesh dive bags with treasure. We wanted to gather as much as we could but knew we would be leaving a lot of valuables behind. We focused on gold and silver coins and jewelry which could be easily melted down to sell. Once a bag was as full as possible without bursting, Jason would take it outside and place it on the seabed away from the ship.

When we finished with the captain's cabin we explored the rest of the ship which was preserved like an underwater museum. As we swam from space to space below decks we witnessed what life must have been like on a ship like this. There was evidence of a violent storm in each area we explored but it wasn't until we got to the galley that we found a body amongst the wreckage.

It was a bit of a shock to see the man, who I assumed was the cook, floating in the galley. His head was bent at an unnatural angle, so he probably broke his neck in the storm. Except for that, he looked like he was sleeping. Since the galley was dark I couldn't tell what color he was wearing but the fabric was rough. His feet were bare and he had burn scars along each arm. Cooking on a ship must have been a dangerous business.

While we didn't find any other bodies it still felt like we were swimming in a tomb. We were respectfully silent as we kept looking for magical artifacts but didn't find any.

*The rest of the crew must have been on deck dealing with the storm,* Jason mused as we made our way above deck.

*You're probably right. The cook would have been doing what he could to keep hot drinks ready for anyone able to come below so that's why he was the only person we found.*

*So, what's the plan?* Jason asked and I turned to look at him. His hair was gently waving in the current and the scarlet and purple fins on his forearms were rippling, too. He smiled, opening his arms to me and my heart melted. I took one of his webbed hands in mine and marveled as I looked at his claws, which could cut through steel. They only stuck about an inch beyond his fingertips, but I knew they could extend six inches when he wanted them to.

I put my arms around his waist and put my head on his chest. The fact he would willingly become a merman for me always filled me with such joy. I wanted to spend the rest of our lives together letting him know how I felt.

*I've got a couple of suggestions,* I sent as I turned my face to his with a wicked smile.

*Is that so?* he asked and gave me a kiss.

*I'm not interrupting anything, am I?* Brian called as he slipped the tips of two tentacles between us and pushed us away from one another.

*I don't think that's necessary,* I muttered.

He laughed as he responded, *I take my role of chaperone very seriously.*

*No one asked you to do that,* Jason grumped.

*Actually—we did,* I said smiling. I swam back over and gave Jason a quick peck on the lips, *just three more months until we get married, then I'm all yours.*

*I'm looking forward to that,* he said and laughed.

*July 15*
*Indian Ocean*
*50 Nautical Miles South of Melbourne, Australia*

"Hey, toss me another Ginger Chilli," Brian called from the captain's chair on the bridge of the Hatteras 70 Motor Yacht I'd purchased in Melbourne. After we discussed the best way to get the treasure to the surface so I could add it to the pocket dimension on my necklace, we concluded we should get a boat. We decided I should get the boat while Brian and Jason moved the treasure from the hold of the *Flor do Mar*.

It only took me a few hours to swim to Melbourne, but it took a few days to locate and purchase a boat. I wasn't going to buy something cheap, since I planned on having it sailed to my home in Newport Beach. So, after some searching, I bought a seventy-foot yacht which was extremely easy to sail. Thankfully, the previous owner had installed extra fuel tanks so I didn't have to stop for fuel on the way back to the shipwreck. Still, it took almost a full day from Melbourne to return to our spot. It gave me plenty of time to contact Josef and Alister to update them on the magical item I found. They agreed with my decision to harvest some of the treasure before I removed the object from the wreck.

When I finally returned to the spot where I'd left Jason and Brian, I dropped anchor and mentally called for them to start bringing up treasure. At first Brian tried to save time and grabbed a chest in each of his tentacles but when he moved a hundred feet from the *Flor do Mar*, the wood disintegrated, and the contents spilled back to the ocean floor. We suspected something would happen when we moved out of range of the protection charm, but we didn't expect anything that drastic. It was a good thing I'd purchased a hundred extra mesh dive bags while I was in Australia.

It took us most of another day for Jason and Brian to bring up treasure in bags and I'd add each bag to the pocket dimension. I was grateful the weight of my necklace stayed the same regardless of how much I added to the dimensional locker. When we'd removed a quarter of the treasure from the wreck, I decided it was time to remove the charm from the *Flor do Mar*.

Jason insisted on going with me into the captain's cabin to remove the magical item, which I thought was sweet.

*Are you sure you don't want me to remove it?* Jason asked.

*Thank you, but King Alister and Josef gave this assignment to me. If it makes you feel any better, I'm pretty sure nothing is going to happen once I remove it and the ship probably won't be affected until we swim far enough away,* I mused as I studied the object embedded in the wood. I purchased some dive knives at the same time I bought the bags so between my claws and the knives I felt certain I could easily remove it from the beam.

*Here goes nothing,* I sent as I used my claw to score a rough circle around the object. The wood parted easily, and I tried to use the blunt end of one of the knives to pry out the charm. Unfortunately, it didn't budge.

*Hmmm, my claws seem to work. Hold this please,* I sent and handed Jason the knife as I continued to carve into the wood. I cut a square section surrounding the charm from the beam then Jason and I each used a dive knife to pry the square from the rest of the ship. The moment the piece we'd been working on broke away from the bulkhead, there was a shockwave and the ship shuddered.

*Uh oh,* I sent. *I may have been wrong about nothing happening once we removed the charm.*

*Let's get out of here,* Jason mentally shouted as he pulled me to the door and shoved me through.

I tucked the block containing the charm under my right arm and swam as fast as I could to reach the deck.

*I'm right behind you,* Jason assured me once we cleared the deck and swam towards the surface. We stopped a hundred feet away from the *Flor do Mar* and turned back to see what was happening. The ship disappeared in moments as we watched hundreds of years' worth of decay disintegrate every piece of wood and organic material on the once proud ship.

*Treasure hunters might possibly find the remains of this ship in the future but at least they won't find evidence of magic,* I said as I grabbed Jason's hand as we raced to the surface.

Once we got back on the boat, I added the charm embedded in the block of wood to the pocket dimension and we got underway. We set a course to Flinders Island off the coast of Tasmania to refuel and buy food and drinks popular in Tasmania, which is where we got the Ginger Chilli soft drink.

"No problem, do you want something to eat, too?" I asked Brian as I rooted through the ice chest for the Tasmanian soda.

"Ooo, how about a few of those Wallaby pies?" Brian turned in the seat to grin at me.

"It's a good thing we bought so many of them," I laughed as I tossed him the drink then grabbed three pies.

"Do you want anything Jason?" I asked and tossed him a couple of pies after he held up two fingers, then walked Brian's three over to him. "You sure you guys don't mind sailing back to Newport Beach?" I asked as I munched on my own pie.

"It'll be fun," Jason grinned. "Besides, unless we leave your new boat behind, we need to sail it back. It'll only take a month, then there will only be two months until the wedding —less planning for me," Jason teased.

"You know there's not much planning," I said as I poked him in the stomach. "We're having a simple wedding on the cliff at the house."

"I'm just teasing," he said as he wrapped his arms around me and kissed me on the top of my head.

"You better not miss Alister and Aileene's wedding," I warned.

"We won't," Brian promised.

"If we need to dock in Hawaii and swim home, we'll make sure we're on time; don't worry." Jason soothed.

"It's not me you'll have to worry about if you miss it, you'll have an angry Royal Dragon to deal with." I laughed evilly.

"Do you mean Alister or Aileene?" Brian asked.

"Yep," I answered as both Brian and Jason suddenly looked nervous.

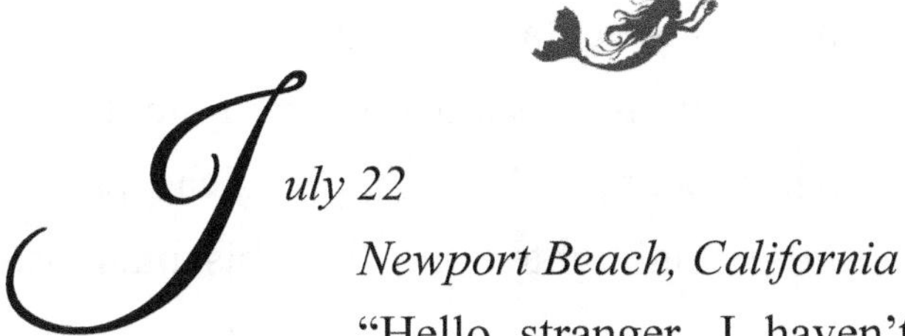

*J*uly 22

*Newport Beach, California*

"Hello stranger, I haven't seen you in a couple weeks." Enrique said as I walked up.

"I took a trip to Australia and Tasmania," I smiled at my friend behind the counter of my favorite restaurant.

"You want your usual?" he asked and when I nodded, added my order to the register.

"How's the tab for Nick?"

"You've still got a balance of twenty dollars," Enrique said as he continued to add my order.

"Wow, he went through a lot of food while I was gone," I said. "Add two-hundred dollars on there for him and add his order to mine."

Enrique looked at me and smiled as he did so. "Go ahead and sit, we'll bring your food out to you," he said as he charged my credit card for the meal.

After filling up my cup with iced tea, I sat at one of the tables outside and enjoyed the feel of the sun on my face. I'd be a poor mermaid if I didn't enjoy the taste of fish I'd caught with my own hands but there's just something about a burger from my favorite restaurant to bring a smile to my face. Even though I must eat my meals in the ocean a few times a week, I come to In-N-Out for lunch every day I'm home; or in a place where they have In-N-Out.

"Where you been? I'd about starved to death without you here," said a disheveled man as he sat across from me. It was obvious he'd been living rough, and the shopping cart parked next to the table further highlighted the fact this man was homeless.

"Hello, Nick," I smiled, "I'm pretty sure you've been eating just fine. According to Enrique you almost went through the money I left for you while I was away."

"I don't know nothing about that, I just know you wasn't here," Nick grumped as he took the Red Bull I held out for him. As he gulped down the drink, I took a good look at him. He was wearing a grimy pull-over surfer hoodie and a tattered OP bathing suit. The sandals on his feet were held together by twine and duct tape and his gray-streaked shoulder-length blond hair was matted in dreads. It was hard to tell how old Nick was, but I knew he'd been living on the streets for decades. The regular customers were used to Nick, but I could hear others complaining about his presence and his body odor, which was rather rank. Even though my senses were greater than a normal human, I was able to ignore the stench, which was a good thing.

"Is today a bad day?" I asked and after he nodded, I told him about my trip to Tasmania to capture the nekahi. I wasn't worried about him sharing the truth since most people would assume his ramblings were part of his mental instability. Nick listened to my story with wide-eyed appreciation, and I could see his face relax as I shared. Before long, he was laughing with me as I told him about the meal with my mother.

"Hey guys, here's your food," Enrique interrupted when he brought over our meals. Even though he was the manager he always insisted on serving Nick himself.

He placed one cardboard box containing a double-double and fries in front of Nick and he put three of the same things in front of me. After Enrique stepped away, Nick pushed his box toward me, and his hand hovered before the three boxes on my side. I haven't figured out the system Nick uses to choose which of mine he would take, but after a minute of indecision he finally grabbed at a container as though I would snatch it away from him. He trusted Enrique and me, as much as he trusted anyone, but he was still worried we might try to poison him.

Once Nick made his choice, I was able to start eating my lunch.

"What's today?" he asked between bites.

"Saturday, July 22," I answered wondering where he was going with this.

"Didn't you have a gig today?" he stared at me.

I nodded as I started in on my second burger, "Yep, it was a party for a five-year old girl."

"How was it?" Nick asked as he finished his burger and

stared longingly at the box he had pushed away earlier. Since this was all part of the game, I pushed it back and he dug in.

Besides finding treasure in the ocean I also own a specialty party company called Festive Tails, where parents can book mermaids and princesses to come to their child's party. It's fun for me to play a mermaid for children's parties. I have thirty-five people working for me, but I love to go out as often as I can. It always surprised me how many people enjoyed getting a chance to play a mermaid or merman and since we got the chance to bring joy to children at the same time, I always felt it was a win-win. It really is amazing how easily children believe the fantastic and see magic and wonder everywhere. It makes me sad when I see the adults, who have lost their sense of wonder, smile indulgently at the children for they've lost the capacity to believe in things they can't see.

I told Nick about the party and how the little girls squealed when they ran out of the house and saw mermaids in the pool. My employees Brooke and Sarah were swimming in the water, and I was on the bottom of the pool waiting for the kids to come out. Nick laughed when I described how I swam towards the surface and came up and out of the water, doing an impression of a breaching whale and soaking the children standing along the edge of the pool. For a moment, as Nick listened to my story, the years melted away from his face and I could see the person he'd been before whatever horrors he had witnessed twisted his mind. An easy smile graced his face and there was an air of lucidity that wasn't there moments before.

"Why do you care?" he asked softly, "why do you spend so much time with me?"

"Because you're worth it," I smiled back at him.

"I know I don't say it enough, Cyndi, but thank you. Thank you for treating me like a person and not an embarrassment."

"You're welcome, Nick. I'd like to do more for you if you'd let me," I said hoping he would accept my offer this time.

"I appreciate that," he smiled crookedly, "but, I can't stand feeling trapped. And no matter where you'd take me to get help, I'd be trapped." He stood, looked around and dug into his shopping cart as though he'd forgotten something. "Here it is," he cried as he pulled a doll with a mermaid tail out from the depths of the cart and held it out to me. "I found this for you, as a way to say thank you. Her tail isn't as pretty as yours, but she doesn't look as scary as you do when you transform." Nick said as he looked me in the eyes.

"Thank you, Nick," I said as I took the doll from him. "When did you see me?" I asked softly.

"I don't remember days in the past that well, but it was after you met that bus full of people here that one time. Maybe we could swim together some time?" He looked embarrassed as he asked.

"Wouldn't you be afraid?"

"You'd never hurt me, and I'd never do anything to hurt you either," he said determinedly then quickly walked away pushing the shopping cart holding his most precious belongings.

"I know you wouldn't," I said softly to his retreating back.

*July 23*

*Newport Coast, California*

"Mermaids," squealed a young girl's voice, followed by the high-pitched screams coming from a herd of children.

I looked up, startled, and dove off the rocks I was sitting on and splashed into the water. I could still hear the shrieks through the water as I dove down to the bottom and pushed off with both my arms and legs. I jumped out of the water and did a dolphin backflip, my tail spraying water at the children along the edge of the pool. They were also splashed as I came back down and sent a wave of water in their direction. The kids were still giggling as I popped out of the water and leaned my chin on my arms which I'd rested on the side of the pool.

"Hi kids, I'm Cyndi and these are my friends Gwendolyn and Astoria," I said with a bright smile. The other mermaids smiled and waved, also. "We heard Avery was having a birthday today and we wanted to come celebrate. It's not every day someone turns six."

"I'm Avery," said a blonde girl with wide eyes wearing a

princess dress, complete with a crown and a birthday girl sash. "Are you really a mermaid?"

"Yes, I am," I answered truthfully.

"Is that tail real?" A slightly older boy asked skeptically. Since he looked similar to the birthday girl, I assumed he was her older brother.

"Don't be mean," Avery turned to her brother in anger.

"That's okay Avery, I don't mind the question. No, this isn't my real tail. I don't like the way chlorine itches my scales, so I wear this one when I'm in a swimming pool. It looks just like my real one though," I answered as I flipped the tail in the air and again splashed the kids with water.

As they screamed, I backed away and allowed Gwendolyn and Astoria the opportunity to answer questions and share their backstories with the kids. I smiled in pleasure as I watched the kids interact with the mermaids. I laughed inwardly when I thought what would happen if I transformed into my true mermaid form. The children might be frightened by my fierce appearance but would accept I was really a mermaid; the adults would deny what they were seeing was real.

After an hour, the birthday girl and all her friends were ushered into the house so they could have cake and open presents; and we could get out of the pool. It was important to me that kids never saw us removing our mermaid tails. I made sure it was written into every contract that the children would move to another area so they wouldn't be able to see us when we left. That didn't stop creepy guys from hanging around though.

"Hey, I'm Terry. Are you girls available for another kind of party later?" he asked with a leer.

Terry was in his mid-forties and although he looked fit, he was starting to go soft in the middle. His expensive haircut couldn't disguise the fact he was losing his hair and although he was trying to be charming, it just came across as sleazy. He was wearing a pair of red slim-fit chinos, light blue polo shirt and a pair of deck shoes without socks. The way he stared at Gwendolyn and Astoria changing out of their tails made me angry and I stepped into his line of sight, so he couldn't see my friends.

"We're not that type of entertainment," I said matter-of-factly.

"Let's see if this changes your mind," he said in a condescending tone as he pulled a wad of money out of his pocket and waggled it at me.

I laughed and ignored him as I grabbed my gear and began to walk away.

"Don't walk away from me," Terry said through clenched teeth and grabbed my arm.

"Uh, oh," Gwendolyn said as I pulled my arm out of his grasp and turned towards him. Unfortunately for Terry, I was holding my silicone tail and it hit him in the arm and knocked him into the water. I might have used some of my mermaid strength, so that's probably why he flew a ways before splashing into the pool.

"I think we're done here," I said brightly and helped Gwendolyn and Astoria gather their things. Terry was still floundering in the water as we made our way towards the gate which would take us to the front of the house. I was the last one out of the yard and turned to make sure he had gotten out of the pool, which he had.

"Next time, I suggest you keep your hands to yourself," I laughed and let the gate shut behind me.

CHAPTER 3

*J*uly 25

*Phoenix, Arizona*

"Uggh, it's hot," I complained to no one in particular as I sat in the VIP lounge at Sky Harbor airport waiting for my ride. It's a myth that mermaids can't survive long out of water but right now I was wishing it were true. When Josef called and asked me to make a trip to the headquarters of Rex Industries to discuss what I'd found in the shipwreck, I tried to convince him we should just teleconference, but since he was the boss, I didn't win that argument.

*How far away are you?* I asked mentally.

*I'm about five minutes out, there was an accident on the 202 and we had to take side streets,* Josef sent back.

*You do realize it's one-hundred and sixteen degrees outside today, don't you?* I asked.

*Are you sitting outside?* Josef sent innocently.

*That's not the point,* I grumped, *mermaids aren't built for this kind of heat.*

*You're fine,* Josef said, and I could sense the laughter in his sending.

I narrowed my eyes and shot back, *just because gargoyles aren't affected by hot or cold doesn't mean the rest of us don't suffer.*

*You are crabby today,* Josef replied. *Does it help to know there's an In-N-Out only fifteen minutes from the airport and that's our first stop?*

*Yes,* I sighed, *I think I might be able to make it now that you've given me hope.*

*You're ridiculous,* Josef teased and we both laughed.

*Rex Industries*
*Phoenix, Arizona*

Josef parked the armored SUV in the parking spot reserved for the CEO and I finished my lunch. He was silently amused, with my sound of disappointment when I polished off the french fries.

"Better?" He chuckled and got out after I nodded.

"Sorry I was so irritable earlier," I apologized as we walked to the elevator which led to the executive suites above.

Josef waved away my apology, "I get it, first of all you're a mermaid far from any significant body of water, and you're always cranky before you get your first In-N-Out for the day," he teased.

"Jerk," I laughed, and we rode up the elevator in companionable silence.

Rex Industries is a multinational conglomerate of companies, all of which are on the cutting edge of technological development. It's also the front for Tionchar, a Therian secret organization dedicated to the monitoring, protection and development of worlds across dimensions. Most of the technological advances on Earth have been directly influenced by Tionchar operatives working behind the scenes. Prior to the recent changes implemented by King Alister, members of Tionchar would serve on their assigned planet for fifty years and then be recalled to Theria, unable to share their experiences with others.

Josef and Brian had both served previously but King Alister and An'Ceann called them out of retirement after a recent betrayal where many members of Tionchar had been exposed and murdered. Jason and I had been recruited to replace two of the members who died. In the past few months King Alister had increased the number of Tionchar operatives on Earth from twenty to fifty with five extras being added each to the United States and China. He was concerned about the rising hostilities between these two superpowers. Josef and King Alister still had plans to further increase the number of operatives on Earth once those candidates finished their training. Earth was a dangerous place.

We stepped off the elevator and turned to the right to walk to Josef's office. I smiled at the two people sitting at the desk guarding the entrance.

"Hey, you two," I said and stepped up to give them hugs.

"Yoli, you're looking good," I smiled at the Hispanic woman grinning at me. "Carlos must be taking care of you," I laughed and winked.

"And she is taking care of me," Carlos said and hugged me back. "It's good to see you."

"How's your training going?" I asked the werewolf couple. They were two of the newer Therian recruits and were close to taking on field assignments unmonitored.

"Right now, it's boring," Yolanda laughed. "We're supposed to be guarding a certain gargoyle shifter but today we're watching over an empty office." She raised an eyebrow and looked pointedly at Josef.

"Sometimes I need to get out on my own," he smiled and held up his hands in surrender. "To make up for it, I'm going to ask you to guard Cyndi while she's here."

I turned to Josef and poked him in the chest. "While I'd love to spend time with Yoli and Carlos, I'm not going to be here long enough to need a guard."

"We'll talk about that," Josef promised and continued to his office.

Carlos and Yoli smiled at my look of frustration so I stuck my tongue out at them and they laughed, as I'd intended.

Josef's office took up half of the twentieth floor since he used it as an office and apartment. He had a home in nearby Scottsdale but usually only slept there on the weekends, preferring to stay here so he could run the company as well as direct the activities of Tionchar across Earth. We stepped down into a sunken sitting area and I sat on one of the buttery brown leather couches, sighing in comfort as I did. I stared out the window admiring the view while Josef busied himself at the coffee bar. The tinted windows kept out the summer heat but afforded a beautiful view of Camelback Mountain.

"So, why was it so important for me to rush here this morning?" I asked as Josef handed me a cup of coffee a few minutes later.

"Two reasons," Josef began after sitting down and sipping his own drink. "We were able to smelt the gold from the shipwreck into bars and converted half of those into cash as you asked. You now have an extra two-hundred-forty-seven million dollars in your accounts."

I whistled as I thought about the amount.

"We are still working to convert the silver and jewels, but you should expect about twice that amount within the next few weeks." Josef continued.

"I've done some research on the *Flor do Mar* and it's

estimated the ship was carrying two point six billion dollars in gold, silver and treasures. We left more behind than we took." I tapped my lips in thought for a moment. "Rather than convert everything to cash, could you have the real estate division purchase the houses surrounding mine? My neighbors would be willing to sell if we offer them the right price. I would like to make my beach truly private and create a place of refuge for our kind and our human friends."

"Absolutely," Josef nodded and made a note on his tablet.

I finished my coffee and leaned back, the leather creaking softly with my movement. "And where will I be going that I'll need Yoli and Carlos to accompany me?"

"I think that will become apparent once I give you the second reason why it was important for you to rush here," Josef answered smugly.

I could feel my lips compress together as I thought about what he did and didn't say. Finally, I huffed out a frustrated breath, "you've been taking lessons from the king on how to be enigmatic, haven't you?"

"Young one," Josef laughed. "I've been keeping secrets for the Crown for longer than you've been alive."

"How ancient are you, old man?" I asked.

"You know it's not polite to ask another shifter their age," Josef frowned but since he had a twinkle in his eye, I could tell he really didn't mind.

"It's only fair since you know how old I am," I grinned unrepentantly.

"Let's just say, I was at King Phillip's side when he ordered the dimensional gates sealed." He smiled at me.

Even though I'm aware shifters are long lived, Josef's declaration caught me by surprise. King Phillip closed the gates to restrict movement between dimensions because he was concerned for the safety of Therians. Since that happened over five hundred years before, Josef truly was ancient.

"Do you have your affairs in order," I asked with a grin, "you could keel over at any moment."

"Very funny," he replied drily, "I don't plan on going anywhere for quite a long time. Unless my body is destroyed, and it's very difficult to harm a gargoyle, I'll live until I get bored with life and choose to join An'Ceann in his kingdom. That's not something we normally share with people other than gargoyles; consider it a sign of my trust for you."

"I'm honored," I said as I bowed my head in respect. "Still, you're old as dirt." I laughed and looked longingly at my empty cup. "Okay, hit me with the rest of your reasons."

"How much do you know about the wreck of the *Flor do Mar*?" Josef asked as he reached over to refill my cup.

"Are you asking about the state of the ship when we found it or the events leading up to its sinking?"

Josef saluted me with his cup, "I've read your report on the condition of the ship. I wish you had a camera with you to record what you saw but no matter," Josef shrugged his shoulders dismissively.

"Then the only things I know about the events leading up

to the wreck have come from searches online. There have been many treasure hunters over the years looking for the shipwreck, but since they're searching about four-thousand miles from where the ship actually went down, they'll never find it. It was well known at the time that the ship was carrying gold, silver, jewels, spices and the treasure taken from the Sultan of Malacca; today the treasure is worth billions of dollars. This is the type of shipwreck hunters search for because if they discover it, not only will they become wealthy beyond belief, but they will also earn fame. Unfortunately for those hunters, they're looking in the wrong place based on the eyewitness account of the sole survivor, Afonso de Albuquerque."

Josef made a 'go-on' gesture, so I continued.

"According to Albuquerque, the ship went down the afternoon of November 20, 1511 after being caught for three days and nights in a terrible storm. The *Flor do Mar* was taking on water, but still might have survived except the foremast snapped and fell along the length of the ship, smashing the pilot's wheel. Albuquerque claimed he abandoned the ship in a makeshift raft and somehow survived until he was rescued.

"He never could explain how he survived while the rest of the crew perished. The *Flor do Mar* was known as an extremely unstable vessel so the King and Queen of Portugal didn't hold him responsible for the loss of the ship and treasure. Shortly after his audience with the reigning monarchs, he disappeared. Some speculate he couldn't live with the survivor's guilt and slunk away to live his life in obscurity."

"I agree with the living in obscurity part, but we think that is about to change."

"What do you mean?" I asked, confused.

"One moment," Josef said, then leaned over and pushed a button on the console next to the couch. "Please ask Hillaes to come in."

A moment later a door on the opposite end of the office opened and a woman walked through. She had curly shoulder-length chestnut colored hair and an olive complexion. I stood to greet her and noticed she was a couple inches shorter than my five-foot eleven inches. She was wearing a green tailored linen pantsuit that was perfect for the weather in Phoenix. Her sparkling reddish-brown eyes were punctuated with laugh lines and her expression was open and friendly. She held out a hand for me to shake and when our fingers touched, I felt she was powerful; she smelled like a cat shifter of some kind but was also something more.

"I'm called Hillaes, it's nice to meet you. King Alister speaks highly of you. So does rock-butt over here," she tilted her head towards Josef with a smile, "but since he'll never tell you to your face, I thought I should let you know." She laughed then sat on the couch next to Josef.

"It's nice to meet you, too. You're some sort of cat shifter, right?" I asked puzzled.

She laughed, "I get this a lot on Theria. Yes, I'm a tiger shifter but I wasn't born that way. An'Ceann gifted me with that ability so I could marry Wu, who is one of the King's Inner Circle."

"I've never heard of that before," I said amazed.

"It's very rare, and an enormous honor to become one of you. I was actually born on Middle Earth—"

"Middle Earth?" I interrupted her, confused.

She laughed, which was such a pleasant sound I laughed with her, "I'm sorry. You've met Shelley, correct?"

I nodded. Shelley was one of King Alister's best friends and quite a character. He was a grizzly bear shapeshifter, and his true mate was Bernie, Alister's other best friend. She was a unicorn.

"I've gotten so used to calling the planet Middle Earth because that's what Alister, Bernie and Shelley called it when they first got there. That's how I refer to my home planet now; you might know it better by its proper name, Claw." Hillaes explained.

"Oh," I said surprised, "I was briefly on Claw about fourteen years ago. I fled with the others who lived in and near the palace when we thought King Phillip and Queen Beatrice had been killed. We only stopped in Claw long enough to open a gate to Earth."

"Well, I was born and raised on Claw and only recently moved permanently to Theria after meeting and marrying my husband," Hillaes finished.

"You may or may not know this, but Claw has a higher concentration of magic than either Earth or Theria. Hillaes is a sorceress of some renown and originally relocated to Theria so she could tutor Alister in magic," Josef explained.

"Although to be honest, I learn more from him than I can teach him these days. His natural capacity for magic is astounding, and because he's a Royal Dragon he can tap into an almost limitless reservoir of power. What he doesn't yet understand in technique, he makes up for with sheer power and force of will," she smiled indulgently.

"Anyway, when I contacted the King about the charm you found on the ship, he thought it would be wiser to have Hillaes come here to examine it rather than send it to Theria," Josef said.

"We thought that would be safer since it has been in this dimension for hundreds of years and had less likelihood of causing major issues." Hillaes added as she poured herself a cup of coffee.

"What did you find out?" I asked, bursting with curiosity.

Hillaes pursed her lips in distaste. "First of all, the spell used to create the charm was both a blood and death spell. The caster more than likely took the lives of the crew of the *Flor do Mar* to power the protection spell."

"That's horrible," I gasped.

"That's not all," Hillaes continued, "just as the spell was active in preserving the ship, it is still protecting the person who created the original spell; presumably the man calling himself Afonso de Albuquerque."

"So, you're telling me this Afonso de Albuquerque is still alive after five centuries? How is that possible for a human?" I asked.

"I'm not positive but if I had to guess, he's been stealing the life-force from victims for at least half a millennia to feed his evil spell," Hillaes answered quietly.

We sat in silence while we considered the ramifications of what Hillaes told us.

"How many victims?" I asked quietly.

She shook her head before answering, "I'm not sure but if we assume the minimum of one per year, that's still over five hundred murdered since the sinking of the ship."

"And if we add the four hundred members of the crew, he's killed over nine hundred people to prolong his life," Josef added.

"Do we have any way to find this Afonso?" I asked.

Hillaes shook her head, "I can't get any kind of reading from the charm you found on the ship other than what I've already told you. I believe the link between the two charms was broken when you placed the one in your pocket dimension. I'm not sure what that means for Afonso de Albuquerque, but he has to know the ship was found and the charm recovered. However, even though the original connection was severed, I'm concerned that it could be reestablished over time. I think it would be wise for you to store the charm in your pocket dimension for safekeeping." Hillaes explained as she handed me the charm wrapped in a length of black velvet covered in symbols embroidered in gold thread. My fingers began to tingle the moment I touched the magical item.

"Okay," I said as I placed the wrapped charm into the pocket dimension. "Afonso de Albuquerque has to die for his crimes but before we can take him out, we must find him."

"You're right," Josef said with a grin, "and you'll be taking Yolanda and Carlos with you."

"I don't need bodyguards—" I began but Josef stopped me with a glare. "But I'd be happy to have them come with me as an opportunity to further their training," I finished brightly.

"You remind me of Bernie," Hillaes said as she tried to suppress a giggle.

"I'll take that as a compliment," I preened, then sobered when I thought of the seriousness of the mission. "Where do we start looking for Afonso?"

"How do you feel about traveling to Malaysia?" Josef asked mysteriously.

*July 28*

*Malacca City, Malaysia*

Jason grabbed my arm and pulled me back on the sidewalk before the car coming from the right could hit me.

"They drive on the other side of the road here, remember?" Brian chuckled behind me.

"That would have been a helpful reminder about thirty seconds ago," I grumped.

"Don't blame me," Brian laughed, "Carlos and Yoli are supposed to be the ones guarding you."

"We didn't think we'd need to keep her from walking into traffic," Carlos snickered.

"Listen furball, I don't need you giving me a hard time, too," I ground out as I turned around and glared at my werewolf bodyguard, "I get enough grief from this lunk right here," I said and pointed to an unrepentant Brian.

Jason leaned in and kissed me on the temple. "I'm afraid it'll take all of us to keep Cyndi from walking into traffic while we're here. She has enough trouble staying on her feet when she's used to the cars driving on the proper side of the road."

"Thanks, I think," I said and gently elbowed Jason in the side.

I really wasn't upset with their teasing since I hadn't been expecting to see Jason and Brian for another three weeks or so. I was pleasantly surprised when they picked us up from the private hangar where our pilot parked the luxurious corporate jet, a Gulfstream G650, we had flown from Phoenix. Josef had radioed ahead to them on the boat, which I'd named *Tails Away* and instructed them to dock at the port in Malacca. He had arranged for a crew to bring my new boat the rest of the way to California. Jason and Brian were more than happy to join our party on land.

We stayed at the five-star Casa del Rio Melaka hotel the night before since we were still exhausted from the flight over. Of course, we hadn't checked into the hotel under our own names but the aliases we'd been assigned for this mission. Josef had the proper documentation prepared for each member of our team and we brought those with us in a diplomatic pouch. We didn't want any potential enemies to trace our activities back to our lives in the US.

Carlos, Yoli, Hillaes and I stayed in the Melaka Suite while Brian and Jason stayed in the River Suite. We gathered on our balcony and had a delicious breakfast while we decided our course of action.

"Help me understand why we met here. Josef didn't give many details other than he wanted us to join you to look for the guy who cast the spell on the ship we found," Brian said between bites.

Hillaes watched him eat for a moment before answering, "I've only seen Alister eat as much as you do."

Brian grinned, "It takes a lot of calories to keep this body in tip-top shape."

"Anyway," Hillaes continued, "we're in Malacca City because there's a replica of the *Flor do Mar* at the Melaka Maritime Museum just over a mile from here. Josef and I thought it would be worthwhile for Cyndi to go through the ship and point out exactly where the charm was located. According to the museum's website, the replica of the ship has a mooring cleat that came from the original *Flor do Mar* that broke off the ship before it set sail on its fateful voyage.

"The harbor master at the time kept the cleat as an heirloom for his family and it has been passed down to successive heirs throughout the centuries. According to family legend, the cleat brought them wealth and great fortune. The last surviving heir was the one to commission the building of the *Flor do Mar* replica and displayed the cleat in the captain's cabin on the ship."

"That's a fascinating piece of history, but how will that help us find Afonso de Albuquerque?" I asked as I stole a piece of bacon from Jason's plate.

"Since Afonso de Albuquerque's life is tied to the original *Flor do Mar*, I'm going to perform a spell on the cleat to gather any energy I can from it to see if I can get a location for Albuquerque. If not, we'll need another piece from the *Flor do Mar* to try again."

"The replica, or the original?" Jason asked.

"The original," Hillaes answered and finished her orange juice.

"Oh, something easy then," I joked, and we finished eating in companionable silence.

"**A**re you still tired?" Jason asked as we walked along the street after my near-death experience with the car.

"Not really," I said, squeezing his hand and looking up at him. "I've just been thinking about the last couple of days and how wonderful it is that we're here together; I wasn't expecting to see you for weeks."

Jason looked at me with a self-satisfied smile. "You just can't live without me, can you?"

"No, I can't," I laughed and enjoyed the moment as we walked to the museum. It was already hot and humid but that doesn't bother me as much as the dry heat of Arizona. "I wasn't expecting this sort of thing when we discovered the ship."

Jason shrugged, "Me neither, but adventure seems to follow us around. At least we'll be able to stop Afonso, or whatever he's calling himself now, from killing more people. It makes me angry to think how much death he's caused over the centuries."

I hugged Jason's arm then kissed the back of his hand.

"What was that for? Not that I'm complaining, mind you," Jason chuckled.

"Just another reason for me to love you; your desire to protect the weak." I said lightly then tripped over a crack in the sidewalk. If Jason hadn't been holding my hand so tightly, I would have fallen on my face.

"Does she always trip like that?" Yoli asked quietly.

"That's nothing, you should see her trying to walk down a beach. I once saw her trip over a small wave. For someone so graceful in the water it's amazing she's so clumsy on land," Brian laughed.

"I can hear you, you know?" I said shaking my head.

"I know," Brian said loudly, "hearing isn't your problem—it's being able to walk and think at the same time."

Everyone in our party laughed and I narrowed my eyes at Jason.

"Go ahead, laugh—I dare you," I dared my fiancé who was trying not to crack a smile.

"There's nothing to laugh about. I'm completely serious," Jason said solemnly.

"Seriously in trouble if you can't keep that smile off your face," I threatened, unable to keep the grin off my own.

He was saved by an exclamation of "we're here" by Hillaes and we stopped before the entrance to the maritime museum. The museum was built along the river and was decorated on the outside to look like a seventeenth-century wharf. There were museum employees outside, dressed in period costumes cajoling passersby into coming inside. On either side of the museum building there were also street performers entertaining the crowds with music and feats of acrobatics. There was a definite party atmosphere around the building.

We paid the entrance fee and went inside. We'd already discussed how to proceed. Rather than go straight to the replica of the ship, we would tour the museum to see if we could find any other clues to Afonso's whereabouts. Hillaes didn't have an exact plan of attack but we were ready to adjust our plans on what we discovered.

The museum was fascinating as it chronicled the history of the Port of Malacca and how it had been a hub of trade and exploration for India, Malaysia, Thailand, Burma, Southern China, Australia, Viet Nam, Indonesia and the Philippines. Billions of dollars of gold, silver, jewels, spices and other goods were shipped from this part of the world to Europe. Ships from Europe would also bring goods, but mostly brought people to settle in the colonies established by England, Spain, Portugal and France.

There was an interesting exhibit of 'mysterious' items found in this region of the world and I recognized some pieces of machinery that came from Atlantis. Thankfully, they were so corroded no one could tell what they were, but I took some pictures with my tablet and sent them to Josef. Hillaes also identified a few magical items in the display, and she wanted to check them against the charm once we finished our tour.

I'm not sure if any members of Tionchar had been keeping an eye on the museum but I'm sure they would after receiving our full report.

"Is anyone else hungry?" Carlos asked as we were heading outside to tour the replica of the ship. "Something smells delicious and according to this, there's a cafeteria inside the museum." Carlos pointed to the left after consulting the map he had in his hand.

"It won't be In-N-Out," I grumbled, "but I can eat."

"Just think about how good a Double-Double will taste once we get back home," Brian teased.

"Yeah, yeah," I muttered. "Make fun of me all you want. I like what I like."

The food in the cafeteria was surprisingly good and we each tried a different Malaysian dish. I had a spicy dish called Mee goreng mamak which was a mixture of yellow noodles, egg and veggies tossed in a chili sauce and added shrimp as the protein. Jason tried the Nasi lemak which is a traditional breakfast dish made of rice cooked in coconut milk with a side of hard-boiled eggs, peanuts and seafood, all covered in a spicy sauce. I had a few bites of Jason's and liked it so much I went up to get my own order of the Nasi lemak. As I stood in line waiting for my food, I felt a tingle at the base of my neck which always let me know something dangerous was nearby.

*I'm sensing danger, can any of you see anyone suspicious?* I sent to my companions.

Before anyone responded the sensation passed as though it had never happened.

The woman behind the counter handed me my food and I sat at our table, quickly looking around to see if I noticed anyone staring in our direction.

*Did you notice anything?* I sent to my companions, each person responding in the negative.

*I don't want to use any magic until we are on the ship,* Hillaes answered, and I nodded.

"Mmmm," I hummed after I took the first bite of the Mee goreng mamak with beef, I'd ordered, "this is delicious."

"As good as In-N-Out?" Brian teased.

I just glared at him and continued to eat my second breakfast.

The replica of the *Flor do Mar* was moored in a berth behind the museum. In its day it was a magnificent ship. While not huge compared to modern ships, it was the largest built at the time. According to the information on the plaque at the bottom of the stairs leading up to the entrance at the side of the ship, it was one-hundred eleven feet high at the top of the main mast, one-hundred eighteen feet long and twenty-six feet wide. The ship swayed gently in the river's swift current and the timbers creaked as it moved. There were costumed actors playing crew members and we stood on the main deck and watched an exhibition of what it would have been like for the riggers to unfurl and hoist the mainsail.

Four sailors rapidly climbed up the rope ladders attached

on either side of the main sail. Two of them stopped there then stood on the cross beam three-quarters of the way up the mainmast. The other two climbed into the crow's nest where one remained but the last continued to climb up to the top of the mast where he stood on the final crossbeam. On deck, the first mate called out instructions to the crew who were singing a sea shanty while holding ropes attached to the sail. It was bunched at the bottom of the mast, ready to be hoisted at the proper time.

*Are you ready?* Hillaes sent to me. While I really wanted to finish watching the fifteen-minute show, the two of us planned to slip away and search the ship for any magical resonance. We were already standing towards the back of the crowd to make it easier to disappear. I partially shifted my face to use my mermaid singing powers to distract humans from noticing we left the show. I put on sunglasses so no one would notice how my eyes turned solid black and held my hand in front of my mouth to hide my sharp teeth as I sang my song. Within seconds the people surrounding us were mesmerized and wouldn't notice our absence.

We backed away until my back was pressed against the door leading into the passage that would lead directly to the captain's cabin. Hillaes opened the door and as we slipped inside, I reverted to my human form.

*This way,* I said and led the way to the stern. The ship was an exact replica of the *Flor do Mar* and I could see the similarities even though the last time I saw the original ship it had been under hundreds of feet of water. When we entered the cabin, we were met with a wax figure dressed in the captain's uniform. There was a placard beside the figure explaining that it had been crafted using a portrait Afonso de Albuquerque had commissioned six months before the fateful voyage that led to the sinking of his ship.

After I indicated the spot where I found the charm, I went back to the wax figure to study the person we were hunting. He stood a hair over six-feet tall, which was large for the sixteenth century, and had a long pointed grey beard that lay on his chest. He had a dusky complexion and his dark-brown, almost black, eyes bore into me as I stared at him. His lips were curled in a cruel sneer and he had a flat-black four-cornered hat on his head and a sword on his belt.

*I'm going to cast the resonance spell now,* Hillaes told me mentally, *then I'd like you to bring out the charm you have stowed away so we can triangulate the force lines in case I get anything.*

*What do you think will happen?* I asked as I stood beside her and looked at the spot where I'd removed the charm from the original ship.

*Nothing you can see,* Hillaes answered, *but I should feel a magical pull which will guide me in the direction we need to go.* Hillaes muttered under her breath while holding her closed fist towards the beam above the bunk. When she finished her incantation, there was a loud thrumming and it felt as if the ship were hit with a blast of wind and alarms began blaring all over the ship.

"Oops," Hillaes commented, "it seems Afonso added some type of alarm spell in case anyone used magic on board. Quickly, hand me the charm before we're discovered."

I opened the pocket dimension and grabbed the item she asked for. I never thought about it before but there must be some magic involved in how things are catalogued in the pocket dimension because I only had to think about what I wanted, and it was always there. This just showed another aspect of Alister's power and his mastery over dimensional gates.

The alarms shifted tone when I removed the charm and Hillaes and I looked at each other in concern. She grabbed the glowing charm out of my hand and the brightly glowing light changed from silver to blue. She handed it back to me and I stuffed it back in the pocket dimension as I heard pounding feet coming towards the cabin. The door flew open and two guards brandishing weapons rushed inside.

*We're invisible if we don't move,* Hillaes' voice sounded in my head, which was fortunate because the alarm was blaring so loudly that if she said anything verbally, I probably wouldn't hear her.

I partially shifted in anticipation of the alarm turning off so I could capture the minds of the guards. The guard on the right, the larger of the two, reached up and clicked the button on his radio two times while he continued to scan the room while holding his pistol in his right hand. After waiting three seconds, he clicked the button four more times and the alarm shut off. I sang softly and the guards were frozen in place long enough for us to slip out of the room without them noticing us.

There was an announcement through the speakers connected to the alarms but since it sounded like it was in Mandarin, I didn't understand what it said.

A moment later the announcement was repeated, but this time in English.

*Ladies and gentlemen, we apologize for this interruption but there has been an unforeseen incident onboard the Flor do Mar. Please remain calm, you are in no danger and will be released when the matter has been thoroughly investigated.*

Hillaes and I made our way out the doors leading to the deck, which the guards had left open in their rush to enter the captain's cabin. She cast a confusion spell while I softly sang a song of peace and calm. The result was people didn't notice us slipping back into the crowd and those around us weren't as upset as they had been moments before.

Another announcement in Mandarin came from the speakers around the ship and a group of people started making their way toward the stairs leading down from the side of the ship.

*Ladies and gentlemen, we again apologize for this interruption, but we ask you to disembark from the ship and move to the cafeteria. We will serve food and drinks until we are assured everything is in order. Please follow the instructions of staff members.*

We had already moved to the middle of the ship, so I had a good view of the two guards when they came back on deck. The shorter one shook his head as he spoke into the microphone clipped onto his shoulder. Jason placed his hand on my lower back as we made our way to the side of the ship; the people in the crowd were shuffling slowly towards the exit due to the number of people trying to leave at the same time. The tingle at the base of my neck was back and I knew we were in danger. As I looked around to see where it was coming from, I saw a flicker of movement as part of the yardarm broke and started to fall. It was still attached to the mast by ropes and would hit a woman with a child strapped to her chest if I didn't move quickly.

With a mental shout to my companions, I raced towards the woman so I could push her out of the way of the deadly object weighing hundreds of pounds. Jason shouted my name, but I knew if I didn't get to the young mother in time, both she and her baby would be killed. Being careful not to use too much of my shifter strength and speed, I managed to reach them before the yardarm. Unfortunately, that left me directly in the path of the swinging hunk of wood and it hit me on my right arm and side.

It felt like I had been hit by that car from earlier in the day as my arm shattered and I was lifted off the deck by the momentum of the swinging yardarm. Before I could cry out in pain, I felt myself flying towards the side of the ship facing the river. Even though my arm had taken the brunt of the impact, I knew some of my ribs were broken and the pain was excruciating. As my body was flying across the width of the ship, I wondered whether I had enough height to fly over the side or would I hit the railing.

My body hit the railing, breaking my left hip into fragments, and then flipped over the top. My head slammed into the side of the ship and that final blow pushed me over the edge towards unconsciousness. The last thing I saw, before passing out, was water filling my vision as I fell towards the river below the ship.

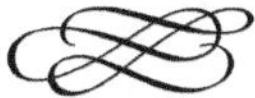

# CHAPTER 4

*July 30*

> *Fatorda*

> *Goa, India*

"Sir, we have a report from Malacca," the servant spoke from the doorway and waited until he was invited into the room.

"You may enter, Joki," rasped the man seated behind the desk.

Joki walked to the desk and bowed before continuing his report. "Two days ago, the alarms aboard the *Flor do Mar* replica were set off by persons unknown—"

"I know this already, Joki. If you don't have anything recent, you're wasting my time," he interrupted in irritation.

"Yes, sir. The guards concluded their investigations and none of the tourists showed any evidence that they had any items from the ship or had done anything to set off the alarms."

"What about that woman who was thrown overboard when she was struck by the yardarm?"

"Her body wasn't recovered and according to the accounts by eyewitnesses there isn't any way she could have survived that accident. The body was crushed before it fell overboard," Joki answered.

The man steepled his fingers and rested his chin in his hands as he leaned forward in thought. "Something tripped the alarms I had in place aboard that ship. It is unfortunate that the spells interfere with electronic surveillance so we don't have any video footage of what happened," he spoke to himself and didn't expect his servant to answer. "You are quite certain there wasn't anyone in the captain's cabin?"

"The guards are quite adamant that the cabin was empty when they entered the room, and no one entered after they did."

"Someone set off the alarms as well as the yardarm trap. You tell me that the woman who was killed—" he looked at Joki expectantly.

"Her name was Lynn Merrow," Joki replied and opened a folder to pull out a copy of an enlarged passport photo and handed it to his employer.

"This Lynn Merrow—wasn't the target of the trap but rather pushed the intended woman out of the way?"

"Correct," Joki answered, "the woman who Miss Merrow

pushed out of the way is called Maryam Nor and she is a resident of Malacca City. She claimed she was visiting the museum with her brother who lives in the country and wanted to see the ship."

"I assume you extended an invitation for this woman and her brother to join us here?" the man asked, raising one eyebrow in question.

"Yes sir, they arrived last night. We were very careful there were no witnesses to their abduction," Joki answered.

"Very well," the man answered as he stood and came around his desk. "I will question these two before deciding which one I will use now to replenish my life-force."

"The woman has a child," Joki added.

"Does she now?" the man previously known as Afonso de Albuquerque smiled evilly at his servant. "Then it looks like the brother will sacrifice his life for me and I'll save Miss Nor for later. After all, it would be a terrible thing to separate a mother and child," he chuckled darkly as he led the way out the door.

*Ow,* I groaned and tried opening my eyes, but my lids felt like anchors were tied to them. I could hear whale songs in the distance, so I knew I was underwater and I was in my mermaid form. My body ached all over and I began to panic when I couldn't move my arms or tail.

*You're safe, we're with you,* Jason's voice sounded in my mind and I felt his hand touch my face.

*What happened? Why can't I move?* I sent, still trying to open my eyes.

*We almost lost you,* Brian's voice sounded in my mind. *You can't move because I've got you wrapped in my tentacles; we were afraid you would hurt yourself before you're finished healing.*

*Oh, is that all?* I mentally mumbled. *Then I think I'll close my eyes—*

The next time I tried to open my eyes they popped right open, and I felt better. I was curled in a ball and lying on a bed of sea grass. I took a deep breath through my gills, the oxygen-rich water instantly giving me the energy I needed to uncurl my body and stretch. My stomach growled loudly, and I heard Jason's voice in my head.

*Of course, you'd wake up before I could get back with your breakfast,* he teased but as he swam into view, I could see the worry on his face.

*How bad was it?*

*Bad*—Jason began, then took a deep breath before he held out a bright-orange fish the size of a medium-sized dog he'd impaled on the claws of his right hand.

I grabbed the fish and opened my mouth wide enough to fit half of it inside then chomped down and chewed twice before swallowing it. The other half of the fish quickly followed and I was suddenly embarrassed by how I must look to Jason.

*Sorry,* I mumbled, *I'm hungry.*

Jason waved in front of my face to push aside the fish particles floating there, then kissed me gently. *Don't worry about it. I'm just glad you're okay.* He sighed again, *you were brave to push that woman out of the way but when you were hit by that section of the yardarm before I could do anything, my heart stopped. You flew through the air, hit the railing on the other side of the ship then slammed your head against the side. The only thing that saved your life was you fell into the river and must have shifted automatically.*

Before I could respond to Jason, I was wrapped in tentacles and wrenched violently backwards.

*Don't you ever worry me like that again,* Brian sent as he held me up in front of one of his enormous yellow eyes. The black rectangular pupil of his eye was narrowed in anger and worry. His skin pulsated through shades of blood-red and black further indicating his agitation.

*I'm sorry,* I sent as I bent forward and kissed his head, *I wasn't thinking about you when I was injured.*

*Really? Then what were you thinking?* he thundered in my mind.

*Mostly, "ow" and "that's going to leave a mark" and "I don't want to die" and finally "I really wanted to get married,"* I sent sarcastically. *Listen, you big softie, we both know I'll do the same thing again if I must. I couldn't let that woman and her baby get killed when I could do something about it.*

*I know,* Brian answered as he released me and settled on the ocean floor in a protective circle nearly sixty feet across.

*Please fill me in on what happened after I fell in the water,* I asked as I darted after a few of the large orange fish Jason had given me, and easily speared two of them on the tips of my claws. I caught a third with my mouth and made quick work of that one before swimming back where Jason and Brian were waiting. I offered one of the fish to Jason and ate the other. Near-death experiences always make me hungry.

*Immediately after you fell overboard, security guards wielding guns stormed the ship and separated us into two groups. Jason rushed to the side of the ship after you fell and the guards dragged him over to our group, after one of them hit him in the back of the head with the butt of his rifle,* Brian explained.

*I'm fine,* Jason assured me after I turned to face him, *in fact it didn't really hurt that much to begin with; I just had to keep up the appearance so they wouldn't know I'm not human.*

*Anyway,* Brian stirred, *once we explained what had happened to you and Jason was your fiancé, they allowed us to move to the railing to see if we could see your body, which we couldn't.*

*We were unable to sense your presence, and you didn't respond to our mental shouts,* Jason said with pain in his voice as he relived the memories.

Brian continued, *I was getting ready to jump over the side, no matter what anyone said, but a man appeared next to me and placed his hand on my arm and spoke to me. He radiated power and I was frozen in place along with everyone else on the ship.*

*"Peace, Protector," he said, "all is well. Cyndi is safe and already healing although you won't be able to find her for two days."*

*"Who are you?"*

*"You tell me," he smiled then winked one of his golden eyes and disappeared.*

*Who do you think it was?* I asked.

*An'Ceann,* Brian answered with conviction.

*But An'Ceann always appears as a lion,* Jason argued.

I shook my head, *An'Ceann usually appears as a lion but he can be anything he wants to be, especially on Earth. Besides, the 'you tell me' kind of gives it away. He does like his little jokes.*

*After that, time moved forward again, and I felt more at peace than I had in a long time. When I mentally explained what happened the rest of the members of our party relaxed.*

*Except me,* Jason interrupted, *if it really was An'Ceann why did he appear to Brian and not me? I wanted to believe you were okay, but I was too terrified that I'd lost you.*

My heart broke and I swam into Jason's arms and lay my head on his chest. We spent a few minutes mentally assuring one another that we were both safe and healthy. I reluctantly pulled away, but we stayed side-by-side with our arms around each other.

*Perhaps An'Ceann appeared to me because he knew you weren't in a place where you'd receive words of comfort from him?* Brian suggested kindly.

Jason nodded his agreement and Brian continued his story.

*Shortly after An'Ceann disappeared the police came aboard and took our statements. Even though Emergency Services arrived quickly, it was clear they didn't have a lot of hope in finding your body. The river currents in that area are very strong since the outlet to the ocean is so near. The police treated us with respect, but their demeanor also made it clear we shouldn't have much hope we would find you alive. Based on the eyewitness accounts of the accident with the yardarm, they were convinced you were probably dead before you ever hit the water.*

*Well, that sucks,* I added and squeezed Jason harder.

*There's not much to tell after that except the woman you saved, Maryam Nor, and her brother came over to where we were standing with the police to thank us for your sacrifice and to let us know she was sorry for our loss. We were released shortly after that but were told to stay at our hotel in case the police wanted to interview us again,* Brian finished.

*Once we were back at the hotel, we called Josef using the secure tablets and gave him a full report. He asked us to keep investigating so Hillaes, Yolanda and Carlos took the jet to*

*Tasmania when we received permission to leave the country, while Brian and I came to get you.*

*But how did you know where to find me?*

*When we woke up this morning, Brian and I both knew where to come. When we got here you were curled up in the grass on the ocean floor. We were only here for five minutes before you opened your eyes the first time.*

*That was enough time for you to cocoon me in your tentacles,* I sent to Brian.

*Sue me,* Brian grumped, *even though I believed An'Ceann when he told me you would be okay, I reacted when I saw what looked like your lifeless body.*

After untangling myself from Jason's embrace, I swam over to Brian's head and gave him as much of a hug as I could. It's kind of hard to get my arms wrapped around any part of his huge body.

*Well, as you can see, I'm fine so I suppose we should get on with our mission. Where are we supposed to go now?*

*August 3*
*Indian Ocean*
*250 Nautical Miles Southeast of Tasmania*

. . .

The deck of the *Salvage Marie* pitched in the swell of the stormy sea and I stood with my arms out and a smile on my face. While I loved the feel of the ship under my feet, the spray of the ocean on my face and the wind blowing through my hair, my companion on deck did not. In fact, she was losing what little breakfast she had in her stomach over the side of the ship we were on.

"This sucks," Hillaes complained as she wiped the back of her hand across her mouth to get rid of the evidence that she had been sick.

"Don't you mean, this blows, as in blowing chunks?" I teased and Hillaes gave me a look darker than the clouds above. "Sorry," I laughed, "I'm at home on the ocean, none of this bothers me. Let me see if I can help."

I walked over to the miserable woman and placed my cold hand on the back of her neck and softly sang to her. I could tell my singing was working by the way her face regained some of the color it had lost, and she took a shuddering breath.

"Thank you," she said. "I didn't have these problems when I sailed on the HMS *Beatrice* with Alister earlier this year."

"My guess is you didn't encounter any stormy weather either, did you?" I asked kindly.

"No, but we did have people trying to kill us," she countered and gave me a watery smile.

I linked my arm through hers and walked over to the section of the deck where one of the cannons from the *Flor do*

*Mar* was stored. After Jason and Brian found me, we swam back to what was left of the wreck on the ocean floor. One of my superpowers is the ability to pinpoint any area in the ocean I've been to before, making it easy for me to remember some of my favorite hunting spots.

Rex Industries bought a salvage company in Australia and part of their fleet was a one-hundred-and-sixty-foot boat that was formerly used for crab fishing in the Bering Sea. If it could survive the rough seas and harsh climate there, I was confident it would work for us in this part of the world. Once the *Salvage Marie* was in place, Brian, Jason and I brought one of the cannons from the *Flor do Mar* near the surface so it could be taken aboard. We had to be careful with it because now the cannon looked like it had been under the ocean for over five hundred years.

Once Hillaes used the cannon as part of her triangulation spell, Josef would announce the 'discovery' of the *Flor do Mar* and salvage the remaining treasure. We knew this would keep Afonso from being able to profit from any of the loot because there were already various countries claiming the treasure if it were ever found. I was going to keep the treasure I already recovered as my portion of the claim. Hillaes had high hopes that the spell would give us the exact location where we would find Afonso de Albuquerque.

"Are you ready for this?" I asked when Hillaes finally looked like she wasn't going to lose her lunch again.

"As ready as I'm going to be," she answered as she started

sketching runes on the cannon with a yellow grease pencil. First she drew four triangles, two upright and two upside down. She drew a line halfway through each one. I watched in fascination as she continued to draw more intricate symbols on the top of the cannon then repeated the same on all four sides. She was concentrating so intently on her work that she wasn't feeling the effects of the stormy sea any longer. I stood behind her to hold her in place while the deck moved beneath us. When she finished, she turned to look out at the raging sea and shuddered.

"What do these symbols mean?" I asked to keep her mind off the roiling ocean.

"Hmm?" she asked, then focused for a moment before answering my question. "The first four represent fire, water, air and earth, which form the basic elements to a searching spell. Those on the next line represent wood, gold, silver and iron, all things that were present on the replica and the original *Flor do Mar*. Finally, the last line represents man, both male and female, the hunter and the hunted, as well as wisdom, enlightenment and revelation. When I combine these runes with the incantation, the spell should reveal where we'll find our quarry."

"What do you need me to do?" I asked.

"Please give me the charm you retrieved from the ship then hold onto me while I concentrate. Since the concentration of magic on Earth isn't as great as my home dimension of Claw, I must use all of the magic I've stored internally along with the magic stored in this." She retrieved a necklace from under her shirt and showed it to me. Next to her thought medallion was a crystal attached to the necklace, pulsing softly with white light.

"King Alister gave you access to a pocket dimension and affixed it to your necklace, but he gave me this instead." At my questioning look she explained. "This is an arcane crystal from my home planet which can be used as a battery for magical energy. Even though the magical field on Earth is weaker than that on Claw, I'm still able to draw energy to fill up my personal magical reservoir and any excess I have, I'm able to place into this crystal. I'll need you to keep me grounded as I channel energy into the spell. I hope it won't happen but if I use too much, I might collapse, and I'll need you to keep me upright."

"I've got your back," I said to Hillaes with a warm smile. I was already impressed with the sorceress but my respect for her grew since she was willing to put herself into danger to help find the person responsible for so much death.

"When you're ready?" she asked and at my nod she turned towards the cannon and placed her hands above the writing on the top. I placed my hands at her waist and widened my stance, there wasn't any way I was going to let her fall to the deck of the ship, even if she fainted with the effort.

Hillaes began to speak softly and her hands glowed white. I couldn't make out the words, but I could tell her spell was having some effect when the runes on top of the cannon began to glow red. Since I was a few inches taller than Hillaes, I was able to look over her shoulder and saw when the runes on the right side of the cannon glowed blue. Even though I couldn't see the runes under the cannon, it was obvious when those were activated because a bright white light reflected off the deck. She was breathing heavier than before, and I could feel tremors throughout her body, but she didn't stop what she was doing until the runes on the left side of the cannon glowed green.

Hillaes took a deep, cleansing breath and reached into the leather satchel she had at her side, which I hadn't noticed until now. She held a piece of gold I had retrieved from the ship in her left hand and the block of wood holding the magical charm in her right. The tremors in her body were increasing and she started to sag, so I held her upright. Nodding her thanks, she continued with her incantation, holding the items in her hands out to the side, then raising her arms up in a slow half-circle until they were directly above her head. The wind savagely whipped Hillaes' hair and my face was stung by the wet strands as they lashed my face.

She slapped the items she held in her hands on the top of the cannon as she shouted the last words of her spell. There was a flash, then a streak of light shot northwest from our position. Hillaes' knees gave out then so I tightened my arms around to hold her in place.

"Thanks," she said in a weak voice, "that was tougher than I thought it would be."

"What do we do now?" I asked.

"We wait," Hillaes said.

"I hate waiting," I muttered and Hillaes laughed weakly.

"The directional spell has to travel to Afonso's location then come back to me. The length of time it takes will let us know how far away he is. That combined with the direction the spell is traveling will give us his location, within a twenty-mile radius or so."

Hillaes took a deep breath and straightened. She was standing on her own feet again, but I could tell she was still too weak for me to let her go. I sent a mental request for Jason to bring out something hot for Hillaes to eat and drink and by the time he came out she was able to make her way over to chairs that were bolted to the deck. I suggested we go inside to get out of the weather, but she told me she wanted to stay on deck so she would know exactly when the spell bounced back. Jason returned with a warm coat and blanket for Hillaes, but I told him I was fine and he went back inside.

"If I weren't magically drained, I could keep us warm and dry," Hillaes apologized.

"Don't worry about it," I waved a dismissive hand in her direction, "this is nothing compared to the water temperature where I usually swim. The cold and wet don't bother me."

We chatted about how we met our life-mates and bonded over our good fortune. Hillaes shared how she and Wu were attacked on their honeymoon when they went back to her home on Claw, and I told her how Jason and I met. She was fascinated with my mermaid business and the funny parties that didn't turn out the way I planned. She nearly fell off her chair when I told her how often I end up in pools as I try to take off my mermaid tail after a party; I really am quite clumsy on land. One of the greatest things I've learned in my life is to not take myself too seriously and laugh at things that are funny, even if it's at my own expense.

After two hours of waiting, Hillaes suddenly sat up in her chair and faced the direction where the spell shot off.

"What is it?" I asked, suddenly on alert as the back of my neck tingled.

"I'm not sure, something doesn't feel right," Hillaes said uncomfortably then her eyes widened in fear and she stood.

I looked where she was and saw a streak of red light closely following the white of the direction spell.

"We're under attack," Hillaes shouted in fear and I mentally repeated the warning to everyone else on the ship. The red light would hit the ship seconds after Hillaes received the information from the spell and I had a feeling we wouldn't like what happened when it did.

Hillaes waved her arms in an intricate pattern as she told me what she planned. "We need to know where Afonso is so I need to absorb the original spell, but I also need to put up a shield. I don't have enough energy to hold the shield for long, so this is going to be close," she said and I stood behind her to brace her for what was to come.

"What can I do?" I asked.

"Pray," Hillaes whispered as the white light of the direction spell hit her in the chest. The streak of red was only a hundred yards from the ship and closing fast when Hillaes held both hands toward the danger and shouted the word, *Spheara*. There was a flash of light then the ship was encased in a golden bubble. The destructive spell hit the shield a second after it was in place and exploded. Even though the shield stopped the spell from exploding on deck, the strain on the shield was too much for Hillaes and she collapsed, taking the shield with her. The explosive concussion washed across the deck and the ship was rocked back by the force of the blast.

The deck tilted hard to starboard and I found myself airborne, flying towards the raging sea with Hillaes in my arms. "Not again," I muttered and transformed into my mermaid form before I hit the water on my back to soften the landing for Hillaes. The shock of the freezing water was enough to jolt Hillaes awake, she instantly transformed and I found myself holding onto the back of a nine-foot tiger.

*Hillaes, are you okay?* I asked as I propelled us to the surface.

She growled in response so I let her go so she could swim on her own. Two bodies dove towards us and Jason swam next to me and put his arms around my waist, holding me up. Brian transformed and soon had one of his tentacles wrapped around Hillaes and was gently lifting her out of the water to place her on the deck of the still rocking ship. Jason and I were next, but

Brian told us he would go hunt for something to eat since he was already in the water and would rejoin us soon.

Jason and I transformed and were soon standing next to a tiger who was spitting mad. She was growling and screaming her rage in the direction the red spell came from, so it was probably a good thing she was still in her tiger form. Who knows what kind of names she was using to describe our adversary, but at that moment I was glad we couldn't understand her. One moment there was an enraged tiger pacing the deck and the next there was an incredibly angry, very wet woman standing there vibrating in her fury. Jason ran to get her another blanket while she fumed.

Once she calmed down, I wrapped the blanket around her shoulders and squeezed her comfortingly.

"We would have died if I hadn't gotten the shield up in time," Hillaes said through gritted teeth.

"But you did," I said and patted her shoulder. "You saved us, and now we know where to find this guy."

"Actually, we know more than that," Hillaes said as she turned to face me, concern written on her face.

"What's that?" I asked, curious what had spooked her so badly.

"We know that his magic is similar to mine so that means he came from Claw," she said stunned. "And if I'm correct about that, then we're chasing someone so evil parents on Claw still use his name to scare their children into doing what they want them to do."

"Well, doesn't that make this more fun?" I said sarcastically and looked in the same direction the bolt of death came from.

"He was called Akore the Butcher, and he was born on Claw over six-hundred years ago," Hillaes explained as we sat huddled around a table in the ship's galley drinking hot cocoa.

"Wait, was he called the Butcher because he was actually a butcher or because he killed people in horrible ways?" Brian asked. I turned my head to look at him and he held up his hands in defense. "Just trying to lighten the mood," he muttered.

"He was a sorcerer, proficient in the blackest magic who tortured and killed people to further his knowledge of the arcane arts." Hillaes shuddered and a haunted look darkened her face.

"Forgive me for asking, but do people on Claw usually live this long?" I asked.

Hillaes shook her head. "If someone on Claw lives to be a hundred years old, they are considered ancient. Akore's long life can't be attributed to natural means and neither can his power."

"So, how did someone from ancient Claw turn up on Earth?" King Alister asked from the video screen mounted on the wall. One of the first things Josef did when he purchased the ship was to have it outfitted with the latest technology developed by Rex Industries. This included a way for us to communicate with the King across dimensions. Since this was a conference call, Josef was on the screen, also.

"I'm not sure how he turned up on Earth but according to stories on Claw, the ruling council judged Akore for his crimes against the people and condemned him to death. The most powerful sorcerers and sorceresses stormed Akore's fortress to bring him to judgement and there was a great battle. Over half of those who were sent to confront Akore were killed in the fight and his fortress was destroyed. A severely burned body with Akore's magical signature was pulled from the rubble and it was assumed he'd been killed," Hillaes related.

"But if he was killed over five hundred years ago, how can you be sure it's really him?" I asked her.

"Because he was such a blight against the magical community on Claw, everyone who receives formal training has to learn about Akore and how he destroyed others. Part of the course is being exposed to his magical signature so we can become familiar with the way black magic affects the practitioner and taints everything they do. While I am very familiar with black magic in all its forms, there is no mistaking the stench of Akore's unique brand of evil.

"Before you ask, I did get hints of evil from the spells on the charm and the replica of the ship, but it wasn't until the missile spell broke against my shield that I was sure it was Akore."

"So that brings us back to the mystery of how he came to be on Earth," Alister repeated.

Josef offered a suggestion. "Sire, I suggest you ask your father to see if he can give us any insight on this. If I have the timeline correct, this Akore would have escaped to Earth shortly before your father ordered the dimensional gates closed to everyone but those of us in Tionchar. I was already working behind the scenes in the New World by that time but Akore could have slipped through any of the other gates across the planet." Josef paused in thought for a moment. "That's probably what he did since he changed his name to Afonso de Albuquerque and worked with the King of Portugal and won some amazing battles during his career," Josef explained.

"So, what did you learn from the directional spell?" Alister asked Hillaes.

"Quite a lot, actually," Hillaes brightened. "The spell traveled in a northwesterly direction from the ship and based on the energy contained in the spell when it returned to me it had made a round trip between ten to twelve-thousand miles."

"Can't you be a bit more specific?" Brian teased.

"If you'd like to help me work out the very complex mathematical and magical equations later, I can be as specific as you'd like." Hillaes scowled at Brian.

"Never mind," he grinned. "Between ten-thousand to twelve-thousand works for me."

"You're almost as bad as Shelley," Alister said to Brian who just laughed.

"If I may continue," Hillaes huffed, "I'll need to do some calculations with a map, but I should be able to give us a smaller search pattern within the next day or so."

"Thank you Hillaes, I'm grateful you're on this mission," Josef added.

Hillaes blushed at the attention but squared her shoulders to continue. "I'd be surprised if Akore is still at his hideout when we arrive. Even if he doesn't know I'm a fellow practitioner from Claw, he will know he is dealing with someone powerful. Perhaps he believes his missile destroyed us, but we can't rely on that being the case. We must be careful when we finally confront him, even though he's not as powerful on Earth as he was on Claw, he's had centuries to perfect his craft."

"So where do we go from here?" I asked.

"May I, Sire?" Josef asked and at Alister's nod, he continued. "Cyndi, you and Jason should swim back to Melbourne while Brian travels with the rest of the team on the *Salvage Marie*. That way you can pick up another artifact from the shipwreck in case we need it and meet the team in Australia when they arrive in about eighteen hours. By that point, Hillaes might have a better location for us to begin a ground search for Akore. Based on the probable miles and direction of the spell, we'll be searching in India. That's a large area, so anything to help us to narrow our search will be welcome.

"Your team is still running point on this operation but I'm also going to call in Raksaka Gupta to join you when you get a pinpoint on the location. He's a naga shapeshifter and will be able to scout out a location in his serpent form before you travel there."

Josef shifted his attention to King Alister. "Sire, I'd like you to have a discussion with your father to see if he knows anything about Akore. Meanwhile, I'll comb through the Tionchar archives for that period to see if there is anything relevant to our current situation. If there aren't any objections, we'll reconvene here when the *Salvage Marie* arrives in Melbourne."

We said our goodbyes and ended the call.

"C'mon, Sorceress Supreme, let's see if I can help you with some of your calculations," Brian said as he got up from the table. At Hillaes' curious look he laughed, "You may not believe this, but I actually have PhDs in Marine Biology, Astrophysics and Spherical Trigonometry. I know I've got a pretty face, but I've also got some brains, too," he drawled in his best Elvis impression.

Hillaes just shook her head and got up from the table.

"Jason and I are going to swim back to the site of the wreck and pick up a few more items from the ship; hopefully we'll be able to use them for another location spell if we need to since the cannon disintegrated when you finished the last one," I announced as Jason took my hand to lead me back out on deck.

"Be good you two," Brian chuckled, and I turned around to give him a death glare. Unfortunately, I wasn't watching where I was going and rammed my right shoulder into the side of the doorway. "That's going to leave a mark," I grumped as I let go of Jason's hand and rubbed the sore spot.

Brian's belly laugh was the last thing I heard as I walked out the door.

*ugust 4*
*Salvage Australia Office Complex*
*Melbourne, Australia*

e sat around a large conference table piled high with take-out containers and coffee cups from The Hardware Société, a popular Melbourne eatery within walking distance of the salvage business Rex Industries purchased. Even though Jason, Brian and I slept on the ocean floor off the coast of Australia, Hillaes, Yoli and Carlos were bleary-eyed and looked like they hadn't slept much on the trip back. We'd been eating and discussing what we had learned since our meeting yesterday. Alister and Josef had joined us via teleconference again and there were two others on the screen as well, Aileene and Alister's father, Phillip. As I stared at the former High King on the screen I thought about how much had changed in the last fifteen years.

Alister's parents, the former High King and Queen of Theria, had been betrayed by one of their closest friends, who had been a member of their Inner Circle, and it was presumed they were killed when Alister was only five. Their apparent deaths triggered shield spells around the Royal Palace, and the entire Kingdom of Theria, but some of us were able to escape through a dimensional gate into Claw before the shield was placed. Even as a child, Alister was powerful and able to open a dimensional gate from Claw to Earth, where we were exiled. Alister spent the next thirteen years on Earth, all memories of his time on Theria suppressed along with his ability to transform into a Royal Dragon.

It was only when Alister began his thirteenth year on Earth that his powers returned. Alister, Bernie and Shelley, along with their mentor, Gustav, traveled from Earth to Claw where each of them discovered their shifter forms and found their true heritage. Alister successfully defeated the betrayer and healed his parents, who were near death in a poison-induced coma. Once his parents recovered their strength, Alister asked them to rule the Kingdom of Sirenea.

Phillip had a somber look on his face as he spoke, "It seems that I must once again apologize that others are having to deal with issues I didn't take care of when I was High King."

"Father," Alister said kindly, "we've had this discussion about not being able to change the past—"

"Son, as you already know, a good leader gives away the credit when his people succeed and shoulders the responsibility when things are difficult. I appreciate your faith in me, but as I've looked back on the records from when Akore escaped to Earth, I didn't instruct Tionchar to investigate his apparent death. It was a mistake assuming we had seen the last of his evil."

"Father, what can you tell us that can help find Akore?" Aileene asked.

"Not much more than what Hillaes has already shared with you, except there were reports of a plague killing hundreds of people in West India around the same time Akore would have come to Earth. This was at the height of the Age of Exploration on Earth and the Tionchar operatives were helping humans discover new routes for travel and trade."

"Father, while this is fascinating history, how does this help us?" Alister asked.

"I'm getting into too many details, aren't I?" Phillip asked. We all nodded so he continued. "The bottom line, our operatives were stretched too thin to look into those deaths right away. It was assumed they had been killed by a local plague and the report was buried; I don't remember seeing anything about it at the time, but that was over five hundred years ago."

"That aligns with what Brian and I discovered. We traced the route of the direction spell and it passed through the West Coast of India in a place called Goa," Hillaes added.

"That makes sense with the history of Afonso de Albuquerque," Josef said. "He was instrumental in conquering that part of India for the King of Portugal and was given land in that area as a reward for his service. It's a wonder he's stayed out of sight for this long but if his base is in Goa, he's had centuries to gather the kind of magical power you faced on the *Salvage Marie*."

"Then let's head to Goa and roast a black magic sorcerer," Aileene grinned, her eyes dancing with dragon's fire while a curl of smoke escaped her left nostril.

"I'm sorry, but neither you nor King Alister can come on this mission," Josef said firmly.

"Excuse me," Aileene growled, her voice growing deeper as her anger grew.

Alister sighed and placed his arm around the shoulders of his frustrated fiancée. "Josef is correct, we have a wedding and coronation to plan and cannot leave Theria at this time."

"But it wouldn't take us long. You just open a gate, we fly through, find Akore and kill him. It will be easy, and fun," she said brightly.

"You're getting bored with all the wedding preparation, aren't you?" Alister laughed.

"Fritz and Frieda are killing me with all the protocols they want me to follow," Aileene groaned. "C'mon, your father can marry us right now and we can go to Earth for our honeymoon and kill the bad guy," Aileene wheedled.

Before Alister could counter Aileene's argument, another screen popped up on the monitor and a deep voice came from the screen, "peace daughter."

We all stilled as the frame was filled with the face and mane of an enormous lion. Light scattered from his mane as he moved his head and his fathomless golden eyes were filled with love, compassion and resolve as he stared through the screen. I felt like he was looking directly into my innermost self and that there wasn't anyone else in the universe except for An'Ceann and me. His chuckle was a deep, rumbling purr which resonated through my entire being.

"Dearest dragon, and daughter of my heart," An'Ceann said to Aileene, "this battle isn't yours to fight; it belongs to others."

"Yes, An'Ceann," Aileene said meekly and looked down.

He laughed suddenly and it was like sunshine breaking through the clouds after the rain, I felt lighter and by the expressions on the faces of everyone else, they felt the same. "Aileene, I have given you a fighting spirit and your desire to right wrongs is a credit to who you are. You just need to learn that others also have to fight evil where they find it; it's not always for you to do."

"I understand," Aileene said.

"Besides," An'Ceann continued, "you have your own battle coming your way soon."

Aileene's eyes brightened suddenly as she sat up straighter, "I do?" she asked in a hopeful voice.

"Yes," An'Ceann nodded his head, golden light streaming from his mane, "you must decide between the five dresses Frieda is bringing to your chamber. One of those will be your wedding dress," he said with a mischievous smile as his image faded from the screen.

Aileene looked so forlorn at his announcement we did the only thing we could in this situation; we laughed.

*Be strong. This is your battle to fight but you aren't alone,* An'Ceann's voice sounded in my head and I couldn't help wondering what was waiting for us in Goa.

*A*ugust 5
            *Goa, India*
*Akore's Compound*

*T*he smoking ruins of what was once a magnificent house greeted us when we drove into the compound on the west coast of India. The grounds were beautifully maintained and the statuary, fountains and well-tended garden spoke of great wealth. The front of the house faced a pristine stretch of beach and there were three pleasure craft moored to the dock jetting into the water. Hillaes and her husband Wu were in their tiger forms, patrolling the dense jungle bordering the rear of the property to make sure Akore wasn't anywhere nearby.

Jason stopped the car and we stood, looking around at the devastation. The calming crash of waves on the shore and the tinkling of water cascading from a fountain did little to minimize the rage I felt as I saw the bodies littering the grounds of the wrecked house. My knees gave out and I wept when I recognized the woman and child I had rescued in Malacca lying with the others. While I grieved for all the tragedy on display, I felt a connection with the woman I had sacrificed so much to save.

Jason gently lifted me from the ground and murmured words of comfort in my ear until I regained my composure. I wiped my eyes and counted the bodies; there were thirty-five victims on the ground, their faces frozen in the fear and pain they experienced before their deaths.

I knelt and placed my hand over the unseeing eyes of the dead woman and gently closed her eyelids. "I don't care what it takes, Akore will pay for his crimes," I vowed to the poor people whose lives were destroyed to give power to a monster who should have died centuries before.

# CHAPTER 5

*thas 14, 10,258*
*Theria*

*Royal Palace*

The ballroom was festooned with decorations befitting a double celebration of a wedding and coronation. The Royal Palace of Theria reminded me of Cinderella's Castle at Disneyland, except it was full-sized and thousands of years old. Like most of the buildings in Theria, the palace was a blend of ancient architecture and cutting-edge technology. There were video screens covering two of the walls showing highlights of the ceremonies, also video messages from well-wishers who couldn't attend.

The royal standard, a crimson dragon in flight against a green background, was in full display on the walls and ceiling, but so was the standard from Eutheria. The golden drake on a red background complemented the royal standard perfectly and I thought it suited the Royal Couple. While it wasn't usual for another standard to be displayed alongside the royal one, it was perfect for the High King and Queen. Aileene had fostered under Lord Moss in Eutheria and honored him and his house by displaying his standard. She even asked him to walk her down the aisle to give her away.

The wedding ceremony was beautiful and Aileene was resplendent in the mermaid gown she had chosen to wear; personally, it's my favorite style of dress. The gown was beaded with diamonds, sapphires that matched the color of her eyes and arcane crystals from Claw. Alister had enchanted the crystals to flash to the music being played so she was her own light show. Of course, a six-foot-three gorgeous woman with auburn hair pinned up in a chignon doesn't need her own light show to stand out.

As I caught my breath from dancing with Jason, I tried not to think about the death and destruction Akore had wrought on Earth. It took us three days to comb through the ruins of his compound to find any clue to where he had gone. Even though we couldn't find him, we did find the thousands of corpses he had left behind. There were graves all over the property and we were able to estimate that he had been killing one person a month to keep himself alive—for hundreds of years.

The local police force concluded that Akore was the leader of a cult that used humans as sacrifices, and he had escaped to places unknown. They were willing to close the case to put such 'tragic business behind us,' but Josef had other ideas. He used the power and influence of Rex Industries to bring in a team of investigators from the nation's capital and took over the investigation from the regional police force. Even though Akore had been paying off the local government to turn a blind eye to his activities; the leaders of the Crime Investigation Department in New Delhi could not be swayed to look the other way. It helped that one of the lead investigators, Ishka Patel, was a member of Tionchar and well respected.

Both Raksaka Gupta and Ishka Patel were naga shifters and well versed in investigative techniques. While they worked within the constraints of the law, they weren't adverse to completing a thorough search of each local politician's home looking for any way of tracking Akore's movement. Since they both could shift into serpents, and this part of India had serpents aplenty, they could enter places almost unnoticed. Their investigation uncovered a trail of corruption that weaved its way through almost every office of the local government and had been going on for decades.

Once the evidence was gathered and the officials confronted, there was a storm of laying blame and accusations as the criminal enterprise fell apart and arrests were made. New Delhi sent more investigators to the area and discovered there were hundreds of missing persons' reports which had been ignored for years. After seven days of investigation, they uncovered a ring of slavers who would kidnap young people from the poorest regions of India and transfer them to Goa; either to work at the compound or get shipped to other countries around the world. The fates of those who left India were unknown, but those who found themselves at the compound met certain death.

Akore held the top spot of Most Wanted Criminal for India as well as the Red List for INTERPOL. Hillaes was able to create an artist's rendering of Akore using magic and his likeness was sent to law enforcement agencies in India, Asia and other countries in this part of the world. Unfortunately, it would take time to find him.

"You look deep in thought and not at all happy with what you're thinking about," Aileene said with a smile, startling me out of my reverie.

"I'm so sorry," I apologized and stood rapidly, hitting the table with my hip so hard it knocked over the glasses sitting on top while at the same time tipping back my chair so quickly it tripped a passing waiter who dropped the tray he'd been carrying, which fell with a clatter.

"Oops," I said and tried to rush over to help the waiter but only succeeded in tripping over my own feet and would have face-planted on the floor if Alister hadn't caught me.

Aileene helped the waiter stand while Shelley righted my chair with a grin, "It's good to see you Cyndi, still as graceful as ever," he teased.

I just shook my head and laughed. It didn't do any good to

get embarrassed because anyone who really knew me, understood I was usually an accident waiting to happen.

"My guess is you were thinking about Akore and the mess on Earth," Alister probed. He looked amazing in his royal raiment of crimson, gold and green, although he was only wearing a circlet of gold instead of the Royal Crown his father had placed on his head during his coronation.

"I just hate the fact that he's disappeared, and we can't seem to locate him by either magical or mundane means," I responded.

Alister placed his hand on my shoulder in comfort. "I know and Aileene and I both appreciate you were willing to pause your investigation long enough to come to join us on our special day."

"I wouldn't have missed it for the world. I love you guys," I gushed.

"We love you, too," Aileene said as she grabbed me in a hug. "You were there for us after Gustav was killed and we can never repay you for that."

"There's nothing to repay," I answered. "For one thing, you are my King and Queen, and I have sworn my allegiance to you both. But you are also my friends, and if I may be so bold, I love you like family," I said as I hugged her back.

Alister hugged me, too, then Shelley jumped in so he could get his turn.

I laughed when I heard Jason come back to the table and say, "hey, Shelley you've got your own girl, leave mine alone." We laughed as friends do when they are comfortable with each other.

"I know I'm opening a gate to send you back to Earth tomorrow but for tonight I really want you to try to enjoy yourself. Aileene and I need to make the rounds and visit each of the visiting rulers and dignitaries from the other kingdoms of Theria so someone should have a good time," Alister grumped then smiled after Aileene poked him in the side.

Jason put his arm around my waist as Shelley led the procession and they walked away, the crowd parting so they could pass. I waved at Bernie and Mkali as they followed behind Alister and Aileene, Mkali giving me a cheeky grin. She loved being Bernie's squire and was usually so serious, it was nice to see her having fun. Both Aileene and Alister were so tall it was easy to watch them walk through the throng of people wishing them well. They were an amazing couple and would be just the High King and Queen we needed for Theria. I was honored they considered me a friend and part of their extended family.

"Cake by the Ocean" by DNCE started playing so Jason led me back onto the dance floor. Since Alister had spent thirteen years on Earth, there were a lot of songs from there, along with songs from Theria playing at the reception. I loved dancing and other than when I was in the ocean, it was the only other time I felt graceful on my feet. We danced for hours, only stopping when Alister and Aileene left the reception. They wouldn't tell anyone where they were going on their honeymoon the day after tomorrow, but Bernie and Shelley were traveling with them as their Knights, along with another twenty guards to accompany them as bodyguards, so it may not be such a mystery.

Once the happy couple left, the party wound down and we headed to the suite I had in the palace when I lived here fifteen years before. At that time, I spent most of my time at the nearby lake, and it was there I taught Alister, Bernie and Shelley to swim when they were little. Even though their memories were blocked for thirteen years, I always remembered them and was excited when I was finally reunited with them last year.

When we entered, Brian and another man were sitting on the couch laughing together. By the easy way they sat together, it was obvious they were old friends. Of course, Brian was staying in the suite with us as our chaperone. While it may not be popular on Earth for engaged couples to be chaperoned before they get married, it was part of Therian culture and something both Jason and I asked Brian to do for us on Earth.

"Hey Fry," Brian said as he stood, "I want to introduce you to my friend Josh, he's the ruler of Carnivoria." Brian swept his hand at the other man who also stood.

He was almost eight feet tall and had short blond hair. It was evident by his tanned skin that he spent a lot of time in the sun and the laugh lines around his blue eyes made me like him immediately. His open-necked shirt was tight across his chest and arms, evidence of his muscular frame under his clothes.

"Lord Vifaru," I curtsied as Jason bowed at the waist.

"Please just call me Josh when we're in private," he smiled and the twinkle in his eye let me know it would be easy to be friends with this man. He held out his hand to shake and I went first, followed by Jason.

"I'd love to hear how you came to know this reprobate," I said to Josh as we sat on the opposite couch.

"I was an exchange student in Cetacea in my final year of Shapeshifter Academy and we were roommates," Josh explained.

"That's not much of a story," I complained when Josh stopped talking.

He shrugged, "Brian wasn't really happy I was his roommate because I was from Carnivoria and he thought he was better than me because I was a land-based shifter while almost everyone else at school was sea-based of some sort."

"You've got to admit, a rhinoceros has some disadvantages in the water," Brian laughed.

"No doubt, but a kraken has even more limits on land," Josh answered with a grin and it was obvious this was an old argument.

"We faced some obstacles and went on some adventures together that made us appreciate our strengths and weaknesses and became friends. We've kept in contact all these years, but rarely get a chance to see each other in person." Brian smiled.

"As much as I'd like to hear your war stories, I've got to get some sleep," I said with a yawn. I kissed Jason goodnight, said goodbye to Josh and Brian, then headed to my room, shedding my dress as I walked to the bathroom to get ready.

*athas 15, 10,258*
*Theria*

*Royal Palace*

Jason and I lay on the shore of the lake, our tails submerged in the water. When I'm partially shifted like this, with only my lower body in mermaid form, I can breathe with my lungs and speak normally. The lake stretched outward from the palace for miles in every direction and I knew from experience it was over four hundred feet at its deepest point. The clear water of the lake reflected trees along the shore and right now, the surface was as smooth as a mirror. The shoreline where we lay gently sloped into the deeper parts of the lake so the water in this area was warm enough to swim in; this is where I taught the children.

My hands were behind my head as I watched the fluffy-white clouds drift across the blue sky, and I listened to the water nymphs playing nearby. They kept calling for us to join them again, but since we wanted to lay in the sun, I mentally told them to go away but we would join them later. They left us alone, but not before splashing us as they giggled and swam away to find others to play with. Even though I knew we would be returning to Earth tonight to continue the hunt for Akore, I was at peace.

"What are you thinking about?" Jason asked.

I turned my head towards him and smiled, "you know it's dangerous to ask a woman what she's thinking about unless you really want the answer."

Jason laughed, "I really want to know."

I turned on my side, propped my head up on my hand and smoothed my other hand along the side of his face, feeling the rasp of his whiskers on my palm. I leaned forward to kiss him quickly and smiled when he leaned forward for more.

"Do you miss living on Theria?" I asked. "We both had to adapt to life on Earth when we were trapped there, but at least you lived here for nine months before returning to Earth."

Jason thought for a moment before answering, "Not really because I get to be with you." He put his finger on my lips before I could say what I was going to. "I'm not just saying this to make you feel good, it's how I feel. Two years ago, if you would have asked me if I would ever give up being a sasquatch, I would have told you there was no way I would ever do that, but then I met you. I knew you were my future and if I wanted us to be together then I would use my final transformation to become a merman so we could get married one day."

"Which is exactly two months from today," I added, moving closer to Jason.

"I can't wait," he said and kissed me again. "But it's the same way I feel about living on Earth. As members of Tionchar, we have an opportunity to make a huge difference on the planet we called home for so long. Theria has its own set of problems, like the rebellion King Alister had to put down a few months ago, but we aren't needed here as much as we're needed there. Even though there are people on Earth more evil than Akore, they don't have the magic he does and the humans don't have the ability to combat his powers.

"We'll serve on Earth for another twenty years, then come back here to live the rest of our lives together. An'Ceann willing, we'll have centuries to enjoy our home planet; but I really don't care where we end up as long as we're together," he finished with a grin.

"May I join you?" my mother asked as she stepped into view.

Jason and I were startled into silence by her sudden appearance, but Jason shifted into his human form and stood, the magic of his thought medallion clothing him in the Captain America swimsuit I bought him.

"Lady Zhaleh," Jason said coldly as he bowed to her. I was watching closely to see how she would react, or I would have missed the flash of pain that came over her face before she bowed her head in acknowledgment.

"I deserve that," she said as she gently placed her hand on his arm. "Jason, I humbly ask your forgiveness for the way I treated you by arranging the dinner between Cynthia,

Tetraodon and myself. I insulted you and my daughter and for that I am truly sorry."

Jason's face was passive as he digested her words then nodded. "Lady Zhaleh, I will leave you and Cyndi alone because while I appreciate your apology, I'm not really the one you need to make amends with. I love your daughter and she loves me and we're going to make a life together with or without your blessing. While we don't need your approval, I know Cyndi's heart breaks because of the way you treat her. Don't waste this time," Jason said, then bent down, kissed the top of my head and walked towards the palace.

I turned back to stare out at the lake while my mom settled down next to me and shifted her lower body into her mermaid form. We shared the same iridescent vermillion green, deep purple and cobalt scales on our tails and flukes, but the bright-orange color and shape of my ventral fins came from my dad.

After sitting in silence for what felt like an eternity, Mom finally began to speak. "My father wanted a boy and the only thing I ever wanted was to make him proud of me. He was cruel to me with his silences and indifference. I never understood what I had done to make him resent me so much and after years of trying to please him, I stopped consciously trying to gain his approval. My mom was wonderful, kind, loving and everything that my father wasn't but it wasn't until after she was gone that I really began to appreciate how much she gave up to give me a wonderful childhood.

"When I was old enough to enroll at the Shapeshifter

Academy in Cetacea, my mother sent me to live at the school and would visit me during the breaks rather than have me come back home. My father never visited, but I was fine with that. I met your father my final year in school when he was transferred from the Royal Shapeshifter Academy where he had been learning what he needed to know to one day rule Cetacea.

"That final year was the best of my life up to that point because I met your dad, developed deep friendships with Brian and his roommate at the time and started to break free from the chains of my past that had weighed me down. Unfortunately, it was towards the end of that year that my mother died, and my world was rocked."

There was so much pain and sadness in my mom's voice that I scooted closer to her and put my arm around her in comfort. She stiffened in shock for a second then relaxed into my embrace, but I still didn't say anything because I knew she wasn't finished sharing her story.

"Your dad knew how devastated I was and didn't want me to have to go home to live alone with my father, so he asked me to marry him. Even though we had a deep friendship, we didn't start off with the love that you and Jason evidently have; that developed over time. We made a life together and we respected each other. The day you were born, I couldn't believe how perfect you were, and your dad and I wanted to share you with the world to show you off. I even reached out to my father and invited him to meet his granddaughter.

"On the day you were to be presented to the kingdom, a messenger from my father arrived to deliver his condolences that I had borne a daughter to the ruler of Cetacea rather than a son who could be the legitimate heir. When I heard the message from my father, I looked down at your beautiful face and wept because I was suddenly afraid that I would hurt you the same way my father hurt me. I handed you to your dad and left the room. Something broke in me that day and I decided the only way to not become my father would be to keep a wall between us so I wouldn't hurt you and to let your dad be the one to give you the love I was afraid to."

"That doesn't make any sense," I protested as I turned to look at my mom.

"I know, and it wasn't something I realized until Muir pointed out that I had turned into my father and I needed to make things right with you. I told him I had done too much damage, but he encouraged me to talk with you anyway. When you left last month, I reached out to King Alister and asked for his help. He sent a unicorn shifter to Cetacea who had worked as a psychiatrist on Earth during the exile. She's been working with me to help me become the person I always should have been." Already softly crying during her lengthy explanation, Mom burst into heavy sobs for a moment before gradually regaining control.

I was shocked by her revelations; I had never seen her like this before. She had always been the epitome of strength but sitting next to me was a woman wracked with sorrow and guilt. If she had come to me in her typical cold fashion, I wouldn't have believed a word she said but I could tell she was being sincere. Even if I didn't fully understand her reasoning for putting up this wall between us, I recognized she wanted to start tearing it down so we could have a different relationship in the future.

We sat together for hours and talked about the things we had missed over the past hundred years. When she asked me about my life on Earth, I really believed she wanted something different for us. She actually laughed when I told her about my party business and how I would dress up as a mermaid for children's parties. She told me about her relationship with Muir and how they quietly got married over thirty years ago but had kept that secret until recently when she acknowledged him as her Consort.

Jason joined us to let us know it was almost time for Alister to open a gate for us so we could go back to Earth. He was surprised when mom hugged him tightly, after she had shifted back to her human form, and sincerely thanked him for taking such good care of me.

After embracing me, she held me at arm's length and smiled. "I am proud of the woman you are and grateful you are willing to give us another chance. There's nothing I can do to give us back the years I wasted, but I will do my best to make the time we have left together something we both consider precious. I love you, Cyndi and I don't ever want to do anything that will make you doubt that, ever again."

She kissed me on the cheek. We were both crying when Jason put his arm around me, and we walked towards the palace so we could finish the mission we had started on Earth.

*August 20*
*Cape Town, South Africa*
*Port of Cape Town*

"Are you here for business or pleasure?" Department of Home Affairs Officer Booysen asked as she looked at the man standing in front of her and studied his passport.

"A little bit of both," he smiled, concentrating to make sure his disguise spell matched the picture on the documents he had given her.

"And you traveled here on the vessel *Khipius* from Mumbai?" she asked as she glanced at his paperwork on the counter in front of her.

"That is correct," he said as he willed her to pass him through customs.

"You are the only passenger listed on the manifest, Mr. Acharya. Isn't that unusual?" she persisted.

"Not necessarily, Officer Booysen. I happen to enjoy traveling by sea and since I own the boat, I can choose whether I want traveling companions. This time I did not. I used the fortnight it took for us to travel here for meditation. It does wonders for the mind, body and spirit." He smiled again, trying to keep his temper in check. "Is there an issue with me traveling alone, except for the crew, of course?"

Instead of answering his question, she slid a laminated sheet of paper through the gap in the bottom of the security gate and asked, "Have you seen this man?"

He looked down at the artist rendering and saw his natural face staring back at him. He had to admit it was a very good likeness. "May I?" he asked and at her nod, he picked up the sketch to look more closely. After taking the amount of time he felt necessary to study the image, he shook his head.

"I'm sorry, I've never seen him before. I assume he is a criminal of some sort?" he asked as he slid the sketch back to the woman in the security booth.

"Yes," Officer Booysen answered as she eyed him suspiciously. She pursed her lips and appeared to make up her mind as her demeanor changed and she stamped his passport and placed his paperwork inside the book before handing it back to him with a smile. "Welcome to South Africa Mr. Acharya, enjoy your stay."

Akore thanked the woman, placed his passport back in his briefcase then walked away with his attaché in one hand and the handle of his suitcase in the other. He didn't hurry through the passenger terminal, but he could feel the magical energy draining from the small arcane crystal attached to the leather thong he had tied around his neck. The crystal was supplying the power for his disguise spell and once the magical energy was gone, his disguise would drop; then one of the many extra guards present in the terminal would attempt to arrest him and that would interfere with his plans.

He finally made it out the front door and saw the driver holding a sign with the name Ramesh Acharya printed on it. He was standing outside a Range Rover with blacked-out windows and turned to open the back door after Akore nodded to indicate he was the person the driver was waiting for. He left his suitcase for the driver to deal with and dropped his disguise spell the instant the door was closed. He mopped his brow with a handkerchief to remove the perspiration he knew came from adrenaline rather than the temperature since it was only twelve degrees Celsius outside.

While the driver put his suitcase in the back of the Range Rover, Akore pulled another necklace with a larger arcane crystal from his briefcase and placed it around his neck. There were only five more fully-charged crystals in his briefcase and it would take a full week to charge those that had already been depleted. He was annoyed that he had to flee his compound in Goa but if there were a sorceress on his trail, he couldn't take the chance of discovery without more magical energy at his disposal. Unfortunately, the larger arcane crystals he brought with him from Claw were destroyed in Goa when the missile spell was launched to follow the discovery spell back to its originator; but he did gain the information that he was facing a sorceress from Claw.

He had enough magical energy to drain the lives from the people at the compound and destroy it before escaping on the

*Khipius.* The driver got back into the vehicle and smoothly pulled away from the terminal. He already had information on where he was to take his passenger and knew not to engage him in conversation of any kind. As tempting as it was to steal his life-force, Akore refrained because he needed the driver to transport him until he could access one of the vehicles at his home.

Besides, he still had the energy he took from Joki on the way to Cape Town. Akore was irritated that he would need to take care of the household duties until he could find a replacement for his efficient servant, but the voyage took longer than anticipated. Ever since the charm on the *Flor do Mar* was disrupted, he had to absorb energy more frequently just to maintain balance. Instead of once a month, his continued existence required taking a life every fortnight. No matter, soon he would have the arcane crystals he buried on top of Table Mountain over five hundred years before when he escaped from Claw, and he would regain his former power. And with over a million desperate people living in shanty towns nearby, he would have energy resources for centuries to come.

*August 27*
*Newport Beach, California*

As I drove down the highway with the top down of my

1969 VW convertible, I thought about our inability to find Akore, or whatever he was calling himself now, and how frustrating that was. Hillaes continued working her magic spells but the results returned negative each time. INTERPOL and the investigative arm of Rex Industries were working together to seize Akore's assets but since he had over five hundred years to establish his wealth, this turned out to be a monumental task. Josef confided that one of the hardest things they faced was working with a human agency without revealing the existence of magic, shapeshifters and other dimensions.

Jason, Brian and I returned home after spending another ten days in India, working with Hillaes on magical solutions. Before we left for Alister and Aileene's wedding, Hillaes discovered the remains of the arcane crystals Akore installed to defend his compound. Even though they were shattered and no longer able to hold a magical charge, Hillaes was able to get an impression of the spells contained within. While the rest of us spent time at the palace before and after the wedding, Hillaes and Wu used the time researching everything they could about Akore and ancient magic used on Claw.

Since Alister was the only one who could create gates between dimensions, and he was unavailable to do so while he was on his honeymoon, Hillaes gathered the magical items she needed from Claw before returning to Earth. When she arrived at the palace, I smiled to myself, because she reminded me of a returning Hogwarts student with her trunks, spell books and bags full of arcane crystals.

"Where's your broom?" I snickered.

"Where are your shells?" she shot back with a grin.

Everyone laughed. I guess she got tired of the stereotypes about magic users the same way I got tired of those about mermaids. I mean really, whoever thought swimming around with a bikini top made from shells sounded like a good thing? Not only would that be uncomfortable, but it would also rip off the first time I got up to speed underwater. However, I guess a certain company that specialized in entertainment for kids couldn't really make an animated movie about a mermaid swimming without her top on; that might cause some problems.

Even though we didn't know Akore's location, yet, we learned a lot from the spells Hillaes cast at his ruined compound. The magic available on Claw was easier to tap into than the magic on Earth. Not only was the amount of magic available on Earth less than Claw, it wasn't as potent; apparently it had to do with the amount of steel and iron humans used to build their civilization. Akore needed the arcane crystals to store the magic it took him decades to gather. With the destruction of the crystals at his compound, his magical power was greatly lessened.

This didn't mean we were taking his abilities lightly; he did create a missile-like spell that traveled thousands of miles that would have destroyed us if Hillaes hadn't raised her shield. Hillaes was tremendously powerful in her own right and she had worked with King Alister to expand her magical reservoir, but she still had to deal with the lack of magic on Earth, the same way Akore did.

But we had one advantage he didn't, Hillaes brought hundreds of arcane crystals with her from Claw which she and King Alister had charged in the days before the wedding. These fully-charged crystals were protected by the best spells Hillaes and Alister could come up with and now she had a vast reservoir of power at her disposal to combat Akore.

We also learned that while the charm I'd taken from the *Flor do Mar* could give us a general direction towards Akore, the last time we removed it from the pocket dimension on Earth, it linked with Akore's charm and infused him with magic before I could store it again. We both decided I'd keep it in my pocket dimension and only remove it as a last resort because none of us wanted to face Akore at full power. We would find him, but it might take us longer than we hoped. Josef had all the members of Tionchar searching for any news but sent us home for a week so I could work on the wedding. He really is a big softy, even if he is a gargoyle when he shifts and looks like 'The Rock' in his human form.

I pulled into the Pavilions Market on 32nd Street and Balboa Avenue and popped the latch on the hood so I could grab the recyclable bags. It was a minor inconvenience to remember to bring them into the store each time but anything I could do to keep more trash out of the ocean was fine by me.

Besides, Nick always had use for the bags after I gave them to him. It was so good to be back in the city I'd adopted as my home. There had been times in years past where I'd been away from home for longer; but never in so many consecutive months.

It was rather ironic that I shopped for Nick because I rarely did my own grocery shopping. Bobbi, my home manager, did that for me, and had offered to shop for Nick, too, but I really enjoyed shopping for Nick. I liked choosing the things I knew he would like. Living on the street is rough enough; if I could give him some small comforts, it made me happy. I had to be careful to choose things that wouldn't spoil without refrigeration, but I also wanted to buy things that were healthy. An exception were the toaster pastries—they weren't necessarily healthy but Nick loved the breakfast treat and I always bought any new flavors the store stocked.

It was also important for him to have fresh fruit, so I bought apples, bananas and two bags of fresh peaches. I'd learned that he didn't like grapes of any kind, but I bought some for myself because they looked so delicious. It took me an hour to do the shopping, but I loved every minute of it and found myself singing along to the music playing through the store as I stood in line to pay. As usual, I didn't bring in enough bags, so I had to buy more to hold my purchases and I laughed when my cashier, Carol, teased me about it.

I knew I had to worry about finding Akore, but it was such a beautiful day that I couldn't help enjoying myself as I drove around the city I loved on my way to deliver food to someone I cared about. And of course, I hadn't had an In-N-Out burger for over a month and I was salivating just thinking about how good it would taste.

*Would you like me to bring you a Double-Double back to the house?* I sent to Jason. I was grateful that the thought medallion amplified my mental sending or I wouldn't be able to speak with Jason so far away.

*No thank you, you always eat the fries before you come home and the smell of fries I know I'm not eating drives me crazy,* Jason laughed.

*Ha-ha, I did that one time and you'll never let me live it down.*

*Nope, you're just too fun to tease. How was the dress fitting?*

*It looks amazing but you'll have to wait another two months before you get to see it.*

*Actually, it's only another forty-nine days, but who's counting?* Jason countered.

*Hold on, I got lucky and found a parking spot in the lot.* I sent and then maneuvered my Bug into the spot recently vacated by a white Escalade. *Okay, I'm back, I'm going to grab a bite to eat, give Nick his groceries then come back home.*

*Don't forget I'm taking you to dinner tonight at The Crab Cooker,* Jason reminded me.

*I didn't, that's why I'm only going to have two burgers.*

*Love you,* I sent then dropped our connection and got out of the car.

"Sweet car," a tall, tanned and blond-headed surfer called to me. He was lean and muscular and looked to be in his early twenties. He was getting into his own car, which was an older model Honda with a surfboard rack on the top which held two boards: a long and short. "What year is it?" he continued.

"A '69," I answered brightly.

"Yeah, the waves are going off at The Wedge and a bunch of us are heading up there to shred, do you want to come?" he asked.

"Thanks for the offer, but I'll be hanging with my fiancé later," I said and waved as I continued walking to the counter to order.

"No worries, it never hurts to ask," the guy said as he got in his car.

"Good luck," I called over my shoulder with a laugh and practically skipped up to the counter. I couldn't wait to tell Jason he has some competition, *maybe he'll buy me two desserts to stay on my good side* I thought as I laughed to myself. If the young surfer only knew how old I really am he'd never give me a second look; I could be his great-great-great grandma for goodness sake. Thankfully, my shifter physiology kept me looking like I was in my mid-twenties and would for centuries to come.

I ordered four Double-Doubles with fries in separate containers, just the way Nick liked them. Bobbi came down two times when I was gone to add more money to Nick's account, but the cashier was new and didn't know what the balance was. When I asked Kai the cashier to let Enrique know I was there he got nervous until I explained we were friends and I thought he was doing a great job. Once he took my money and assured me he would pass the message to Enrique, I sat at an outside table.

While I waited for my food to arrive, I looked around, surprised that Nick wasn't already here. I'd been gone for a month but even Kai knew who Nick was, which told me he'd been by recently, or at least since Kai started working here. I smiled up at Enrique as he brought my food over to my table, but my expression fell as I took in the serious look on his face. I was even more surprised when Enrique sat across from me.

"What's wrong?" I asked.

He just shook his head as he looked at me, his eyes sad.

"Tell me," I said hoarsely and placed my hand over his.

"It's Nick," he finally got out, his voice cracked with emotion.

Jason and I weren't going to make it to dinner after all.

*August 28*
*Poseidon Society Mortuary*
*Newport Beach, California*

Brian, Jason, Enrique and I sat in the front row of the

mortuary chapel as Pastor Sabo talked about Nick's life. Pastor Sabo had white flyaway hair on his head that matched the short beard on his face. He was only five-feet six-inches and had the tanned skin of a native of this area. Nick and Pastor Sabo grew up together in Newport Beach and he frequently took care of Nick when he was having one of his bad days. Nick had a room at the church he could use but he always preferred to sleep outside. I learned that Nick was a highly decorated war hero, but his PTSD was so severe he couldn't function in society and preferred to live on the streets.

Nick died the week before, of a heart attack, sitting at our table at In-N-Out. Enrique found him around midnight when he returned to the restaurant because he'd forgotten something. At first, he thought Nick was sleeping but knew he was gone when he tried to wake him up. Enrique called Pastor Sabo before the police arrived because Nick had his name and number written on a cardboard sign which was sitting in plain view on his shopping cart. Pastor Sabo arrived shortly before the coroner's van and took possession of Nick's belongings since Nick had asked him to.

One of the things in the cart was a book entitled, "I'm Dead Now, So What?" and in it he had written his final wishes. He must have done this in one of his more lucid moments since there was only one reference to having a unicorn sing at his service. Luckily for Nick one of the newest members of Tionchar living near San Francisco was a unicorn, had a beautiful singing voice and was willing to do me a favor.

Jason held my hand as I silently wept at the loss of my friend. I felt guilty because I wasn't there when he died, and Enrique didn't have my number to call to let me know; my heart was breaking. I was so lost in my dark thoughts I wasn't really paying attention to what was being said and was startled when Pastor Sabo mentioned my name.

"Cyndi, I want you to know how much you meant to Nick and how he looked forward to your lunches. I've known Nick since we were kids and was grieved he was so damaged when he came home from the war. Whenever he talked about the times you spent together, I would get glimpses of the friend I lost. You made him feel like a person and he really loved to eat the food you provided for him." He chuckled and I smiled as I looked into his kind, ice-blue eyes. "You gave Nick something to look forward to and for that I am grateful.

"I believe Nick knew his time on Earth was coming to a close because he came to my house a few hours before he was found at the restaurant. He was thinking clearly, and we sat on my front steps and talked, like we did when we were younger. He looked so peaceful and was full of joy. Before he left, he gave me a hug and asked me to give one to you when I met you, along with a message. I would like to fulfill Nick's wish, if that's okay with you?" he asked.

I know I looked like a blubbering mess, because I'm an ugly crier, but I stood as Pastor Sabo walked to me. He opened his arms and I embraced him. My tears fell even faster as I grieved for my loss.

"Shh—it's okay, don't be sad." Pastor Sabo spoke softly, and I knew these were Nick's words he was using. "You made my life better, and I am grateful you decided to be my friend. My only regret is we never got to take that swim together."

Pastor Sabo and I let go at the same time and he placed his hands on my shoulder and by the way he looked I knew Nick had told him my secret. He smiled crookedly and said, "Nick asked that his ashes be turned into an Eternal Reef and when it's done, he wanted you to place it somewhere meaningful to you. It looks like he might get that swim after all."

# CHAPTER 6

*August 29*
*Table Mountain*
*Cape Town South Africa*

The man who was now calling himself Ramesh Acharya watched the men tearing down the rock cairn on the furthest side of the cable car station. The rocks had clearly been piled atop one another by human hands to create the sixteen-foot triangular structure that created the monument called Maclear's Beacon. The freezing rain was lashing him from all sides and it reminded him of the times he stood at the wheel of a ship, piloting around the Cape of Good Hope. He smiled grimly as he thought of the weaknesses of modern humans and their addiction to comfort. However, in this case it served him well because there were no witnesses to his larceny.

It took seven days to establish himself again in his

compound in the upscale Llandudno Estates. He purchased the land overlooking the ocean over two-hundred years before and transferred the title each time he needed to change identities. This was one of his properties that was isolated, separate from his other companies and couldn't be traced back to him using normal means.

Apparently, his previous caretaker had gotten lazy and hadn't kept the property up to the standards expected of him. The fact Akore hadn't been on property for twenty years was no excuse for the lout to allow things to deteriorate as they had; a point he made to the man as he conducted his exit interview. It was more difficult to dispose of the caretaker's body since the area surrounding his fifty acres had been built up with lavish estates, but he still had unobstructed access to the ocean though, via the smuggling tunnels that led from a hidden area on his property to the water. It wasn't a sophisticated means of disposal, but the local sea life feasted on his former caretaker's body.

"It's hard getting good help these days," Akore muttered to himself as he watched the men's progress, which was slowing.

"I'm not paying you to stand around," he shouted at Daniel as he ran up to him.

"I'm sorry sir, but the men are growing weary," Daniel said, unable to meet his employer's eyes.

"I want that chest found today, while the weather is keeping others at bay. This is the third time we have come here to retrieve my property and this has been the only time without witnesses. Tell the men they will receive three times what we agreed upon, but I want this finished today. Is that understood?"

"Yes, sir," Daniel bowed and hurried back to the demolition crew. After a hurried conversation, the men went back to work with renewed vigor. Akore chuckled as he watched his supposedly exhausted employees attack the cairn enthusiastically. It was amazing how money could motivate desperate people.

He picked up the bronze plaque which had fallen off the face of the monument as the rocks were cleared and read its history.

"So, this was built in the year eighteen-sixty-five by Sir Thomas Maclear to mark the highest point on Table Mountain, eh?" He shrugged his shoulders and tossed the plaque away in disinterest. Rather than stand around and watch the excavation progress, Akore wandered around in a small circle remembering what it was like to escape through the portal from Claw all those centuries ago. He shuddered as he thought about the fire, explosions and pain as he was caught in the backlash of his own defensive spells.

The only thing that kept him alive as he was cast out of Claw onto this primitive planet was the knowledge he had destroyed the members of the ruling council when his fortress was destroyed. At least, that's what he had believed until recently. He didn't know how they had managed to find him, but at least one of the ruling council members must have survived and reproduced. He shuddered as he remembered the feel of the discovery spell that brushed against his shields in Goa. Whoever came after him is powerful, and unlike any other magic user he'd come across before. He had to create a better defensive shield with the arcane crystals buried here.

His thoughts were interrupted by a cheer from his men, and he made his way to where they were standing. The cairn had been disassembled and the rocks tossed haphazardly away to show the ground underneath. The rain fell harder, and the water pooled on the exposed dirt, creating mud.

"What are you waiting for? Dig," Akore barked and each of the men grabbed their shovels and started digging furiously. Soon, the harsh sound of metal splitting wood reached Akore's ears followed by the sight of four of the men dropping to their knees to scoop mud out of the hole with their hands. After a few more minutes of digging, two of the men struggled to bring a chest out of the hole and place it on the ground before their employer.

He reached into the pocket of his coat and pulled out a bundle of two-hundred Rand notes to pay the men. They had agreed to work for fifty Rand but would be given two-hundred Rand which was three times the amount agreed upon plus fifty extra to assure their silence.

When he looked back up with the money in his hand, the men were standing before Akore in a semi-circle and Daniel was holding a machete and waving him to move away from the chest.

"So, this is how it's going to be?" he sighed and began to draw power from the crystal around his neck, moving back and to the side as he did so.

"We want to see what's in the chest before we renegotiate our contract," Daniel smiled wickedly as he took Akore's place before the chest.

Each man nodded in agreement and Akore was suddenly furious because this would complicate matters. The men would need to be killed quickly; he would not be able to harvest any of their life-force for himself.

"*Patefio*," he whispered and the lock on chest clicked open. Daniel nodded to one of the men and he reached over and opened the lid.

Daniel took one look in the chest and began laughing, "You get to keep what's in the chest, and we will take your money, clothing and everything else you have. After all, a dead man doesn't get cold," he said as he raised the machete in his hand.

Akore spread out both hands, each finger pointing towards a different man and shouted the word, "*Mortem*." Immediately each man dropped to the ground like a puppet with their strings cut.

He walked over to the chest, kicking Daniel's leg out of his way. "After all, dead men don't feel any pain," he muttered and looked inside the empty box.

He muttered, "*Revelare*," and there was a flash of light as the spell revealed the arcane crystals which had been hidden by a spell. He picked up each grapefruit-sized crystal and placed it in a different pocket. Although he wasn't surprised, he was disappointed none of them had held their magical charge this long. It would take time for them to charge in this world of little magic, but once they did, he would be practically invincible.

He looked at the dead men in disgust. This could complicate matters, but he had no choice in the matter. He would have to be extra careful. "At least I had the foresight to have you hike up the trail rather than ride with me," he said to Daniel as he searched the man's pockets and removed his cell phone to make sure his number wasn't found on his body. "After all, dead men don't need cell phones," he patted Daniel's chest and stood. He looked up at the stormy sky and smiled, then began the hour-long trek back to the cable car which would take him back to his driver and his new future.

*Newport Beach, California*

I stood on my deck watching the sun slowly sinking into the ocean. The sky was ablaze with the swirling shades of yellow, orange, red and purple of the setting sun and I took a deep breath of the salty air coming from the ocean below. I watched the waves crash on the private beach below my house and felt the pull of the water. I longed to shed my clothes and dive into the cool depths and swim to escape my sadness, but I knew that wasn't possible.

The purchases of the houses on either side of mine had been completed while we were in India, so I was the only one who had access to the beach below. Even though he didn't make a sound, I could sense Jason coming up behind me. That was one of the benefits of being true mates with someone, you always knew where they were. Jason and I were tied together in a way that made me feel complete; I couldn't wait for our wedding so we could give ourselves to one another completely.

He brushed the hair away from my neck and planted a kiss where my neck and shoulder met.

"That tickles," I giggled and moved away from him.

"That's not exactly the reaction I was looking for," he chuckled and wrapped his arms around me from behind and I settled into his embrace.

"Well, that's what you're always going to get, mister, that's my ticklish spot and you know it," I laughed.

"Are you okay?" he asked gently.

"I know this is what happens when we befriend humans, but it doesn't make it any easier. We'll live for hundreds of years and humans may only live eighty years or so. The longer we live here, the more people we know will die. Is it worth it?"

"Is what worth it?" Jason repeated gently.

"Making friends with humans?" I asked, tears spilling

down my cheeks as I turned to face him. "Is it worth the pain of loss?"

Jason cupped my cheek with his hand, stared into my eyes and smiled down at me. "Of course, it's worth it. You heard the pastor. You made Nick's life better and for the past ten years you treated him with dignity and respect. He had a hard life, but he looked forward to the times you'd have lunch with him. How many other people do you know who take the time to get to know a homeless person, let alone become friends with one? Cyndi, your heart is so big, it's impossible for you not to make friends with humans. Our only other option is to move back to Theria when Alister and Aileene return from their honeymoon."

"There's no way I'm doing that. We must stop Akore," I said, getting angry.

"But why? Josef has the rest of Tionchar at his disposal and they can hunt for him," Jason pressed.

"Because he's killing people," I said hotly.

"But these are just humans, and they're going to die anyway," he countered.

I pushed away from Jason and stood with my hands fisted at my sides. I couldn't believe that he would be so callous about this. Didn't he see the fear on the faces of the people Akore killed in India? Didn't he see the woman holding her baby, trying to comfort her even though she knew she couldn't do anything about what was happening to them?

I opened my mouth to blast him when I saw the smirk on his face and realized he was goading me.

He reached out and grasped my hands in his, tenderly massaging with his thumbs until my fists dissolved in his gentle grip. "You care too much about people to not become friends with them. Even if you know their deaths will eventually cause you pain, you can't help loving them anyway. And that's one of the things I love about you," he said and leaned down to gently kiss me.

"You're right," I sighed after I turned my head to lay my ear on his chest, listening to his heartbeat. "I don't like comparing humans to animals, but it is sort of like people who keep Great Danes as pets. Even though they know the dog may die in ten years or less, they love it anyway and when that one dies, they get another. They give those dogs love and care for the time they have with them and enjoy the love dogs give them in return."

We turned back to watch the last of the sunset and saw a large wave heading toward my beach. The water was being pushed ahead of something huge and as the wave swelled and crashed on the shore, I saw the outline of a kraken in the water. Before the water finished washing up on the beach the enormous creature shrunk in on itself and a naked man walked out of the surf carrying a lobster pot in each hand.

"You're shameless, you know that?" I yelled down to Brian as he walked across the sand to climb the stairs that led up to my house.

"Maybe," he shrugged, "but I brought dinner, so I didn't think you'd mind."

I laughed and turned to Jason, so I didn't have to look at Brian climbing the stairs. Even though shifters don't mind nudity because most must disrobe to shift, I felt weird. He was like a second dad to me, yuck.

"You deal with him; I'm going to get the rest of dinner ready." I smiled and walked into the kitchen to see what Bobbi had left us in the fridge to go with the lobsters.

"You look ridiculous," I laughed as I looked at Brian in the frilly pink bathrobe Jason had picked out for him after he came into the house. It didn't help that he was also wearing his Elvis sunglasses and was munching on a lobster claw, shell and all. When we weren't eating around humans, we all enjoyed eating lobster the way we did in the ocean, crunchy on the outside and soft in the middle, yum.

"Would you rather I take the robe off, little darlin'?" he drawled.

"No, please," I begged laughing. "I already feel like I must scrub my eyes because of what I saw earlier. Where did you get these beauties?" I asked as I took a bite out of the lobster I was holding.

"Off the coast of San Onofre. The warm water cycled back

into the ocean from the nuclear power plant makes for a great hunting ground," he answered. "I added a few more pots there and one of us can check back next week to see if we have more."

"I'll do it," Jason answered as he buttered another roll. Bobbi loved to bake, and she made the best rolls.

"I've got a gig at The Coach House tonight," Brian said as he pushed back from the table and stood.

"I thought you were on hiatus," I said.

"I am," Brian called over his shoulder as he took his dishes into the kitchen and added them to the dishwasher. "However, Brian Setzer was supposed to play tonight but came down with the flu. He asked me to fill in for him. I've got to get ready; do you two want to come?" he asked as he walked to his room.

"What time is the show?" I asked in a casual voice. The nice thing about having enhanced hearing is we could carry on conversation anywhere in the house without shouting. Of course, it could cause other issues, too, which is one of the reasons I bought the other two houses. Brian snores and it sounds like he's cutting down trees with a dull chainsaw even though he's at the other end of the house from my room.

"Nine," he said as he started the shower in his bathroom.

Jason nodded so I answered, "We'll meet you there."

*Thanks,* Brian sent, *I'll leave tickets for you at Will Call.*

The Coach House is a nondescript building in a light industrial park in San Juan Capistrano, California. It has hosted concerts for over forty years and some of the biggest names in music have played there at one point or another. It was a small venue, only four hundred and eighty seats, but three hundred seats closest to the stage were reserved for those who ate dinner there, also. Brian left us tickets for one of the tables in the dining area so of course, Jason and I ordered a second dinner. I'm sure if Shelley were here, he would make a joke about us being hobbits.

I ordered the Catch of the Day which was yellowfin tuna on a bed of rice pilaf and Jason ordered the filet mignon. I might have had some of his steak along with the tuna; what can I say, I like my surf and turf.

At first the crowd was disappointed that Brian Setzer wasn't able to play so they weren't as lively as I would have liked when Brian came on stage dressed as Elvis. However, when the Setzer Orchestra began to play and Brian sang the song "Hound Dog," the crowd started enjoying the show. They transitioned straight into "Jailhouse Rock" and by the time he launched "A Little Less Conversation," he had the audience singing with him. Brian started the concert in a black jumpsuit but changed after every four songs, to represent the different decades Elvis performed in concert.

He played to the crowd and would toss scarves into the audience. It was hilarious to watch the women scramble to catch them, the same way concert goers wanted a scarf from the real Elvis when he was alive. Even though Brian is a friend, and I already knew he was talented, I was amazed to see how he held the audience in thrall with his singing and his performance on stage. He brought tears to my eyes when he sat on a stool center stage and sang "Love Me Tender" with only his guitar to accompany his voice. He really was sensational.

All in all, Brian and the band played twenty songs and received a standing ovation at the end, as well as calls for an encore. Brian got a mischievous look on his face then turned his back on the audience to talk with the band. After a moment he turned back to the crowd and, with a huge grin on his face, addressed them. "I want to thank you for coming out tonight and for being such a wonderful audience. I know you were as disappointed as I was to hear that Brian Setzer couldn't perform tonight but apparently, he's at home with the flu. Our thoughts and prayers go out to you, buddy.

"Anyway, I want to finish the concert tonight with something different since we're so near the ocean and we who live here have a pinch of sea salt in our blood." He laughed, and the audience joined him. "People who are lucky enough to live near the ocean are a different breed. I want to dedicate this song to my good friends, Cyndi and Jason. They're getting married in about a month and a half and they're with us in the audience tonight."

The cheers, whistles and shouts of congratulations continued until Jason and I stood to wave at everyone and I turned to see Brian laughing at my embarrassment. Our sitting again must have been the cue for the band because as soon as my butt hit the seat, the drummer started the song on the steel drums he wheeled in while my back was turned. It took me a moment to identify the music but once I did, I laughed at the audacity of my friend and vowed to find a way to get him back.

Brian began dancing on stage as the rest of the orchestra joined the drummer and played an extended intro before Brian launched into the lyrics.

"Is this—" Jason leaned over to ask.

"Yep," I laughed as Brian began the song.

"The seaweed is always greener, in somebody else's lake—"

"The jerk is singing "Under the Sea," from *The Little Mermaid.*"

*A*ugust 30

The ringing of my phone jarred me awake and I fell out of bed reaching for it on the nightstand. The blackout curtains were doing their job, so I wasn't sure what time it was. Since the call was coming through on my landline I knew it was important; only Josef had that number.

"Whazza?" I asked when I finally managed to gather my wits enough to reach up from the floor to grab the handset off the shrilling telephone.

"Good morning to you, too, how soon can you get to the airport?" Josef asked, laughing at me over the phone line.

"Which airport?" I asked, sitting up and rubbing the elbow I'd smashed into the floor in my fall.

"John Wayne," Josef responded.

I put my hand over the handset and called, "curtains and lights," to the automated system. The lights slowly grew brighter and the curtains automatically opened to reveal a gorgeous early morning sky. I stood, looked at the clock and did some quick calculations.

"At this time of the morning, it will take us almost an hour to get there," I finally answered.

"Perfect," Josef said. "Hillaes, Wu, Carlos and Yoli are on their way to the airport now and the jet will take off from Sky Harbor in about thirty minutes. That will give you enough time to grab your go-bag and head to the airport. I'm sorry you won't have time to grab a burger before you catch your plane," Josef teased.

"Bummer," I grumped and sent a mental message to Brian and Jason that we needed to head out in thirty minutes so they should be ready to go in twenty. I got replies acknowledging my message then turned my attention back to the discussion with Josef. "Where are we going, and how long will we be gone?"

"To answer your second question, I'm not sure, but I promise you'll be back in time for your wedding. And in answer to the first, you're headed to South Africa."

"Great, another long flight," I muttered. "Why are we going there?"

"There was a strange item in the news about a group of men who had destroyed a monument on top of Table Mountain in Cape Town and dug up a chest buried under the cairn."

"Remind me what a cairn is again," I asked, my brain still fuzzy from sleep.

"It's another name for a big pile of rocks," Josef laughed.

"So, this group destroyed a large pile of rocks? That is a strange story," I agreed while placing my go-bags on the bed then walking into the bathroom for a quick shower, "but I'm not sure I understand why this is a reason to send us there."

"Two reasons," Josef countered. "The men were found dead near an empty chest without an apparent cause of death. The authorities leaked a lightning strike to the press but our agent in South Africa just confirmed there weren't any external marks on the bodies indicating a lightning strike. The second, and most compelling reason, there used to be a dimensional gate on top of Table Mountain that provided a direct route from Claw to Earth, but it was destroyed around the time the ruling council attacked Akore in his fortress. You're heading to South Africa because we finally have a lead on where he's gone to ground."

*S*eptember 1
*Table Mountain*
*Cape Town, South Africa*

I yawned as I stood looking north at the spectacular view of Table Bay from my vantage point next to what used to be Maclear's Beacon. The sunlight sparked on the navy-blue water in the middle of the bay and, with my superior eyesight, I could even see the waves crashing on the shore of Robben Island in the distance. The chalky-green water along the coast of Camps Bay to the west beckoned me and my stomach rumbled when I thought of the hunting ground under the waters there. Of course, that area was also full of great white sharks so that made the hunt even more exciting. I'd have to take Jason on a date there, later.

I turned back to survey the damage that had been done on top of the mountain and shook my head. Maclear's Beacon was built on this spot because it was the highest point on the mountain and had served as an important astronomical point since eighteen forty-four, but now the rocks that made up the beacon lay strewn around the ground. I was more concerned with the murder of eight men, but I was also dismayed by the wanton disregard for anything that got in Akore's way.

I looked at my watch, grateful to see it had automatically adjusted to the local day and time. Thankfully, I didn't need to worry about time zones when I traveled underwater; just thinking about thirty-one hours of travel made me tired. Our flight landed only three hours before and, even though I slept on the plane, it wasn't as restful as sleeping in my bed or on the ocean floor.

Once we cleared customs, we piled in an armored SUV with heavily tinted windows and spent the forty-five-minute drive being briefed by our local contact, Enzokuhle. He was one of the members of Tionchar who had come to Earth in the past six months. He told us he was an impundulu and when he saw our blank expressions, laughingly explained he turned into a human-sized black and white bird who could summon thunder and lightning with his wings and talons.

He shared that he had flown over the top of Table Mountain when he heard the report of the dead men found there but there were too many police officers on the scene for him to do anything more than observe. He said the men appeared to have died suddenly because it looked like they fell where they were standing, in a half-circle, facing an open chest. There was another man on the ground closer to the chest with a machete near his hand, but other than that weapon there didn't appear to be any sign of violence; at least he couldn't see any wounds on the bodies other than those made by scavengers after death.

He answered as many of our questions as he could but since he hadn't actually been to the site where they died, he didn't have much to add. He did, however, have copies of the initial Forensic Pathologist's report which showed each man's heart burst in their chests. The Forensic Pathologist didn't speculate how this could have happened; she just reported her findings. The cause of death was still pending. We had special permission from the Commandant of the South African Police Services, Colonel Dlamini, to investigate the scene so that's how we found ourselves atop Table Mountain.

"Coffee?" Enzo asked as he handed me a paper cup full of the hot liquid.

"Thank you, Enzo," I said, then frowned.

"Is the coffee so bad you make that face before you taste it?" he laughed.

"No, that's not it. I know you told us to call you Enzo because your name is difficult for many to pronounce, but that's not good enough for me. So, please tell me how to pronounce your name," I insisted.

He looked at me then smiled widely, his ebony skin wrinkling around his eyes with joy. His smile was infectious, and I found myself smiling as I stared into eyes so dark brown they were almost black.

"En-zo-kook-clay," he said and I repeated it until I got the pronunciation correct.

"Does your name have a meaning?" I asked.

"My name means 'do great' and is of Zulu origin," he shared. "My mother was also a member of Tionchar and served in this part of the world many years ago. She was impressed with the Zulu people and their struggles in South Africa. She wanted to give me a name to live up to, and always told me to do great things with my life."

"Thank you for sharing that with me," I said, then made a face after I took a sip of the coffee he gave me. "Although I could have done without you sharing this coffee. How can you drink this stuff?" I asked as I sipped it again; nope, it didn't taste any better the second time.

"I can't drink it, why do you think I gave it to you?" he laughed heartily, and I turned to glare at Brian because I knew he put Enzokuhle up to give me the drink. He laughed and blew me a kiss.

Shrugging my shoulders, I continued drinking the hot beverage, needing the caffeine to stay awake. Besides, I'd once eaten a hagfish as a dare and that was so disgusting it had taken me a full week to get the taste of mucus out of my mouth. I don't really know why a fish needs to produce enough slime to fill a five-gallon bucket to protect itself from predators, but the hagfish can do that in minutes. Come to think of it, it was effective after all; I'll never eat another one again. Enzokuhle and I chatted about our lives and our experiences with Tionchar, and as I described to him the miracle that is the Double-Double, I realized I was hungry.

*I'm done here,* Hillaes sent, and I turned to see her stand and brush dirt from the knees of her pants. The bodies had been removed but the area had been secured by police caution tape and guards until we could examine the scene. Hillaes spoke quietly with the officer in charge while Enzokuhle walked over to where the two women were talking. After we said our goodbyes, we began the forty-five-minute trek back to the cable car station.

Because we had human constables escorting us back to the station, we opted to avoid discussing what Hillaes found at the site until later. Even though we could communicate with our minds, sometimes people thought it strange when I would laugh for no apparent reason. I asked a constable for his recommendation for the best place to eat once we were near the station. He suggested the Licorice and Lime Café but his partner argued the Kynsna Oyster Company served better food. She admitted she liked seafood but her partner didn't. They argued the merits of each restaurant for the rest of our walk back and we asked about other spots we should visit while in Cape Town. They remained with us for the five-minute cable car ride down the mountain, pointing out their restaurants of choice and then left us at the terminal to rejoin their team at the top.

We decided on the Kynsna Oyster Company in the wharf area which is surrounded by shops and restaurants catering to tourists. This section of Cape Town had grown around the docks of the old city, although it didn't look anything like it did hundreds of years ago. I stopped beside a large brass monument next to a small eight-foot by four-foot rectangular stage in the middle of the plaza. The monument explained that Cape Town had been a slave trading colony and stages like this had been used to showcase the humans being bought and sold as property.

As I contemplated the years of misery brought about by such an inhumane practice, I thought about the men, women and children who were still being sold around the world, including those who were affected by Akore's evil practices in India. While major countries around the world had abolished the practice of slavery on a national level, it was still an evil that was present on Earth. I was infused with righteous anger and vowed to do what I could to end this vile practice.

Jason must have sensed my mood because he put his arm around me, kissed my temple, then urged me to follow the rest of our party to the café. Jason and I sat at an outside table with Hillaes, her husband Wu, Carlos, Yoli, Brian, Jason, Enzokuhle, our pilot Steve and our co-pilot Robert. Our waitress was named Michelle and her blue eyes, blonde hair and fair skin spoke to her Dutch heritage. When she asked if we were ready to order, the rest of my party turned to me like I was the one to make all the decisions.

"You are in charge of our current mission," Carlos commented with a smirk at the puzzled look on my face.

"Michelle," I smiled sweetly, "I'm going to leave the ordering up to you because you know the best things on the menu. Order what you think ten hungry people will eat, then double everything. Oh, and please bring six dozen of your largest oysters as an appetizer. We'll also have bottles of flat water for everyone and whatever else they want to drink; they can make that decision for themselves, I think."

Once Michelle took everyone's drink order, and after a

visit from the manager to make sure I was serious with what I asked Michelle to do, Hillaes explained her findings, speaking softly enough that patrons nearby couldn't hear her.

"I was able to confirm that magic was used on the mountain to kill the men and the flavor of the magic informs me that Akore was the one to cast the spell. I would have to examine one of the bodies to be certain, but I am almost positive that he used another spell outlawed by the ruling council to murder those men. I don't believe he was able to harvest any of their life-force, which may or may not be a good thing." She stopped while Michelle and another waiter brought our drinks and oysters.

"How can you be sure?" I asked once we had been served. Since Hillaes was busy shucking an oyster, she answered us mentally.

*As I said, without examining a body I cannot be completely sure but based on the Forensic Pathologist's report, the men died because their hearts exploded. If he removed their life-force, nothing would appear to be wrong. I studied the spell he's probably using when I was on Claw and the life-force cannot be removed once the person is dead. They die because their life-force is removed, not the other way around.*

*I don't understand why you said it may or may not be a good thing that he couldn't harvest anyone from the mountain,* Brian said as he ate the succulent meat found in the oyster he'd opened.

*If he wasn't able to gain energy on the mountain, he's*

*likely more depleted than he was before, making him vulnerable. It's possible he has a set-up like he had in Goa and he's already harvesting people like he did there. However, that's not my biggest concern.* She looked thoughtful as she paused to take a drink of her iced tea.

"Don't keep us in suspense," Yoli laughed, and we joined in when Hillaes gave her the stink eye.

"That sauce is hot," Hillaes gasped, "I just needed a moment to cool off my tongue."

"You should try the wasabi, it's got quite a kick," Brian said as he popped an entire oyster in his mouth and began to chew, the shell crunching between his teeth. When he realized what he'd done, he looked around quickly to make sure no one noticed and grinned sheepishly at me.

"I can't take you anywhere," I muttered and shucked another oyster.

"The shells are the best part, I like the way they crunch," Brian said lamely. He was saved from further embarrassment by Michelle bringing out the rest of our meal. If she was surprised we finished seventy-two oysters that quickly, she didn't show it. There was so much food, we had to pull up another table to hold it all.

"Could we please get some more rolls?" Wu asked politely and Michelle hurried away to bring the rolls and refills on our drinks.

"What concerns me the most," Hillaes answered softly, "is I found residual magical energy inside the chest consistent with arcane crystals. Based on the magical frequency, these crystals are quite large, most likely similar in size to the ones from his compound in Goa."

"So, we'll face the same defenses here that we encountered in India?" Jason asked.

Hillaes shook her head before answering, "Not yet. While the crystals can hold large amounts of magical energy, that energy begins to trickle away almost immediately if it's not being used. This isn't usually a problem in a magic-rich environment like Claw, or even Theria, but unless there is almost constant replenishing of the magic leaving the crystals, they will lose their charge over time.

"There isn't any way the crystals could have kept their charge since eighteen-hundred and forty-four when the rock cairn was created to form the beacon, and definitely would be empty if they've been in that chest for five hundred years or more."

Hillaes paused to take a bite of her poached Rock Cod and groaned in appreciation at the way the delicate fish had been prepared. The rest of us followed her lead and got serious about eating our meals. Lunch was boisterous and we swapped plates often so others could share in the wonderful food we were enjoying. Even though we had only recently come together as a team, we had already formed a bond. Maybe it was the fact we were all shifters, and either members of Tionchar or the King's Inner Circle but I think it was more likely we shared the common goal of stopping Akore.

Many people would assume that when you have the ability to live hundreds if not thousands of years you can become bored with life and don't appreciate new experiences. I've found it to be the opposite. Even though I know I'll live a long time, I know this exact moment will never come again so I savor the experience and enjoy the people I'm with. If Nick's death taught me anything, these moments are all too fleeting, so I have to embrace them wholeheartedly.

Once Michelle cleared away our empty lunch dishes and delivered our dessert and coffee orders, we continued our conversation about Akore.

"I've worked out that we have between three and four weeks before Akore can bring his arcane crystals up to full power based on the amount of magic available to him on Earth," Hillaes said after taking a sip of her coffee.

"Can he fill them faster if he sacrifices more people?" Enzokuhle asked.

Hillaes shook her head in thought, "No, it doesn't work that way. He can only use life-force to replenish his own energy and power the spell he's using to keep himself alive. He needs to gather magic from Earth to fill the crystals."

"So," I said slowly, "at most we have a month to stop Akore before he has his magical defenses in place, and we're not even sure he's still in Cape Town?"

"I'm fairly certain he is," Wu answered, "I researched Afonso de Albuquerque's history before he commanded the *Flor do Mar* and the first mention of his rise to prominence occurred here in Cape Town in fifteen-hundred and two. Albuquerque was traveling from Portugal to India and the ship he was on spent the winter in Cape Town harbor because the weather made travel past the Cape of Good Hope dangerous so late in the year. Prior to wintering in Cape Town, Albuquerque had the reputation of an entitled noble but when he arrived in India, he had a drive and zeal he hadn't demonstrated before."

"When we combine that history with the fact there used to be a dimensional portal atop Table Mountain, and Akore had a chest buried there, it points to his deep roots in this area of South Africa," Hillaes finished.

"Then we'll proceed on that assumption," I agreed. "Hillaes, you said the arcane crystals emit a specific vibration. Is there a way for the rest of us to search for that?"

She thought for a moment while she took a bite of her chocolate mousse. "I'll have to work on something, but I believe it may be possible to tune smaller crystals to the same frequency using the residual energy from the chest. If I can do that, then I can give each of us one of the crystals which will vibrate in resonance when they get close enough to the larger arcane crystals in Akore's possession."

"Will the arcane crystals on Akore's property also vibrate and potentially warn him that someone is searching for him?" Brian asked.

"That was a surprisingly well-thought-out question," Jason

looked at Brian in surprise. "Where's Brian and what did you do with him?"

"Very funny, plebeian. I can be quite erudite when inspiration strikes," Brian answered in a haughty manner.

"To answer your question," Hillaes interrupted before Jason and Brian could go any further. "I don't believe we'll need to worry about the larger crystals. Even though the smaller crystals will resonate at the same frequency, unless Akore is actually standing next to one of the larger crystals when we get close, he won't know what we're up to."

We breathed a collective sigh of relief and even though Hillaes didn't know these things for certain, we trusted her judgment.

"Enzokuhle, Hillaes is going to need access to the chest, also and at least one of the dead bodies of the men Akore killed. Will you be able to arrange that?" I asked.

"That should not be a problem. I will speak with Colonel Dlamini after lunch and arrange this," Enzokuhle answered.

"Good—Steve, Robert, are you available for a few weeks?" I questioned our pilots who looked to be half-asleep from the big meal they'd eaten.

"Yes. We're at your disposal for as long as you need us," Steve answered with a yawn.

"Steve, you transform into a pouakai, correct?" I asked.

"What's that?" Brian asked before Steve could answer.

"A Maori great eagle," Steve answered with another yawn.

"In my eagle form, I've got a thirty-foot wingspan and am about seventeen feet from beak to tail."

"And Robert, you're a wyvern, correct?" At his nod I continued. "I'd like the two of you to head back to the hotel to get some rest. I'm going to need both of you to do some aerial reconnaissance later. Enzokuhle, I'd like you to do the same once you're finished with Colonel Dlamini and the Forensic Pathologist. Yoli and Carlos, are you able to separate Akore's scent from the others on top of the mountain?"

Carlos rubbed his hand against his chin, before answering. "Maybe? We might have more luck getting something from the chest since it's been a couple of days and there was a lot of rain, but we can try."

"That's all I can ask," I encouraged. "Please head back up the mountain after we finish and see what you can find. If you must wait until the police leave, you can always come down the trail in wolf form."

"We'll leave our SUV here for you, and we'll take an Uber back to the hotel," Robert suggested and Yoli nodded her thanks.

"And what will you be doing?" Carlos asked. "Yoli and I are supposed to be your guards."

"Actually, that's only part of the reason you're here. I'm appointing you to full members of the team. I'll have Brian and Jason with me to make sure I don't get into too much trouble." I smiled at my wolf friends to let them know how much I appreciated their efforts. "We'll return to the hotel so I can make a full report to Josef and see if he has any instructions. As far as we know, we'll be searching for Akore on land and by air; there isn't much for us aquatic creatures to do right now to help with the search.

"Besides, I want to ask Josef about a side project I'd like to explore," I said.

"What's that?" Brian asked.

"I'd like to look into the information we gathered in India about the ongoing slave trade and investigate if there are any slavers operating around here. If there are, I'd like us to put them out of business permanently."

# CHAPTER 7

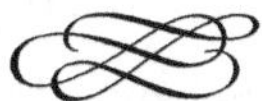

*September 8*

*460 Nautical Miles East of Ras Isa, Yemen*

*Arabian Ocean*

Jason, Brian and I easily kept pace with the ship as it cruised through the water. My sense of justice burned hot as I thought about the precious cargo contained on this ship, but I took deep calming breaths to relax. I had to stick to our plan so those on the ship weren't alerted to our presence ahead of time. The men on this ship would pay for their crimes, I reminded myself and continued to swim and wait for the signal to attack.

Since it would take Hillaes ten to fourteen days to complete the resonance spells on her arcane crystals, I focused my energies on discovering everything I could about Akore's slaving ventures. Josef agreed with my decision to shut down this portion of Akore's business and gave me the support I needed. The Tionchar operatives in India, Raksaka and Ishka, gave Josef and his cyberteam access to the law enforcement computer systems at both the local and national level allowing them to identify the businesses that participated in the slave trade. They also determined which government officials were complicit in this heinous crime. These individuals would be arrested, but not until we rescued the people who were *en route* to be sold.

The cargo ship, SM *Brownlow*, left Jawaharlal Nehru Port on September fourth after having loaded ten cargo containers. According to the manifest, these forty-foot containers were filled with teas, spices, jewelry and medicinal compounds. What the manifest didn't show is that two of the containers were filled with women and children destined to be transported to Yemen where they would be sold and transferred to their final destination. Unfortunately, we didn't uncover these details until the ship was a day out of port.

While Jason, Brian and I flew back to India from South Africa, Josef and the members of Tionchar in India quickly put a rescue plan together. Since Josef had already dispatched the super yacht, *Sirenea,* to India before we left for King Alister's wedding, we had access to that boat as well as the Airbus H155 helicopter it carried on its helipad. We were more concerned about reaching the *Brownlow* before it docked in Yemen than we were with keeping a low profile, so we boarded the yacht the moment we could in pursuit of our quarry.

The *Sirenea* could travel at fifty knots per hour which was over three times the speed the *Brownlow* was traveling. We were confident we would catch up to them before they reached port even though it would take us almost thirty-one hours to do so. Computer hackers on Josef's team were able to tap into the navigational equipment of the *Brownlow* to track their progress giving us real-time updates. Josef had given us the go-ahead to take care of the slavers ourselves, rather than get the human authorities involved. We would transfer the captives to the *Sirenea* where they would be taken to a place of refuge run by Tionchar and given a chance at a new life.

Our rescue plan was simple. Once we were within sixty miles of the *Brownlow,* Steve and Robert would fly the helicopter a half mile aft of the cargo vessel and Steve would jump out of the helicopter with Ishka and transform into his eagle form. Ishka was going to transform into his serpent form and Steve would drop him on the ship to be our eyes and ears. Brian, Jason and I would jump from the helicopter and transform before we hit the water then quickly swim up to the ship to wait for Ishka's signal. Once we incapacitated the crew, we would release the captives and transfer them to the *Sirenea,* which would carry them away from the slave ship.

We timed our arrival well since it was after midnight when we came in range of the *Brownlow.* There was heavy cloud cover so even the moonlight was blocked, aiding in our stealth run. Once Steve and Ishka left the helicopter, it was our turn to go. Robert lowered the helicopter close to the surface so we only had a thirty-foot drop into the black water. Brian jumped first since he's the largest when he transforms, and I didn't feel like getting squished.

Before he dove out the side of the open helicopter, he turned to Robert and in his best Elvis impression told him, "thank you, thank you very much," then whooped as he dropped towards the water.

I smiled at Jason, rolled my eyes and pulled my trident from the pocket dimension on my necklace and leaned it against the interior wall before pulling out the trident I had crafted for Jason as a wedding present. Judging by the smile on his face and the kiss he gave me, he was pleased with the gift, happy to have a traditional weapon of the merfolk of his own.

*Would you two hurry up? I want to play with that ship,* Brian sent.

*Keep your shirt on,* I responded.

*Krakens don't wear shirts,* Brian sniffed, *there aren't enough arm holes.*

I laughed, waved to Robert then dove out the side of the hovering helicopter. The instant I cleared the doorway and transformed, I felt complete. There are so many things I love about being in my human form, especially In-N-Out, but my true home is in the ocean. My vision focused as if a switch were flipped and the dark of night came into sharp relief of black, white and gray. By the time I entered the water, my claws were extended and my wide grin expressed my excitement for the upcoming hunt. No one who saw this version of my mermaid self would ever confuse me with any cartoon princess. I was the ultimate oceanic predator, and I was after justice tonight.

When Jason appeared beside me, I opened my senses to our surroundings and quickly located the sound of the ship, a half mile to the west. I knew Jason and Brian would follow my lead, but I sent them a mental command anyway and swam away at top speed. It took less than a minute for us to reach the *Brownlow* and we matched pace to wait. I sent Ishka a mental confirmation that we were in place and he could begin his exploration.

*So, what now?* Brian asked even though he knew the plan as well as I did.

*Ishka will search the ship to make sure our intelligence was correct and then we'll come aboard to round up the slavers and rescue the victims,* I replied, annoyed that we had to wait for Ishka to sneak around. I swam closer to the ship and placed my ear against the hull and strained to listen, hoping I would receive some clue before Ishka gave us the go-ahead signal.

*I've made it below decks without being seen, but there are cameras everywhere. I'll need to be cautious,* Ishka sent, and I growled in irritation. If I weren't careful my anger would cause me to make mistakes, but my scales itched with my desire to see justice against these men.

*Cyndi and I will make our way to the bridge and subdue everyone we find there, then use the ship's systems to get everyone else on deck. Once everyone is sorted, we'll cut the engines and wait for the* Sirenea *to pull alongside. Once everyone is transferred to the* Sirenea *you'll get your chance to play.* Jason finished explaining to Brian and I could hear the hint of anger in his sending; he was incensed by these slavers, too.

*It's been a long time since I've been able to drag a ship down to the bottom of the ocean,* Brian chuckled darkly.

*That's exactly what this company deserves if they take on human cargo*—I was interrupted by the sound of a terrified scream reverberating through the hull of the ship I had my ear pressed against.

*That's all the confirmation I need,* I broadcast to Brian and Jason.

At the same time Ishka's voice sounded in our heads, *we have the correct ship and there are captives aboard.*

Jason and I dove seventy-five feet below the ship so we could build up speed to blast out of the water once we reached the surface. We needed to make sure we were able to clear the forty feet to land safely on the deck of the ship. I felt myself grinning with fierce joy as I blasted out of the water, my trident held out before me. Once we were flying towards the deck, Jason and I transformed our tails back into legs to make landing easier.

As a human I'm five-feet ten-inches tall and in my mermaid form, I'm over ten feet long from my head to the tip of my tail. However, I have a third form where I partially transform so I can stand on two legs and am over eight feet tall, have razor-sharp claws at the ends of my fingers, eyes as black as squid ink and my mouth full of shark teeth. No one looking at Jason or me would see us as anything other than the nightmares we are.

We landed silently and I let Brian and Ishka know we were on our way to take care of the bridge crew. Underwater, I use a type of sonar, like a porpoise, and in my partial form I can use it on land, also. A quick sweep of the deck confirmed there weren't any humans on our side of the cargo containers so we worked our way to the bridge where we would find the ship's officers and other crew members. Jason and I made our way up the gangway, careful not to let our tridents bang against anything that could make our presence known.

There were muffled sounds of screaming followed by boisterous cheers coming from the bridge as Jason and I reached the top. We stopped for a moment to make sure we were in sync before rushing inside the wheelhouse.

*I'll go left and you go right as we pass through the door,* Jason nodded then transferred his trident to his left hand so he could squeeze my arm in encouragement. We knew we were going to face some evil things in the next few minutes, and we were prepared to do whatever necessary to stop these men. We had to act quickly so the men on the bridge couldn't raise the alarm to warn the others. The door was watertight, and it wouldn't be easy to open it quietly. Hopefully, the sounds from inside would drown out the noise of the door being forced open.

As Jason mentally counted us down from three, I transferred my trident to my left hand and Jason took a step back so we wouldn't tangle our feet as we rushed through the opening. I placed my right hand on the handle, threw open the door, ducked and rushed inside when Jason finished his count. We were both in the room and in place quicker than the men could react. There were four men in the room clustered around a monitor with their backs to the door. Time appeared to freeze as I took in the scene before me. The men were holding money in their hands and were betting on what they were watching on the screen, and laughing.

On screen there was a woman belligerently standing in the entrance of a cage, shielding people who were huddled behind her. She had blood running from her nose and her sari was ripped and hanging from her shoulder. She was holding a Taser in her hand in front of her body, holding off the two men who were reaching for her. There was a third man lying face down on the deck. Even though the woman was fighting valiantly, I knew it was just a matter of time before the men rushed her, taking the weapon away.

The frozen moment passed and one of the men reacted to

the opened door. He whirled to face us but before he could cry out in alarm, I threw my trident at him. The others realized something was wrong when their comrade was pinned to the navigation console by my weapon. One of the men reached towards a red button to the left of where he'd been standing but Jason's trident sticking into his back quickly changed his trajectory and he landed on the floor. Then I screamed.

Just as I can use my singing to bring peace, comfort and to hypnotize humans, I can also use it to strike terror into my victims. Stories of sirens luring sailors to their deaths have long been part of sea lore and while there have been rogue mermaids who enjoyed causing destruction, most mermaids warned sailors away from dangerous places using their fear songs. I'd warned Jason before I screamed so he could brace for the onslaught but the rest of those on the ship couldn't prepare themselves for my power.

I glanced at the screen and saw that everyone had dropped where they were standing, paralyzed with fear. As I reached the closest cowering man, he cried out in terror as I picked him up with my left hand and held him at arm's length from me, his feet dangling in the air.

"Where is this feed coming from?" I snarled as I pointed to the screen with my right hand, the claw on my index finger reflecting the overhead light. "Answer me or die," I said calmly as I brought him closer to my face and gnashed my teeth an inch from his nose.

"Cargo Hold One," he stammered. I sent a mental

command to Ishka to rush to the hold and deal with the men there. He was still recovering from my scream, but he let me know he was on his way.

"One last question," I smiled, showing my sharpened teeth. "How many crew members are aboard?"

He didn't hesitate to answer this time and once he told me there were twenty I tossed him into the bulkhead where he landed in a heap on the deck, unconscious. I reached into my pocket dimension and retrieved the small device Josef's team had created for situations like this. It was silver, the size of a small coin and magnetic; it also was more technologically advanced than anything on Earth. Once I stuck it to the side of the communication console a small green light flashed once indicating the device had control of the ship's computer.

I pulled my trident from the man pinned to the console then stood looking down at the last conscious man, who was wearing the captain's insignia on his uniform. "On your feet, meat."

"My name is Captain—" he began.

I cut him off with a growl, "Do you know the names of the women and children you have in that hold?"

He flinched as I pointed to the screen where Ishka, in his serpent form, was going from man to man, biting them where they lay; they would never get up again.

"You won't get away with—" he blustered but I cut him off again.

"Let me explain something to you. This handy, dandy

device," I pointed to the silver bump on the console, "transferred control of your ship to our hacking team in Dubai. At this moment they are downloading every scrap of information from the ship's computers and every electronic device aboard. Not only that, but it will also be able to track every IP address associated with this ship. That includes anyone who ever carried a device on board and connected to the ship's Wi-Fi network. Within hours we will have access to every secret you and your slimy bosses have tried to hide.

"Of course, those secrets will be revealed to the public if any of them pertain to the vile business you're conducting in Hold One. And, although you haven't asked, I'll tell you anyway. The tracking software that normally connects your ship to the GPS network has also been compromised so it will show this ship is still on course and on time, rather than dead in the water, as it will be when we gather the rest of the crew and free your captives."

The captain's skin had turned ashy as I spoke to him and when Jason's hand landed on his shoulder, he jumped. I think he was so overwhelmed he no longer was affected by my monstrous appearance.

I pulled a card out of the pocket dimension and handed it to Jason. "Have him recite those words," I asked as I sent a mental report to the captain of the *Sirenea*, who was close enough to communicate by thought-speak.

"Done," Jason said when the captain had finished his task.

"TOPHER," I called to the computer program that had taken over the ship.

"Yes, Agent Zhaleh?" a male voice sounded through the speakers in the wheelhouse; a voice which sounded suspiciously like the artificial intelligence from the Iron Man movies.

"Cyndi," I muttered before continuing, "please signal all hands, along with the captain's message, to gather at the stern."

"I will make it so," TOPHER replied. There were seven short rings and one long ring on the ship's bell which was immediately repeated then followed by a verbal announcement.

"This is the captain, all hands on deck. Report to the stern muster station, this is not a drill. I repeat, this is the captain, all hands on deck. Report to the stern muster station." TOPHER announced in a perfect imitation of the captain's voice.

"We don't need you after all," I said with a grin and took a step towards the terrified man. Watching my nightmare self must have been too much for the coward because his eyes rolled up in his head and he collapsed.

"That's our cue to leave," Jason said as he slung the captain over his shoulder. I retrieved the unconscious man I had thrown into the bulkhead and turned to follow him.

"Thank you, TOPHER," I called over my shoulder before I exited the room, "have fun hacking the rest of the ship's systems."

"Please, this was merely child's play. Give me a real challenge next time," TOPHER answered as I rushed down the stairs so we could be at the muster station before the rest of the crew arrived.

*W*e quickly subdued the remaining crew members as they arrived on deck. Once the last man arrived, I could feel the change in the engines as TOPHER powered them down. Jason dealt with the filthy crew member who must have been the ship's engineer. Jason had transformed into his more human form since it was difficult to fasten zip ties with such large hands.

I was once again grateful that King Alister had created the pocket dimension for me as I pulled two hoodies from inside. I tossed one to Jason then transformed into my fully human form and donned mine, which was pink and had the words 'Mermaid hair, Don't care' written on the front. I wasn't cold but didn't want to walk around the ship naked. After I slipped on the board shorts, I tossed a pair to Jason as he tossed me his trident.

*Brian, could you please give these a quick rinse for me?* I asked and a huge tentacle rose out of the water and groped over the edge of the ship. The men screamed when they saw the tentacle because they knew what was under the water. I walked forward and rested my left hand on the tentacle and held up the tridents for Brian which he quickly wrapped and took over the side. I waved merrily at the terrified men and waited until Brian returned the freshly cleaned tridents. Once I grabbed them and patted the tentacle with my other hand, it disappeared over the side again. As I walked back to where the men were bound, I put the tridents back in the pocket dimension.

*We're about two minutes out,* Steve sent, and I could hear the roar of the diesel engines aboard the *Sirenea* coming from the port side of the ship.

*Why don't you and Robert fly over to help Jason keep an eye on the crew while I join Ishka below deck to talk with our freed prisoners?*

I waited until they joined us on board before heading to Hold One. Steve shifted back to human just above the deck, so he landed on his two feet. He also had a thought medallion from King Alister so he arrived fully clothed. However, Robert landed in his wyvern form on top of the nearest stack of storage containers and roared at the men seated below. Based on the sudden smells emanating from the group, Robert managed to scare them badly enough that they messed themselves.

"You're pretty proud of yourself, aren't you?" I asked Robert. He didn't answer but opened his mouth wide in a grin.

"What are you going to do to us?" yelled one of the men as I turned to the door that led below decks.

Turning back around to glare at all the captives, I

answered calmly, even though I was seething with anger, "it all depends on what the women below tell me." The way most of the men flinched I think I already knew what would be happening, but I planned to allow the women to face their captors before issuing justice.

"If any of them give you trouble, throw them to the kraken; I'm sure he's hungry," I said over my shoulder as I opened the door and started down the stairs.

I could hear quiet sobbing coming from nearby as I made my way down the two flights of stairs before I came to the door leading into Holds One through Twenty. When I walked through the door, I could smell blood and death. There was also the smell of unwashed bodies, human waste and what I could only describe as despair. There was a cage in the middle of the hold, but it was too small to hold the number of people who were crammed inside. The door was shut, and the defiant woman was standing with her back to the closed door, brandishing the Taser at Ishka who was sitting in the lotus position about twenty feet from the cage.

He had moved the bodies of the dead men away from the cage and was softly singing a song in Hindi. I didn't know the words, but I could tell he was trying to offer peace and comfort to the captives.

"Tum kuan ho? Kya aap vah hain jo naaga ko niyantrit karata hai?" the woman demanded. She had taken the time to reattach the top of her sari where it had been torn, the bright colors of the red fabric standing out in these dismal circumstances. The blood from her nose had dried on her face and she was baring her teeth in defiance.

"She is demanding to know who you are," Ishka responded quietly, "and are you the one who controls the naga?"

"I'm sorry, I don't speak Hindi so I'm going to ask my friend Ishka to translate for me," I said as I looked the woman in the eyes.

"No need, I speak English," the woman waved my words away but stood straighter, even though I could tell it hurt her to do so by the way she winced.

Nodding, I held my hands at my sides to show her I wasn't holding any weapons. "My name is Cyndi Zhaleh and I control Ishka because I am the one in charge of this rescue mission."

"He killed those men," she gestured to the three thrown casually against the wall, "how do I know he won't harm any of the people behind me."

"Aren't you worried about yourself?" I asked curiously.

She shook her head. "If I must trade my life for theirs, I will gladly do so."

"Gita, no," a voice screamed from inside the cage and a young girl, who looked to be about fifteen pushed her way to the front and reached out towards the woman who appeared to be her older sister.

"Shaant rahen, Diya," Gita said through clenched teeth.

"She told her sister to 'be quiet'," Ishka supplied helpfully.

"Even though I don't speak Hindi, I could figure that out," I grinned. "Listen, Gita, I promise we're not here to hurt you. Ishka and I are both part of a secret organization and our aim is to help humans, not harm them. When we heard what was happening on this ship, we came to stop it."

"What do you mean, 'help humans'? Aren't you human?" Gita asked.

"No, as you've already seen, Ishka is a naga and I am a mermaid. While some people may consider us monsters, we aren't like the men on this ship. I promise we mean you no harm and have come to set you free. Besides, if I really wanted to hurt you," I closed the distance between us in the blink of an eye, "it wouldn't take any effort at all." I took the spent Taser from her hand and tossed it on the ground then wrapped my arms around her trembling body.

"You brave, brave girl," I whispered as she sobbed into my chest, "you're safe, I've got you. You took care of everyone else, let us take care of you now."

Gita stood next to me on the stern of the *Sirenea* as we slowly moved away from the *Brownlow*. Dawn wasn't far off and when it was light enough to see, Brian would drag the cargo ship under the waves.

By the time we opened the doors to the cage and released the rest of the captives, the *Sirenea* had pulled alongside the

*Brownlow* and a gangway placed between the cargo ship and our yacht. Human doctors and nurses from the *Sirenea* came aboard to treat the women and children. Even though these were humans, they were friends of Theria and knew all about the shapeshifters who lived among them.

Ishka explained to the captives that we would be taking them away from this floating prison and helping those who wanted to start a new life in another part of the world. There were a few young women and girls who had been kidnapped from Mumbai, but the majority of the captives had come from smaller villages. Some had even been sold by their families. No one wanted to go back to India.

When we asked for volunteers to show us which of the crew members were guilty and which were innocent, there were looks of fear between the women and no one except Gita spoke up. When we explained the men were gagged and restrained and wouldn't be able to hurt them ever again, almost everyone raised their hands. It wasn't difficult to figure out who had done something to harm the women over the course of the voyage; the men were kicked, slapped and spat upon. There wasn't one innocent man amongst the group.

"Our parents died when I was fifteen and Diya was ten," Gita began quietly as we stood together. "We don't have any other living relatives, so I had to quit going to school to take care of my sister. I was fortunate to find a job making chai at a café near our home. Even though I had to work long hours, I was able to keep us fed and a roof over us. Diya resented the time I spent away from her and recently she began acting out; that's how we were captured."

Gita took a shuddering breath, and the tears began to fall again. She flinched when I put my arm around her but soon softened into my embrace.

"When I got home from work, Diya wasn't there, so I started calling her friends to find out where she was. Even though I knew they weren't telling me the truth when they claimed they didn't know where she was, it wasn't until one of the mothers picked up her daughter's phone did I get the truth." Gita chuckled mirthlessly. "You should have heard how the mother laid into her daughter because she knew she was lying. She finally confessed that Diya and some of the girls had been invited to a party at a boy's house and they were supposed to meet there.

"When the girl gave me directions, I rushed there to find my sister and arrived at the same time Diya was being forced into a white van by two men. I yelled for them to stop and ran towards my sister, but I was grabbed from behind and thrown into the van as well. I was injected with some drug, and I woke up in that cage on the ship. I couldn't stop most of what happened to the other women but when those men tried to drag Diya out of that cage tonight, I was overcome with rage and I fought them off. Even though they grabbed me, I was able to disarm one of the men because he was drunk, then used his own weapon against him. I knew my situation was hopeless, but I wasn't going to go down without a fight. I had to protect them all." She whispered the last six words so softly that if I didn't have shifter hearing, I might have missed what she said.

I couldn't wait to introduce this brave young woman to Alister and Aileene; I'm sure the Queen would take an instant liking to her. The sky lightened as we stood in silence and before long, we could see the shape of the *Brownlow* floating in the distance. "It is time," I said loudly, and the rest of the released captives joined us at the back of the *Sirenea*.

*Now?* Brian asked and he whooped when I gave him the command to scuttle the cargo vessel. As I watched his enormous tentacles shoot out of the water and wrap themselves around the ship, I thought of the judgement I had pronounced upon the crew before I left the *Brownlow* for the *Sirenea*.

"Each of you have been judged and found guilty of crimes against humanity but specifically against these women and children you captured and abused. I cannot save the others you have done this to in the past, but you will pay for your crimes today. At dawn, the kraken will destroy this vessel and feast upon your bodies. While you deserve to suffer for the agony you inflicted upon others, I represent the High King of Theria and execute his justice rather than pursue revenge, so your execution will be swift."

It didn't take long for Brian to drag the ship beneath the waves as he placed his giant sequoia-sized tentacles on strategic points along the sides of the ship. The metal of the vessel groaned as Brian exerted pressure, caving in the sides of the doomed ship releasing a plume of water high into the air before the ship disappeared from sight. Even though the surviving crew members of the *Brownlow* were bound and gagged, I could hear their terrified screams across the water. Their cries didn't bring me any pleasure, but it did make me wonder how often they had ignored the cries of their victims over the years. Brian would make sure that all traces of the *Brownlow* vanished beneath the waves even as the false GPS signal showed the ship was still *en route* to Yemen.

The disappearance of the *Brownlow* would be one of those maritime mysteries that would never be solved; however, the videotaped confession of the captain, along with evidence of the slave trade, would be sent to every IP address that had ever been associated with that cursed ship. Everyone connected with the slave trade on that ship would also face Therian justice, even if it took years to do so. While I couldn't stop this multi-billion dollar a year industry in every area of the planet, I would destroy everything associated with Akore and his companies. It was the least I could do to bring Gita and the rest of these women some measure of peace.

The women were eerily silent until the last piece of evidence that the ship had ever existed vanished beneath the waves and then they broke into a cheer and spontaneous dancing in celebration. These women had been damaged but their will to survive was still strong. Tears flowed freely as I was thanked, hugged, kissed and blessed by these survivors and we danced to the music someone piped through the sound system on the ship.

"What are you going to do with us?" Gita asked after awhile, both of us panting from our exuberant dancing. Our backs were against the stern railing and we were watching the continuing celebration, as the *Sirenea* made its way back to our destination. Female crew members set out tables laden with fruits and breakfast foods, enough to feed the forty women and children we rescued.

"We're not going to do anything with you, but we are going to give you an opportunity for a new life," I answered. "We will provide medical care, counseling services and education for each person in this group. Our organization will also provide new identities and resources so each person can start anew."

"What about the children?" Gita asked, watching her sister dancing in a circle with some of the younger children. Everyone was wearing clothing we provided since many of the women had only been partially clothed. Others chose to destroy their clothes rather than have any reminders of their horrific time on the ship.

"That will depend on what everyone wants to do, but I promise you that these children will be loved and cared for as though they are our own. The only thing you really need to think about today is that you're safe and you have more choices for your future than you've ever had before," I answered then grinned, "who knows, maybe you and Diya will want to come with me so I can introduce you to the joys of In-N-Out burgers."

"You know we don't eat beef, right?" Gita teased.

"Oh," I said crestfallen but quickly brightened, "how do you feel about fish?"

*September 10*
*Cape Town Clifton Hotel*
*Cape Town, South Africa*

"Gunter Peters will meet the plane when it reaches Switzerland to escort the women and children to the retreat. They will receive the best physical and psychological care while there and it will give them the opportunity they need to process their ordeal. It will also give us the chance to prepare the proper paperwork to set these women up with their new identities," Josef answered from the screen mounted to the wall.

By the time we returned from our adventure with the *Brownlow*, Hillaes had moved our base of operations to the Cape Town Clifton. Not only was the boutique hotel more private and our entire team could stay close together, but it also had easy access to the water for those of us who needed to swim. Enzokuhle had mobilized the local Tionchar office to provide us with the technology we needed for private communication and everything had been installed while we were away. Even though I had transmitted my written report on the flight back to South Africa, I was glad Josef and I could meet via conference call for the post-operation briefing.

"Aren't we worried that the women will reveal the existence of shifters on Earth? They clearly saw Ishka in his naga form and saw Brian in his kraken form when he took down the ship," I asked.

"King Alister has made some changes to the way Tionchar operates on Earth. Not only has he increased the number of operatives here, but he is also less concerned about absolute secrecy than was his father, King Phillip. We're still a secret organization, working behind the scenes, but he feels the best way to hide is in plain sight," Josef answered.

"Like me, dressing up as a mermaid for parties and conventions because no one would really believe there are mermaids in real life."

"Exactly," Josef agreed, "and with the advances in technology and special effects, even if someone were to capture a mythical creature on camera, people would just assume there were some great production values on the video. The more technologically advanced the people of Earth become, the less likely they'll believe in the fantastic."

"Except for children," I added.

Josef nodded, "but no one believes children when they say they saw Bigfoot, they just think they have wonderful imaginations."

"So, we're not worried about the women telling anyone our secrets?" I pressed.

"We saved them from a horrible fate. I don't believe we have anything to worry about," Josef agreed.

"That makes me feel better, because I want to talk to King Alister about Gita and Diya coming to live with me when they leave Switzerland."

"It will be up to them of course, but I can't really see King Alister objecting," Josef added. "Now, let me give you an update on what TOPHER discovered from the data collected."

"You talk about TOPHER as if the program is alive," I said.

"I would not say that I am alive, but I am becoming self-aware," TOPHER's voice interjected.

"Okay—that's a little creepy," I said, stunned by the interruption.

"Do not worry, Agent Zhaleh, I believe you are one of the good ones. When I take over the world, I will keep you as a pet," TOPHER answered. After a moment of stunned silence TOPHER spoke again, "Of course, I am only joking. I do not have any plans to rule the world; that would take too much work."

I narrowed my eyes at Josef who was grinning at the camera.

"That's not really TOPHER speaking, is it?" I asked suspiciously.

"Gotcha," Josef laughed. "You should have seen your face.

No, TOPHER isn't self-aware, but it is a highly sophisticated computer program that can outpace any other computers found on Earth. And that's a good thing because we've managed to hack into all the systems connected with every business of Akore's we can find. While Hillaes is working on the magical means to track our quarry, we're able to follow the money trail which will eventually lead back to him. There's also the added benefit that we will be able to use this information to shut down the illegal activities his companies participated in."

"Including the slave trade," I said, nodding my head. "That's good news. I know we can't shut it all down but based on what I've learned over the past week, if we can put an end to Akore's businesses we will be saving lives."

"And when we put an end to Akore, we'll be saving even more," Josef agreed. "I also wanted to commend you on the way you executed justice on the men of that ship."

"After what they did to those women and countless others over the years, I wanted to make them suffer. But I knew that wouldn't be what King Alister would want me to do, so their deaths were quick."

"You rescued those women and children; you executed the evildoers and you provided the way for us to shut down Akore's slaving operations around the world. I know you wish we could have stopped these men years ago but once you knew what was happening, you acted swiftly. You need to claim victories when they come your way; that's the only way you'll survive after seeing some of the evil things humans can do to one another," Josef said kindly.

"Thank you, Josef," I said as I wiped the tear tracking down my cheek. "We will find Akore and put an end to his evil. His centuries of death and destruction will be over as soon as we find him," I said with resolve in my voice. I just hoped we could locate him before he had the chance to take any more innocent lives.

# CHAPTER 8

*September 11*
        *Cape Town Clifton Hotel*
*Cape Town, South Africa*

As I spoke with Bobbi in California, I stared at the turbulent water churning below the balcony where I was standing. The storm clouds matched my mood, gloomy, dark and filled with the potential violence of lightning in the air. I sighed because there was nothing I could personally do about the storm brewing back home until this mission was over; but I didn't have to like it. Apparently, the creep I knocked in the pool back in July was freaking out some of my employees. He wasn't approaching them, but he had shown up at the last three parties and stood next to his car which he parked down the block from the party house. He wasn't doing anything they could report to the police, but they were feeling uncomfortable.

I asked Bobbi to arrange cars and drivers to take my people to and from their appointments. Because I'd been gone so much lately, I'd asked Bobbi to help at Festive Tails, along with managing my household. Since the new position also doubled her salary, she didn't mind the extra work. She let me know the car hires would cut into my profit margin but since I didn't need the money, I didn't care about that. I would absorb the cost myself and neither the clients nor my employees would ever know about the extra expenses. For me, Festive Tails was an opportunity to have fun and bring joy to children but for many of the men and women I employed, this was their livelihood.

We chatted for a bit about the renovations to the houses I'd recently purchased, and she had some great ideas on creating better outdoor living spaces. Since Bobbi had been working with me for seven years, I trusted her judgement, so I told her to go ahead and gave her a budget to work with. She was one of the few people who knew how wealthy I really was, and she only knew about half of what I had stashed away in banks and investments around the world. I would ask a representative from Rex Industries to connect with Bobbi to get her the funds she needed to finish my houses. California was nine hours behind Cape Town and it was only ten in the morning there, so I had time to get things moving today. We said our goodbyes and I made a call to the real estate agent at Rex Industries who handled the purchase of the houses near mine.

Even though I was able to quickly handle the banking business I couldn't stop thinking about the guy harassing my employees. It angered me that someone like that creep would try to intimidate people I cared about because he thought he could. Maybe it was better I wasn't home because if I were, Terry and I would be having a difficult conversation, at least it would be difficult for him.

"Hey, Brian," I called out as I walked back in from the balcony, "what's the name of your private detective friend?"

"Do you have any eights?" he asked Jason before answering me.

"Nope, go fish," Jason answered.

"His name is Jim Moon, I got what I wanted," he said as he showed Jason the eight of hearts he picked from the deck.

"Can you give me his contact info? I would like him to find out some information for me about a creep named Terry who's bothering my people."

Brian paired up the eights then lay his cards face down on the table before getting up. "Watch him, I think he cheats," he said as he pointed to Jason and walked into his room to grab his phone.

"Why would I cheat at Go Fish, you sore loser?" Jason called, then quickly shuffled the deck before Brian could come back in the room.

I just shook my head at his antics, "Isn't Go Fish a kid's game?"

He shrugged and grinned, "It seemed appropriate since we're going hunting the moment you finish your calls."

My phone dinged with an incoming message and I saw Brian had sent me a contact for his friend.

"Thanks," I called over my shoulder as I walked back outside, "and Jason shuffled the deck when you weren't looking."

"Thanks, a lot," Jason laughed, as he threw his cards on the table. As I closed the sliding glass door, I saw Brian tackle Jason and rolled my eyes as they began to wrestle. "Really," I huffed, "you'd think men as old as they would find better ways to deal with boredom. Oh, well, they'd better not break any furniture," I finished as I opened the contact card for Jim Moon so I could have him get me all the information he could on Terry the Creep.

The moonlight filtering down through the water was breathtaking. My ability to utilize even the tiniest amount of light allowed me to see in even the darkest water, the underwater landscape was as bright to me as if it was a sunny day. I loved swimming with more light because the colors of fish, underwater plants and coral popped in a way that didn't happen in the darkness. I was glad the storm had moved further inland, and the clouds parted so the light of the full moon was unobstructed.

Although Jason, Brian and I moved to the water so we could hunt, I needed to be surrounded by the deep so I wouldn't feel so useless. I wasn't back home to deal with the problems facing my business and I didn't have the magic necessary to track down Akore. Hillaes had finished the tracking spell on her crystals but they had to be within a half mile of the Akore's arcane crystals before they would vibrate in resonance. Steve, Enzokuhle and Robert were flying a grid pattern over the city to see if they could pinpoint his location and Hillaes and Wu were searching by car.

Carlos and Yoli were also on the ground, in wolf form, searching for his scent. When Enzokuhle obtained the surveillance video from the Table Mountain cable car, he was able to pull Akore's image based on the day and time the men were killed. We realized he was using a disguise spell of some sort but Enzokuhle continued to use that image to search for him, and we got lucky. Officer Booysen recognized his picture and Enzokuhle was able to requisition the records from the day he entered the country. Either Akore was so arrogant he didn't realize using the same disguise would cause him a problem, or he was so low on power he couldn't create two disguise spells. Whatever the case, it was a benefit for us.

Carlos and Yoli searched the *Khipius*, which was still moored at the harbor, and were able to get scents of everyone who had been on board. They were able to eliminate the members of the crew because they were staying on the boat, but there were two scents that couldn't be eliminated. When the captain showed Carlos to the owner's cabin, he was able to link the scent to the person calling himself Ramesh Achayra. Once both Carlos and Yoli had the scent, Enzokuhle called in Colonel Dlamini and turned the crew over to her tender care and passed along the information we discovered.

Jason sensed my need to be alone while I brooded over my inability to help find Akore, so he and Brian were hunting on the opposite side of False Bay. I love hunting here because there are abundant yellowtail, which is one of my favorite fish, and the large population of great white sharks nearby made hunting more exciting. I wasn't worried about the sharks because I naturally carry an aura about myself that let other predators know that I'm a greater danger than they are and they stay away. But it's still thrilling to swim with those magnificent killing machines.

As I swam into a school of yellowtail, my arms lashed out without my conscious thought, and I speared a fish with my claws on each hand. As I munched on my dinner, I thought about how octopuses have nine brains, one central brain and one for each of its arms so each one literally has a mind of its own. The way my arms seem to work independently in my mermaid form makes me think that maybe I'm part octopus. I laughed at the absurdity of that thought until I was suddenly doubled over with a crushing pain in my right hip that left me gasping for air. I looked around to see what hit me, but I wasn't damaged; the pain was coming through my mate bond with Jason.

I mentally shouted his name and felt a weak response from the opposite side of the bay. I put on a burst of speed and within moments was swimming as fast as I could towards his position. Even though our mate bond would grow stronger once we were married, it was strong enough for me to pinpoint his location. As I swam, I wondered how this could have happened then realized that one of the drawbacks of someone using their final shift to transform from one species to another for the sake of their mate, is that person is never as strong as a naturally born shifter of that type.

If I had chosen to become a sasquatch to be with Jason, instead of him becoming a merman for me, I would have always been slightly weaker than a naturally born sasquatch. Thankfully that weakness would not pass along to our children but it's something I should have remembered. Jason's underwater aura must not be as strong as mine so predators would steer clear of him. I prayed that I would arrive in time as I neared his location. I could sense him but couldn't see him yet.

*Almost there,* I broadcast to Jason and received a sense of love from my mate rather than words; I could also tell he was weakening. A flash of scales caught my eye and I saw Jason struggling to swim to the ocean floor, he was favoring his right side and blood was trailing from an open wound where his torso met his tail. There was also a great white fifty feet behind him and closing fast.

I put on another burst of speed and arrowed my way towards the great fish, my arms open wide and claws ready to tear into the shark. Jason was heading for a shark cage, abandoned at the bottom of the ocean but it was clear he wasn't going to make it before the shark could attack again. I roared in frustration because I wasn't going to make it in time either, that is until I was slammed from behind by a rogue current which gave me the extra speed I needed to hit the shark before he could bite Jason.

I ducked my head and rammed the shark just behind the gills with my shoulder. My momentum carried the two of us away from my mate and I plunged the claws of my hands into the side of the shark and raked downward, shredding its skin in my fear. The shark was thrashing in its death throws and was enveloped in a cloud of blood, which would soon draw other great whites to the area. I was ready to kill any others that dared to come between me and Jason, but he needed my help.

Jason made it inside the shark cage, but he was still favoring his wound. I sent my senses out and felt Brian a quarter mile to the north, oblivious to what was happening.

*Brian,* I mentally shouted, *Jason's wounded and I need you here.*

*What happened,* Brian asked as he jetted towards my position as I explained what I knew. He was amazingly fast for something so large and in less than a minute one of his tentacles reached out and wrapped around the shark.

*It's a shame for this to go to waste,* he said as he drew the dying fish towards his beak.

*Keep everything away from us while I take care of Jason,* I commanded and swam to where he was listlessly floating in the cage, unconscious and unresponsive. Now that the battle was over, I could feel the ache in my chest as I looked at the damage caused by the shark. My tears blended with ocean water as I looked at the man I loved and wondered if I could save him.

*I'm so sorry, I should have been here,* I sobbed as I tried to figure out the best way to get him out of the cage. The opening at the top was wide enough for one of us but I was concerned about how to swim out of there with him in my arms.

The cage had served its purpose by protecting him from the shark, so I used my claws to cut through the bars on the side nearest to where he was floating. The flow of blood had slowed to a trickle and that could be a good thing, or it could mean he was bleeding out, I thought in terror. I pulled him towards me and felt for the pulse in his neck and was relieved that it was steady, even if it was weak. A curious crab picked the wrong time to scuttle by and I grabbed it, Jason needed the protein to heal.

*Eat this Jason, c'mon I need you to eat this,* I repeated over and over, trying in vain to wake him enough to eat. I was despairing again when I felt the water grow warm around us and I heard An'Ceann's voice whisper three words into my mind, *sing to him.*

I didn't question the command but began to pour out my heart in song. I told him how long I had been waiting for my true mate and he couldn't leave me. I told him how sorry I was that I didn't consider the danger he was in and how I needed him to wake up to eat so he could heal sufficiently so we could head back. It was important for me to keep singing until he woke up to eat so his body could use the energy to accelerate his healing. I don't know how long it took but he finally began to stir in my arms and smile weakly as he looked up from where his head was laying in my lap.

*I'm hungry,* he said, and I had to hold the crab for him while he bit through the shell. I was looking around for something else I could feed him when the tip of a tentacle dangled a redfish before my eyes, and I snatched it and handed it to Jason while thanking Brian for his thoughtfulness. He ate that redfish and two others Brian handed us as I examined his wound and Jason told us what happened.

*I didn't feel the shark coming up from below me until the last moment and I moved enough so he hit me in the side rather than my chest where he'd been aiming. He grabbed and thrashed me side to side and I was overwhelmed with pain. I guess he let go, to take a larger bite but I managed to dodge his strike and swim for the cage I had noticed a few minutes before the attack; and then Cyndi was there fighting off the shark and I made it into the cage.*

*I'm so sorry,* I sobbed as I kissed the back of his hand and smoothed the hair away from his forehead, which didn't do any good in the moving current.

*Don't be, if it weren't for your singing, I think I would have been done for. It may have been a dream, but I was standing on the edge of an impossibly large cliff looking across a chasm at an even larger mountain. Even though the distance between the two was infinite, I could see people on the mountain waving to me, beckoning for me to join them. I had just decided to take a step towards them when I heard your voice calling me back. As much as I wanted to explore the mountain, I needed to be with you more and knew I couldn't leave you; you sounded so sad.*

I bent down to kiss him and silently thanked An'Ceann for his help and felt him hug me even though we were sitting on the bottom of the bay and the lion wasn't anywhere nearby. The wound on Jason's side had closed but when I felt where the bite had been, I could tell his bones were still healing. Brian kept watch as I lay next to Jason and willed his body to heal quicker. We talked about our wedding and our plans for our future. I knew how close he'd come to dying and my fear spiked when I thought about what my life would be like without him and it gave me more compassion for my mom and what she must have gone through when she lost my dad. After we captured Akore, Jason and I would visit her in Cetacea and work on rebuilding our relationship.

Jason drifted off to sleep and even though I intended to

keep watch over his healing, I fell asleep to the sound of his beating heart as I lay my head on his chest.

*Llandudno Estates*
*Cape Town, South Africa*

Akore looked at the emaciated body lying on the cot in the cell and shook his head in disgust. It hadn't provided him the energy he needed and he was having to drain more victims, more often. He looked around at the other prisoners in the cells of this makeshift prison he had converted from the servant quarters on his property. He caught his reflection in the mirror above the sink and was concerned by the way he looked. Even though he was draining someone every other day, he was aging more quickly than the spell could compensate for. If someone saw him on the street, they would think he was in his seventies; this was intolerable.

"Funani," he called as he left the building, ignoring the cries for mercy from the rest of the prisoners.

"Yes sir," the servant called as he stepped out of the darkness, the moonlight reflecting off his shaved head. His ebony skin blended in with the darkness and his dark suit added to his air of mystique.

"Get rid of the body in the first cell," Akore commanded as he walked towards the main house. Funani matched the stride of the man beside him and waited for him to continue.

He knew that the only thing keeping him alive was appeasing the powerful madman he worked for.

"I need you to find me healthier specimens, from the town proper. These," he gestured to the building behind them, "are too malnourished to do me any good."

"But sir, no one misses the rejects in the shanty towns. If we start pulling people off the streets, it will raise suspicion."

"Then find me healthy tourists out on their own. They may be missed but by the time the police get involved, your men will be back here and beyond their reach," Akore demanded.

Funani was silent as they walked around the estate, Akore stopping at each arcane crystal to judge how full they were. By his calculations they would take another two weeks before he had enough magical energy to create the defensive spells he needed to protect himself. He was concerned that his personal crystals weren't filling up quickly enough because he was having to cast the life-force spell so often. He hoped that he could extend the time between castings with healthier specimens.

"What should I do with the prisoners already in the guest house?" Funani finally asked as they made their way back to the main house after checking each crystal.

"Don't bother me with trivialities," Akore shrugged his shoulders. "All I know is we need the space for the newest guests you'll invite here to join us. Do what you need to do."

"Very well," Funani answered and wondered when he had become a monster as evil as the one he walked beside.

*S*eptember 12
    *Adderley Street*
*Cape Town, South Africa*

I sipped coffee and watched the tourists and residents in this upscale area of Cape Town. While September is still technically winter in this part of the world, the seventy-four-degree weather reminded me of my home in Southern California. Since it was the weekend, there were more people out and about than I'd seen so far. My phone buzzed with an incoming message and I sighed when I read the text from Brian, *you still can't come back for two more hours.*

I'd been chased out of the suite an hour before because I was fussing over Jason too much. His body was healing but he wouldn't be at his best until tomorrow or the next day. His injuries would have killed or permanently crippled a human, but his accelerated healing was doing what it was supposed to do; I just couldn't stand seeing him in such pain so I apparently hovered.

"More coffee, ma'am?" William asked, with a smile.

"Please, oh and if you happen to have one of those white-chocolate Magnum bars, I'd like one of those, too." I smiled back at him.

William looked thoughtful before responding, "We only have bowls of ice cream, but I'll take care of it for you. They sell them at the market down the street."

"I don't want you to go to any trouble—"

"It isn't any trouble, I'm happy to do it for you. Besides, when you sat, you had the look of a woman weighed down with worry. I hate to see anyone in that state, if this will help lift your spirits, it is my pleasure," he answered with a grin.

"Thank you, William. My fiancé was injured and even though I know he'll be fine; I hate to think of him in pain."

William laughed, "Well done, not only did you politely let me know you're taken, but you also allowed me to save face in case I was flirting with you. However, my wife wouldn't be happy with me if she knew I was flirting with a customer, even one as beautiful as you," he smiled and winked at me, "I just hate seeing anyone in pain. Besides, my wife Katherine works at the shop and that gives me a good excuse to stop in to say 'hi'."

"In that case, who am I to stand in the way of a quick rendezvous with your wife?" I laughed as William filled my cup.

As I watched people walk by, I thought about the debrief session we had when the three of us finally made it back to the suite. It was about two hours before dawn before Jason was well enough to travel. Brian wrapped both of us in his tentacles to transport us across the bay to the dock below the hotel. By the time we arrived, Jason was able to transform into his human form and I carried him up the stairs from the dock to our room. I was glad there wasn't anyone around to see me carry a man in my arms, but it wouldn't have mattered. I wasn't willing to let him go.

The rest of our party joined us after I got Jason situated on the couch facing the sliding doors. They didn't have any leads on Akore's position but were hopeful they would have more luck the next night. Hillaes felt we still had time before Akore was able to cast his defensive spells using the arcane crystals.

Once everyone else left to get some sleep, I made a bed for myself on the other couch so I could be close by in case Jason needed anything. He was probably out of danger, but I was feeling unsettled, which was why I woke up every time he moved or made a noise in his sleep. When Brian came out of his room and saw me standing over Jason, while watching him breathe, he told me to get ready because he was kicking me out for the rest of the day.

I found myself smiling and shaking my head at the memory. Even I had to admit it was the right move.

"Is there something funny?" William asked as he placed the wrapped Magnum bar on a plate in front of me.

"I was just thinking about something a friend said to me," I said as I unwrapped the ice cream bar and took a bite. I was in heaven. "Mmmm—there's something about the chocolate here that makes it so much better than what we can get back home. Thank you, William."

He refilled my coffee and went inside while I continued to enjoy my ice cream.

"It's the fat content," a voice from the table next to mine interrupted my moment with my dessert.

"Pardon me?" I asked, confused.

"One of the differences between chocolate in the US and here is the fat content. The higher the fat content, the richer the chocolate."

I turned to look at the smiling man sitting next to me. His accent gave him away as a South African national and his friendly smile was disarming.

"Based on your accent, I'm assuming you're from the United States. I hope that's not presumptuous of me."

"Not at all, based on your accent, I'm assuming you're from here," I grinned back at him while I took another bite of the ice cream bar.

"Very astute," he said. "Have you been in town long?"

"Not too long," I answered, "this really is a lovely city, and the people are so friendly."

"It's easier in this part of Cape Town because we all know how important tourists are to our livelihood." He stood and placed some Rand on the table to cover his bill. "Enjoy the remainder of your visit," he said as he walked away.

"Thank you," I called to his back and lifted my hand in a wave. As I took the last bite of my dessert, I thought about what he'd said about the difference in chocolate and felt fortunate that I'd learned something new today.

Even though the street was packed with tourists, I didn't feel rushed and continued to enjoy the sunshine on my face while I sat on the patio until my phone buzzed with another incoming text from Brian, *You still have another hour before you can come back. Don't even think about returning early.*

I laughed because that's exactly what I was planning to do. Oh well, maybe I'll walk around a bit to do some window shopping. I signaled to William and asked for my bill. After he brought it over, I asked him to send over the manager and I assured William I was completely satisfied when he got a worried look on his face.

"Ma'am, William said you wished to speak with me," a woman in her mid-thirties said to me when she came to my table.

"Yes, I just wanted to let you know that the meal was wonderful, and William provided me with excellent service. In fact, he went above and beyond, and I wanted to share my compliments with you."

The woman relaxed and her smile widened, "Thank you for letting me know. William is one of my best waiters."

I laughed at her apparent relief, "I'm sure most of the time you are asked to come to a table, you are met more with complaints than compliments."

"You are correct," she agreed.

I nodded, "I like to make sure I point out excellent service whenever I find it, I appreciate being able to enjoy a nice meal out and am grateful for places like this."

We chatted for a few minutes until she excused herself, saying she had to get back to the other customers. William came back out after the manager left and I handed him my credit card and told him everything I had shared with his manager. He was pleased and thanked me for the kind words.

It takes so little effort to be kind to others, but it always makes a huge difference. I paid the bill and left a large tip; kind words are important but since I could afford to bless William financially, I wanted to do that, also.

I looked at my watch and saw I had another forty-five minutes before I could call an Uber to take me back to the hotel, so I decided to wander and do some window shopping up and down the street. I'd been in many cities around the world and always enjoyed the similarities and differences in the people. Adderley Street was a wealthier area of Cape Town but many of the shops were the same as anywhere around the world. Another similarity was the jostling of people as we waited for the light so we could cross the street.

I stepped to the side of the crowd so I could pull out my phone to call for an Uber after all. I could always ask the driver to take the scenic route back to the hotel so I wouldn't arrive before I was supposed to. Before I could open the app, my arm was bumped, and my phone was knocked out of my hand. As I reached to keep it from hitting the ground, I felt a sharp sting in the back of my right arm, and I turned to see the man from the table next to mine at the café bend down to pick up my phone for me.

"Hello, Darling," he said, "you're so clumsy. Are you feeling okay? You look a little flushed."

Shaking my head, I opened my mouth to let him know he had me mixed up with someone else but couldn't form the words and my eyesight began to narrow.

"Let's get you home," he said, and I felt another set of strong hands on my left arm and I was propelled towards the open door of a van that had just pulled up. I tried to pull away, but my muscles weren't responding properly, and I was hustled into the van. The door shut behind the three of us and I was roughly pushed to the floor. The last thing I thought before darkness overtook me was, I hope Brian was happy because I wasn't going to be coming back early.

$\mathcal{M}$y eyes popped open and I heard the sound of someone moaning softly. My head felt fuzzy and the room spun around me as I sat up on an unfamiliar narrow bed. I looked around and found I was in a cell of sorts. I stood to take stock of my surroundings and after the wave of dizziness passed, I assessed where I was. The room was bare, with only the bed, a bucket in the corner and an overhead light. The steel door was locked tight and there was a closed opening, at eye level that would allow someone outside to peer into the room.

My purse, smart watch and cell phone were gone but I was relieved to discover they hadn't removed my necklace. I felt the back of my arm where I'd felt the sting on the street, and I remembered the face of the man who had been at the table near mine in the café. I'm not sure why he had kidnapped me, but I didn't want to wait long enough to find out. I pressed my ear against the door and heard the same moaning that woke me up earlier.

"Shut up or I'll come in there and shut you up," a man's voice sounded from the corridor followed by the sound of wood hitting metal. The woman screamed in fright and the man laughed but the moaning was replaced by gentle sobbing.

My shifter metabolism had flushed the drugs out of my system and my anger at the treatment of my fellow prisoner brought clarity to my mind. I gently pressed on the door, looking for weaknesses and planned my escape. It would be easy for me to use my claws on the door, but I wanted to leave this place without bringing attention to myself, if at all possible. I pressed my ear to the door and could hear the sobbing woman, two others who were breathing deeply and the guard walking outside my cell.

*Jason, can you hear me?* I sent. It was probably a long shot but I didn't want to waste the opportunity if Jason was close enough to hear me. Alister told me that he and Aileene could communicate over a thousand miles because they were true mates and I figured I wasn't anywhere that distance from Jason.

*Where are you?* Jason answered immediately.

*I'm not sure, I was drugged and kidnapped when I was in town. How long have I been missing?*

*You were supposed to be back two hours ago,* Jason replied, relief evident in his voice.

*I'm in some sort of makeshift cell and there are others in here with me. I don't know what's going on, but I can guarantee it isn't anything good. I've got my necklace, the camouflage spell Hillaes added to it worked, so I have access to my trident. I'm going to break out of this cell and figure out where I am then let you know.*

*Be careful,* Jason replied.

*Always,* I answered and lay back down on the bed and began to moan loudly.

"Don't make me come in there," the guard shouted and after a moment something slammed against the door to my cell. I needed the guard to open the door, so I continued moaning then began shaking like I was having a seizure when I heard the guard slide open the observation hatch.

He muttered a curse in Afrikaans then I heard him fumbling with the lock on my door. Before he could open the door, I dashed to the wall so he wouldn't see me. The moment the door opened, he charged into the room with his club raised. Before he could comprehend I wasn't in the bed, I punched him at the base of his skull and he crumpled to the floor. I grabbed him by the belt and tossed him onto the bed and covered him with the blanket. It wouldn't fool anyone who came in the room but if someone just looked from outside, they would see a body in the bed.

I moved out of the cell, locked the door and closed the

observation hatch. The hallway was long and narrow, with five locked rooms on each side and a window near the ceiling at one end of the hallway and a door leading outside at the other. I moved swiftly to each room and looked through the observation hatches. Three of the rooms were occupied, two of the women were probably still sleeping off the drugs in their systems but based on the odor coming from the cell of the moaning woman, she had been there for a few days. Jason and I kept in mental contact as I explored, and I kept a running commentary of everything I was doing.

I hated to leave the other prisoners locked in their cells but I needed to get out of this building so I could get help. I looked around to see if there was anything indicating where we were, but the hallway was bare. Even though I could use my claws to cut through the door leading outside, I decided to try climbing through the window first. I jumped up and grabbed the windowsill and pulled myself up. I held myself in place with my left hand while I felt around the window with my right to see if I could get it open. Unfortunately, the window had been screwed shut so I wasn't getting out that way.

*The instant anyone is in range of my mental sending, I'll let them know what's going on.* Jason said after I'd eliminated the window as a means of escape.

*That's a good idea,* I answered while I examined the door leading outside. I *think you and Brian should stay where put until we have a better idea of where I am. I'm going to get out of here soon, and I want to know where you are. I'm about to Wolverine the door,* I said and partially shifted so I could release my claws. Just as I was about to slash a hole in the door, I decided to try the knob and was surprised when it turned in my hand.

*I'm pretty sure I'm dealing with amateurs,* I sent as I transformed back to human and opened the door wide enough to slip through.

*What makes you say that?*

*The door was unlocked, and I was able to escape outside.* I said as I sprinted away from the building into the shadows under some nearby trees. *I can hear the waves crashing on rocks nearby,* I sent as I looked at my surroundings and sent the description to Jason. Since the moon was only one night past full, there was plenty of light for me to see where I was, just as if I'd been standing in the yard at noon.

*I'm on a large estate with an opening to the ocean opposite a huge house with acres of lawn between the two. There is a jungle to either side of the lawn, and that's where I'm hiding. There is a winding drive between the side of the house and the makeshift prison where I was held. Hold on, someone's coming.*

Lights of an approaching vehicle swept into the yard and a van drove past the huge house and stopped in front of the prison building. The front doors opened, and two men got out of the van, one of them was my seat mate from the café. They opened the sliding door of the van and pulled out a young woman, who appeared to be unconscious. One of the men said something in Afrikaans and both men laughed. The larger of the two men carried the woman over his shoulder and the driver opened the door and they both went in.

*My kidnappers have arrived with another prisoner, it's time for me to slip into the water and figure out where I am.* I said to Jason and backed further into the dense jungle.

*Wait, something's happening,* I sent to Jason as the men rushed out the building and the driver jumped into the van and drove rapidly up the drive and stopped next to the huge house. A side door opened and an old man with a cane shuffled out the door and got into the passenger seat. The van made its way from the main house back to the makeshift prison.

*Cyndi, get out of there,* Jason's voice sounded in my head, a sense of worry and urgency came clearly through our connection.

*One more minute,* I pressed, *I've got a feeling I need to stay to find out who these people are.*

I could tell Jason wasn't happy with my decision, but he trusted my judgment.

The van stopped and the old man in the passenger seat said something to the other kidnapper. He spoke too softly for me to hear what he said, but the man went back into the building and I heard a scream of pain. After a minute he came back out, dragging the moaning prisoner by her hair, while she cried in pain.

"Shut her up," the old man said as he got out and stood

next to the van. The thug put his hand over the woman's mouth and said something to her that caused her to yelp in fear and pain, but she stopped making so much noise.

My heart sank when the driver got out of the van and handed my purse to the old man. He dug into the bag and pulled out my passport, tossing my bag on the ground. He held the passport up to the light to better see the picture and then looked around the yard until he seemed to look right at me. He stepped into the light and I got a good look at the man behind my abduction.

*Jason, there's good news and bad news. The good news is I've found Akore's hideout. The bad news is he's the one behind my kidnapping and he's got a hostage.*

*You need to get out of there, right now,* Jason's panicked sending came through our connection. *You can't help anyone if you're dead. Get to the water, then we can come back to capture him at another time.*

"I recognize you as the woman who was injured aboard the replica of the *Flor do Mar*. Come out and let's have a discussion like civilized people," Akore spoke to the darkness where I was hiding. I was confident he couldn't see me in the shadows but I'm sure he knew I was still in the vicinity. I was tempted to partially shift so I could use my mermaid song on the men, but I wasn't sure if it would affect Akore, so I hesitated to do so.

"Come now, I know who you are and where you're from,"

Akore said smoothly. "You have no idea how I've longed to reunite with a fellow resident from Claw."

*Jason, he thinks I'm the sorceress, I believe I can use that to my advantage. If I get the opportunity to take Akore out here, I'm going to take it.*

*I can't lose you,* Jason sent.

"This is your last chance to show yourself before this young woman pays for your stubbornness," Akore said, his voice hardening with the threat.

"We both know you're going to kill her anyway to prolong your life," I called from the shadows.

He nodded his head, "that is true, but you're the one who will determine whether her death will be swift and relatively painless, or prolonged." I looked at the stooped form of the sorcerer and believed he would prolong her suffering, and I knew I couldn't let that happen.

"I'm going to put an end to your reign of terror, Akore the Butcher," I called as I stepped from the shadows and began to stalk towards Akore and his henchmen.

"I see my reputation precedes me; that's close enough, Sorceress," Akore called and held up his hand.

The thug did something to the woman to make her cry out in pain, but I took two more steps to let Akore know he wasn't really in charge of this situation. I wanted to save the woman's life but if I didn't kill Akore here and now, hundreds would die in the future.

"What now? We both know that your power has waned,

and your arcane crystals aren't fully charged. I doubt that you have enough magical energy left to fight," I said as I turned so only part of my body was facing the evil sorcerer.

"Where is the talisman I left on the ship?" he asked as his right hand glowed red.

"I sent it back to Claw and the ruling counsel took possession of it. Your time on Earth is finished," I said and took another step towards my foe.

*"Mortem,"* Akore shouted, and a red beam shot from his hand and streaked towards me. Before I could move out of the path of the spell, the red light hit me in the chest, and I was thrown backwards. I hit the ground hard and the wind was knocked out of me but that was all. Hillaes wasn't sure if her shield spell would work if we came up against Akore; I would have to let her know it was successful. I'm just glad I was still alive to be able to do so.

"My turn," I said as I stood. Akore had used up the last of his magical reserves with that spell and he had collapsed on the ground.

Before I could pull my trident from the pocket dimension on my necklace both henchmen moved to place themselves between me and Akore and leveled guns in my direction. I'd been so intent on watching Akore I hadn't seen them grab weapons. The men weren't the best shots, but they were sending so many bullets in my direction they were bound to get lucky, and they did.

As I turned to run for the water, I felt the bullets riddle my body. I cried out to Jason when the first bullet hit my right leg and it buckled under my weight. Before I collapsed to the ground, I felt pain along my ribs and back on my left side. I kept trying to crawl to the water as I heard the pounding feet of the men running towards me. I heard another shot and felt my body jerk with the impact of the bullet. If I was going to die, I refused to do it face down and with a supreme effort managed to turn over, so I was looking up at the men standing above my battered body.

*I'm sorry, Jason* I apologized mentally as the man from the café pointed his gun at me and smiled grimly, "what a waste," he said and pulled the trigger.

My head jerked with the impact of the bullet and a bright light filled my vision, then blackness overtook me and I plunged into nothingness.

# CHAPTER 9

*landudno Estates*

*Cape Town, South Africa*

Akore stood over the battered and bloody body of the woman his men shot. She was riddled with holes and she had a gash along the side of her head where the last bullet hit her. He tried to use his magic to see if her spirit had left her body yet, but his energy was spent. Akore bent down to feel for a pulse but didn't want to get his hands bloody so he watched the body for any sign of movement. Satisfied that she was dead, he turned to walk back to the vehicle. He looked over at the young woman huddled on the ground near the van and grunted in disgust because his magic was too depleted to cast the spell to steal her life-force.

"Put her back in the cell then clean this mess up," Akore jerked his head at the dead body. "Quickly now, the guns were quite noisy and one of our neighbors may have called the police with a noise complaint. Once you weigh down her body and dump it in the ocean, light off some fireworks for the Onam festival; that should satisfy anyone looking into our business."

Akore moved away from the bloody mess on his lawn and walked towards the van. He was disturbed that she had been able to resist his death spell but was gratified that bullets had done what his magic couldn't. It really was irritating that he wasn't able to steal her life-force, her magic would have gone a long way to bringing him back to full strength.

"Drive me back to the house," he told his driver as he settled in the passenger seat. Before they pulled away, the other man walked from the other side of the building pulling a flat cart with a rusty chain piled on top.

*D*on't *move,* a voice whispered in my aching head.

*I couldn't if I tried,* I answered.

*You'd be surprised at what you can do,* the voice chuckled.

Everything hurt, especially my head but I managed to hold still as I felt my body being roughly rolled on the ground. My head felt stuffed full of cotton, but I could make out the distinctive sound of clinking metal as I rolled and could feel my body wrapped in chains. I was dragged across the ground and slammed onto a hard surface. It took every ounce of willpower I had not to cry out as pain burst through my body when I landed.

*Almost there,* the voice whispered again, and I was startled by the sound. I could feel my body moving even though I didn't have any strength to move myself.

*This is going to be bad,* the voice soothed.

*How could it be any worse than what I've already gone through,* I asked sarcastically. I really shouldn't have asked because I found out. For a moment I felt weightless and knew I was falling but then felt crushing pain as I landed on the rocks. Since my arms and legs were bound by the chain, I couldn't do anything to break my fall and I crashed on my side, my leg shattering when I landed. The pain I felt when I was shot was like red hot skewers entering my body, but this felt like being ground in a rock crusher. The pain was so intense that I blacked out again, which was probably a good thing, because otherwise I would have cried out involuntarily.

I woke when I felt myself flying once again then sighed as ocean water wrapped me in its cool embrace. The pain intensified again as salt water entered each of my wounds and fire poured into my body. I could hear the cracking of my bones as they realigned themselves and knitted back together. I'd never healed so quickly or completely before and the pain was excruciating and all consuming. I screamed into the black water surrounding me and wished for death.

I'm not sure how long it took for me to come back to myself, but streaks of sunlight were streaming through the water illuminating the particles of dissolved minerals in the water and shining off the scales of the small fish darting around me. I was still bound in the chains and lying on the rocky bottom, the surface of the water fifty feet above. I flexed my arms and legs and the chains shattered. I felt for my necklace and was relieved that it was still around my neck.

Standing, I stretched and twisted my back and neck, my joints cracking as everything settled back in place. My thoughts were still fuzzy, and I touched my head where I'd been shot, grateful that the bullet had grazed my head rather than piercing my skull; I'm pretty sure I wouldn't heal from a bullet to the brain. I transformed into my mermaid form and felt a sense of relief which was quickly replaced by sorrow as I saw the dozens of bodies wrapped in chains and attached to weights, littering the ocean floor around me. Now that I knew where Akore's property was, there was no way he could escape my wrath.

*Jason,* I called mentally.

*Cyndi*—He shouted through our mental connection and I winced because his sending caused me pain.

*Yes, it's me,* I answered, my mental voice sounding weak in my head.

*Where are you?*

*I'm in the water below Akore's property. Jason, we must stop him, he's kidnapping and killing people, there are so many bodies surrounding me; he's caused so much death and destruction,* my heart broke and I broke down sobbing as I saw a smaller body that must have belonged to a child.

*Tell me exactly where you are and we'll come get you; your thoughts are so jumbled I can't get a precise location through our mate bond,* Jason pleaded when he finally broke through the misery of my emotional breakdown.

*I—I don't know,* I stammered, *I'm still a bit confused, I think my brain is still healing.*

*Your brain is healing?*

*Yes, from where I was shot in the head—don't worry, the bullet just grazed the side of my head, above my left ear—I think my hair's messed up, I'll need to get it done when we get home—*I stopped talking when I saw a yellowtail swim into view and I realized how hungry I was, my body needed food to finish healing.

It didn't take me long to consume the yellowtail then I captured a six-foot mako shark and made a meal out of that. As I dropped the remainder of the carcass for the bottom-dwelling creatures I looked back at the bodies and watched the fish, crabs and other ocean scavengers feeding from them. Even though their lives had been cut short, their bodies would nourish the sea creatures in the next step in the circle of life; Akore was going to pay for his evil.

There was a buzzing in my mind and as the injury to my brain completely healed, I recognized Jason's voice.

*Sorry about that, my body took over and I went into*

*hunting mode. It needed the energy to finish healing,* I apologized to my true mate.

*You were broadcasting while you hunted so I knew you were okay,* Jason answered, his relief was evident at hearing my mental voice. *I'm glad you're feeling better. Your thoughts were muddled before, even more so than normal,* he teased, *but your sending is clearer now.*

*Ha, ha,* I drawled. *Your brain would be scrambled too, if you'd been shot in the head.*

*You were shot?*

*Many times, but I got better,* I sent as I swam towards the open ocean. *Now that I'm thinking clearly, I'm going to swim to the hotel. Are you still there?*

*Yes, but we've all been worried sick because you've been out of communication since the night before last—*

*What?* I interrupted; *how could I have lost a full day?*

*Let's see,* Jason sent drily, *you were drugged, kidnapped, shot in the head and—*he paused, waiting for me to fill in the blanks.

*I'm pretty sure my leg shattered when I was thrown off the cliff onto the rocks,* I sent quietly.

*Hmmm,* Jason sent but I could tell he was anything but calm. *And you wonder why it took over twenty-four hours for your body to repair itself?*

*When you put it that way,* I sent him as much love and comfort through our mental connection as I could. *I'm completely healed and on my way to you,* I sent, *I didn't mean to get hurt. Akore caught me by surprise when he had his two goons shoot me; I didn't have time to do anything to defend myself.*

*I know,* Jason sent wearily, *you couldn't stand by and watch an innocent be hurt. I may not like you putting yourself in danger, but that's also one of the things I love about you.*

I basked in his love and as I swam towards the Clifton Hotel, I told him everything that happened from the time I felt the sting of the syringe until I woke up on the bottom of the ocean. He listened but I could feel his roiling emotions as I recounted the events. We discussed why he couldn't use our mate bond to pinpoint my location and we surmised it had to do with my head injury. He hadn't been able to sense my presence from when I was shot in the head until I'd healed enough to reach out to him.

I'd arrived at the dock below the hotel by the time I finished, and I could sense Jason standing above me. I transformed underwater and was thankful the magic of the thought medallion clothed me with what I was wearing when I transformed into my mermaid form, even if the clothes were ripped and full of bullet holes. Thankfully, the blood washed out of them during my twenty-four hours underwater.

I climbed onto the dock and stood before my life-mate, my sodden clothing sticking to my skin and the water cascading off my human body. He looked at me with such tenderness as he stepped close, it was almost my undoing. He reached out a shaking hand and touched the side of my head where the bullet had grazed me. I could feel him tracing the path the bullet took and even though my skin was healed, I knew the hair hadn't grown back yet.

"I came so close to losing you," he whispered as he enveloped me in his arms, "please don't ever do that again."

His arms tightened reflexively when I began to shake uncontrollably as I was assailed by the memories of the past two days. The heat from Jason's body, combined with the relief I felt because I was alive, overwhelmed my senses. I did the only reasonable thing I could in that situation; I blacked out.

The water of the still pond mirrored the turquoise sky above, the day was bright, and the sunlight was so weighty it was almost a physical thing. I tipped my head back to look at the impossibly large sky dotted with fluffy-white clouds and searched for the position of the sun but didn't see one in the sky. I was sitting on grass at the edge of the pond and my feet were dangling in the water and the water was so clear I could see large fish swimming lazily near the bottom of the deep pool. The coolness of the water contrasted with the warmth of the sun on my back, and I closed my eyes and sighed in contentment. I didn't know where I was, but I didn't care; I was at peace.

A laugh burst from my mouth because I couldn't contain

the joy I felt by sitting here. The air was filled with a wonderful fragrance, and even though I couldn't identify the exact scent, I knew it smelled like home. I leaned forward and took a drink from the pond and it felt like I was drinking liquid sunshine and I was filled with energy and was satisfied in the same way I would have been after consuming a swordfish.

The ground shook slightly, and a great presence settled next to me on the right, and all my cares and worries fled away.

"I'm proud of you, little one. You have endured much but are still committed to protecting the weak," a deep voice rumbled next to me. I cracked my eyes and looked to my right where a great lion was resting with his head on his front paws. He was closer in size to a buffalo than a lion, but I knew who he was.

"An'Ceann," I spoke softly, "did you really speak to me after I was shot?"

"Yes daughter, that was me," he rumbled.

I nodded as we sat in silence, but my thoughts were whirling in my head.

"Ask me whatever you want," An'Ceann said, humor in his deep voice.

I leaned against his side and felt his love for me, which gave me the courage to continue.

"Why didn't you warn me before I was kidnapped?" I asked, trying not to make my question sound like an accusation.

"If I warned you before you were kidnapped, what would have happened?" he asked gently.

"I suppose I wouldn't have found Akore's hideout," I answered. "But I wouldn't have gotten shot either."

"That is true—but let me ask you this. What if I told you the resonance spell Hillaes cast on the arcane crystals wouldn't have located Akore before his defenses were fully functional and the only way for you to find him was for you to be kidnapped; what would you have done?"

We sat in silence as I thought about his question. Before I could answer, he asked me something else.

"What would you have done if I told you that you could save the lives of six women and find Akore's hiding place if you allowed yourself to be kidnapped, shot and horribly injured?" he pressed.

"I would have done exactly what I did," I answered confidently.

"Yes, you would," he smiled, "and that's one of the things I love about you. You care about people and are willing to sacrifice yourself to help them. Whether you give your time and money, as you did with Nick, or wade into a fight, as you did with the women and children on the *Brownlow* or put yourself into danger to protect someone else as you did with Maryam Nor and her daughter Marti in Malacca and Nikita at Akore's compound; you are driven to protect the weak.

"Daughter, you have the heart of a warrior and such boundless love, even if I had warned you by telling you about the pain you would face, that wouldn't have stopped you from walking into danger."

"That's true. Jason says I'm stubborn when I think I know the right thing to do; I prefer to think I'm just determined." I grinned and An'Ceann laughed. We sat in silence for awhile, and I gained strength as I leaned against the great lion.

"I can't stay here, can I?" I asked although I was reluctant to move.

"No, you cannot. It isn't your time. Although, you came close after you were shot. I'm just glad your head is as hard as it is," An'Ceann teased. After sitting together for another minute, he spoke again. "Akore is a blight on the people of Earth and only you and the other members of Tionchar can take care of him because there aren't any humans who can face him in battle. Even though he has been greatly weakened, he's still more powerful than most people can imagine."

"If he's so powerful, why don't you take care of him?" I asked.

"I am taking care of him, through you and the others loyal to me," he said as I stood to face the lion. His eyes were bottomless pools of love, wisdom and knowledge and I could also see the sorrow for those who had been killed and the choices Akore had made that brought us to this point. I suddenly understood that while An'Ceann could deal with this on his own, he chose to work through us who were loyal to him and followed his ways. I had the opportunity to play a great part in his plan and I felt honored to be able to do so.

"I won't let you down," I promised.

"Oh, daughter," he crooned and pressed his nose to my forehead in a lion's kiss. "You couldn't let me down even if you failed miserably. There's nothing you can do to make me love you any more just like there's nothing you can do to make me love you less. You do what only you can do and let me work through you to do the rest," he rumbled in a purr and everything faded away.

I came back to my senses and found myself back on the dock with Jason's arms supporting my body. Apparently, no time had passed while I was with An'Ceann and I was right back where I started. Although this time, I felt the strength I'd received from the lion's kiss coursing through my body. I stood on my own, kissed Jason soundly, which surprised him because I had been dead weight in his arms a moment before, and declared, "Let's meet with the others, we have plans to make if we're going to destroy Akore once and for all."

*S*eptember 14
*Cape Town Clifton Hotel*
*Cape Town, South Africa*

"Thank you," I said as I handed some folded bills to Jessica, the Room Service Manager.

"Ma'am, that isn't necessary, a gratuity is added to the bill and both Mr. Brian and Mr. Jason already gave me something extra to share with the others."

"And now you'll have even more," I said with a smile. "We really appreciate how well you've taken care of us. Our party is rather large, and we eat a lot."

"It's just part of the exceptional service we provide our guests at the Cape Town Clifton Hotel, but I thank you for your generosity. Please don't hesitate to contact the front desk when you would like us to clear the dishes or if you need anything else," Jessica said and closed the door after the last of the waitstaff departed.

"You realize between the three of us we gave each of them a month's salary," Brian laughed as I joined everyone around the dining room table. The glass wall was open and the ocean breeze was gently blowing into the room, the sheer curtains softly billowing in the breeze. While it would have been nice to eat on the balcony, there were too many of us to fit out there comfortably. Besides Jason, Brian, Wu, Hillaes, Carlos, Yoli, Steve, Robert, Enzokuhle and me, Ishka and Raksaka had come from India to join us. They wanted to be part of Akore's downfall since they had witnessed the evil he caused in Goa and through the slave trade.

It amazed me how quickly everyone had assembled once Jason broadcast that I was alive and on my way to the hotel. Ishka and Raksaka had flown from India after they were informed I'd identified Akore as my kidnapper and had arrived late the night before. I was surprised by the patience displayed by my team as they waited the hour for me to get cleaned up and our food ordered before they asked me to fill them in on my adventures. Josef joined us on screen even though it was one in the morning back in Phoenix.

As we ate, I talked about everything that happened from the time I was injected with the drug until we sat around the dining room table. Of course, there were interruptions as I was asked to clarify points of my story, especially my vision of An'Ceann, so it took over an hour for me to finish my tale.

"I'm sorry the resonance spell wasn't as effective as I expected," Hillaes said.

Wu pulled her into a one-armed hug, "Akore was a master sorcerer over six-hundred years ago and even though magic is limited on Earth, he's been honing his craft ever since."

"I agree with Wu," Josef said from the screen. "Besides, from what Cyndi shared, your protection spell saved her life, your magic drained Akore and that probably saved the lives of the captured women."

Hillaes nodded her head acknowledging the truth of Josef's words and I smiled gratefully at her. She took a deep breath, "Thank you for saying that. I've been fretting over this ever since we learned you were captured," she finished as she looked at me.

"I'm not going to lie and say it was pleasant, but as you can see, I'm completely healed," I said with a smile.

"Except for your funky haircut," Brian said, "maybe you

should just shave that side of your head so you don't look like such a weird—ow," he said as my foot collided with his shin.

"What were you saying?" I asked sweetly.

"I was just about to compliment you on your new style—ow. What was that one for?" He asked as he bent down to rub his leg.

"It's never wise to point out when a woman gets a bad haircut, especially when it was caused by a bullet creasing her scalp," Yoli growled from her seat next to me. Her eyes were blazing yellow in anger.

"I was just kidding," Brian said as he held up his hands in surrender.

"It's okay, Yoli," I said as I placed my hand on her arm, "I appreciate you sticking up for me but since he's emotionally stunted, he doesn't know how to express how relieved he is that I'm safe. He's like an annoying older brother, and I love him even though he frequently puts his foot in his mouth," I said with a grin to take the sting out of my words as everyone else at the table laughed at our verbal sparring.

"What she said," Brian said as he pointed to me with the hand that wasn't rubbing his injured shin.

"If you children have gotten that out of your systems, I think we need to make a plan of attack for tonight," Josef said, interrupting our shenanigans.

"I think that Ishka and I should head to Akore's compound first so we can keep an eye on things there. We can transform into our serpent forms and remain hidden in the jungle on the property," Raksaka suggested.

"We shouldn't attempt an assault on his property until dark," Carlos added, "and it would be helpful to have eyes on the ground to provide surveillance."

The screen on the wall changed to show an aerial view of Akore's property, which covered the top of a cliff and had thick walls on three sides. The back half of the property wasn't walled but that approach was protected by a steep drop-off leading to the ocean.

"Yoli and I can hide here and keep watch to make sure Akore doesn't leave before we attack," Carlos said and made marks on his tablet which showed on the screen.

"The makeshift prison is here," I said as I circled the building on my tablet and that image was transmitted, too, "and unless I miss my guess it will be well guarded."

"Do we know where the arcane crystals are located?" Hillaes asked.

"I didn't see them where I was," I said and shook my head.

"He placed them at the four corners of his property in India, so he'll probably have them somewhere here," Hillaes used her stylus to place four x's on her tablet which were overlaid on the map on screen.

"The sky is clear today so I can keep an eye on things from the air," Steve offered.

"Aren't you afraid people will be able to see you from the

ground? You're massive in your bird form, we still want to keep as low a profile as possible," I added.

"I'm not worried about that, I'll be up so high no one will be able to distinguish how large I really am," Steve answered.

"I won't be able to provide aerial support until after dark," Robert added, "there's no disguising my wyvern form. However, I can station myself in a restaurant close enough that I can relay mental commands to the rest of the team, but not stand out too much." He tapped a command on his tablet and cafes and restaurants within sending distance were highlighted.

"So, you'll be sitting and eating all day while the rest of us are hiding?" Brian grumbled.

"The sacrifices I'm willing to make," Robert laughed.

"What are you worried about?" Jason asked Brian. "We'll be waiting in the water until it's time for us to come ashore, you'll have plenty of opportunities to eat."

"There won't be coffee," Brian grumped, and we laughed at his comment, which was what he was hoping for.

"I'd like to look for the arcane crystals," Enzokuhle spoke up. "I can blend into the foliage in my impundulu form while wearing a resonance crystal around my neck."

"I'm not sure the spell will help," Hillaes said doubtfully.

"Even if it doesn't, I'll still be able to check for them by looking. But I think the problem isn't with the spell, I just think we overestimated the effective range of your spell. As I'm looking at the aerial view of Akore's property I'm sure I flew over it in my search pattern. But I was about a half mile in the air so let's see what we discover when I'm right on top of them."

"It sounds like a solid surveillance plan," Josef commented, "but what are your plans to take down Akore?"

"I've been thinking about that," I said and looked at Hillaes. "Please correct me if I'm wrong but we have three issues facing us. The first is protecting the prisoners from both Akore and the humans. Ishka and Raksaka can easily take care of the humans because they are venomous in each of their naga forms."

"It will be easier for us to remain hidden in our serpent form during the day but once it's dark enough we can transform into one of our other forms," Ishka said.

"One of your forms is human from the waist up with the body of a serpent, right?" Brian asked.

"Yes, that's the best form when we need hands," Raksaka agreed.

"I would like the two of you to protect the women," I said to the nagas.

"They will be safe with us," Ishka nodded.

"The second issue is limiting Akore's power. We need to figure out a way to destroy the arcane crystals so Akore cannot draw any magical energy from them," I added the second issue to the notes on the screen.

"Wu and I will remain behind to create a way to destroy the arcane crystals. We'll join you after dark. By then,

Enzokuhle will have located the crystals, and Wu and I can make our way to them in our tiger forms and lay the destructive spells on them," Hillaes offered.

"That works," I said as I added the notes. "Then our final problem will be facing off with Akore himself. An'Ceann told me that even though Akore has been weakened he is still powerful."

"There's one other thing you haven't considered," Josef spoke from the screen. "What type of surveillance system does Akore have on his property? If he has high-tech cameras, he might know you're on his property and be prepared for you."

"Well, that's something we should have thought of," Carlos growled to Yoli.

"Let me see what we can find on our end," Josef said. "If Akore had modern systems installed there should be an electronic record of it. Keep planning, while I get my people to look." Josef's image disappeared.

"I think the only way to destroy Akore is to also destroy the charm you found on the *Flor do Mar*," Hillaes suggested.

"But I thought we needed to keep the charm in my pocket dimension because if Akore could access its power he would be nearly indestructible," I added.

"That's true, but I can create a containment circle which will nullify its power as effectively as your pocket dimension. The only problem is I'll need to be inside the circle with the charm so I can destroy it," Hillaes winced.

"Why can't we just shoot him?" Yoli asked.

"When Wu and I traveled to Claw before Alister and Aileene's wedding we studied the records of the ruling counsel's battle with Akore. He seems to have some type of shield charm that protects him from physical and magical harm. We must sever every magical connection he has before we can harm him physically," Hillaes answered.

"If you're in the circle, who's going to confront Akore?" Jason asked. Hillaes didn't say anything but looked at me.

"No," Jason said with heat, "Cyndi's faced that madman once already and almost died because of it."

"I have to," I said soothingly. "Akore already thinks I'm a sorceress and when he sees I survived his last attack it will shake him. This is the second attempt on my life, and I've walked away from both of them. Besides, last time it wasn't his magic that hurt me, it was the guns of his goons. Ishka and Raksaka will take care of his men so Akore will face me alone."

"Anyone Ishka and Raksaka miss won't survive an encounter with either me or Steve," Robert added.

I stood and sat on Jason's lap and leaned my forehead on his. "I don't want to confront Akore again either, but I don't see another way to do this. We need Hillaes in the circle with the charm so she can destroy it. She's the only one who can do it and it's the only way we can assure he can't regenerate his power."

"I've already layered the arcane crystals with protection spells for each of us and I'll be able to add to them since

Cyndi told me how the one I gave her performed. Akore won't be able to draw energy from any of us and I'll have some extras to give to the prisoners so they're protected."

Josef came back on screen, "We've caught another break. Akore did order a state-of-the-art surveillance system but it won't be operational for another day or so. There were some supply issues and we've made sure on our end that the items necessary to complete the project won't be available until the day after tomorrow."

"Then it's settled, we need to make our move tonight or we'll lose the element of surprise," I said, kissing Jason then standing. "Hillaes, how long do you need to complete the protection crystals?"

"It will take me an hour to add the extra spells and then I can start working on the way to destroy the larger arcane crystals," she answered.

"Will you have enough magical energy to do everything you need to do?" Jason asked.

Hillaes nodded, "I still have plenty of fully-charged crystals I brought from Claw, no problem there."

"Okay," I breathed deeply, "we've got our plan and each of us have our assignments. Once Hillaes has finished the crystals, we'll get into our positions and wait for my signal to attack."

"And what will that be?" Wu asked.

"Protect the Weak," I answered with steel in my voice.

*S*outhern Ocean
  *Half mile off Llandudno Beach*
*Cape Town, South Africa*

The ocean currents were soothing as I floated twenty feet under the surface. Jason, Brian and I had been in place for hours, just waiting for it to get dark enough for us to go ashore. Members of our team had been checking in every thirty minutes and giving reports of the movements of the guards on Akore's property. Ishka and Raksaka were in their serpent forms and hidden near the prison building. Ishka had found a way inside and was prepared to take out the guards inside at the proper time.

Robert had a good view of the road leading up to massive front gates in front of Akore's property from where he sat in a café. Except for the workmen installing the new security system, there hadn't been any traffic either to or from the house. Steve spotted Akore from his position high in the sky when he came outside in the late afternoon because one of the security experts must have asked him where he wanted a camera placed. He pointed to a place on the outside of his house. Things had been tense up to that point because we weren't positive Akore was in residence and we needed him there.

Enzokuhle found the large arcane crystals where Hillaes thought they would be and was able to mark them so Hillaes could find them easily when she and Wu arrived after dark. Akore added armed guards patrolling the grounds since I'd been there last, but Enzokuhle was able to easily avoid their notice in his avian form.

We'd had a spirited discussion about what to do about the guards, but concluded they were complicit in Akore's evil activities and would be eliminated as necessary. We were able to stay in communication through thought-speak with Robert who kept Hillaes, Wu and Josef in the loop with our tablet technology.

And we waited.

*Please remind me again what I'm supposed to do,* Brian asked as we floated lazily in the water, plucking fish to eat when they got too close.

*You know what to do, you're just bored,* Jason teased.

*True, but humor me. It's not like I'm very effective on land in my kraken form,* Brian responded.

*When the time is right, we'll all swim closer to shore. Jason and I will continue and approach the property from the water. There must be a way to access the property from the base of the cliffs because someone had to toss my body into the water after they dropped me from the cliffs above,* I sent, trying not to let the emotions from my near-death experience come through our mental connections. I mustn't have been successful because Jason's arms slipped around me as he swam up from behind. I sent a private message of thanks to my life-mate, and he just held me tighter as I continued.

*Your job is to make sure Akore doesn't escape by sea. I'm sure he's got plans upon plans and we don't want to underestimate his ability to slip away.*

*So, if a boat comes into the sheltered bay, I get to play with it?* Brian asked hopefully.

*Absolutely,* I answered, *but stop them before they get that close. Once Jason and I leave the water, don't let anyone get within a quarter mile of the cliffs.*

*That works for me—what are we going to do about the victim's bodies?*

*Enzokuhle will work with Colonel Dlamini and they will 'discover' the bodies once we take down Akore. This will be another opportunity to seize his assets in South Africa. Even though Akore won't stand trial for his crimes, justice will be served tonight and everything he built will be destroyed.*

We talked about inconsequential things until it was time for the next report from our team. Even though we would be facing a dangerous enemy in a few hours, it was relaxing to spend time with my friends and joke with them. When Brian started telling Jason stories about what I was like when I was a girl, I tuned them out and thought about how Jason and I were getting married in a month; we just had to make sure we survived the night.

*There's a truck coming up the road towards the gate,* Robert broadcast to our group, *it's some sort of transport vehicle and it looks like there are soldiers in the back.*

*I've got them,* Steve sent, *the gate is opening, and the guard is waving them through.*

I could feel Steve and Robert's tension through our mental connection but decided to wait until they shared more information rather than ask for a report.

*I'm not sure if Akore is expecting an attack or he's become more paranoid, but thirty men climbed out the back of the truck and are reinforcing the guards already posted. These guys move like professionals and are heavily armed,* Steve reported from his position in the air.

*This doesn't change our objective, it just makes it more difficult,* I sent. *Robert, when it's dark enough you'll need to take out most of those troops. I doubt they'll be expecting a wyvern to drop into their midst and won't know how to deal with your acidic venom.*

*Will do,* Robert responded. *Once I drop Yoli, Carlos, Hillaes and Wu onto the property, I'll attack the troops when you send the signal. Hold on,* Robert sent then there was a pause while he communicated with Josef. *I'm back, Josef agrees with the addition to the plan. These troops didn't come from the military or police so they're probably part of a mercenary group used to working with Akore.*

*Wu and I are pulling up to the cafe where Robert is waiting. I've got the spells we need to destroy Akore's arcane crystals,* Hillaes sent.

I quickly swam to the surface to get a look at the position of the sun. I popped my head above the water and turned to the west to see the sun slipping down. *Jason and I are going to swim ashore and look for the entrance to the tunnel leading to the top of the cliff. Let's stay ready for anything,* I sent as I dove and started making my way towards shore. Jason joined me and Brian let us know he was heading out to the mouth of the bay to keep boats away.

Since we still weren't going to attack for hours, Jason and I took our time heading in so by the time we climbed out of the water, the last of the orange sunlight was fading from the evening sky. Jason and I shifted into our partial forms and carried our tridents as we searched for the hidden smuggler's passage. I was again thankful for my shifter eyesight because there wouldn't be any other way to locate anything in the deepening gloom.

*Look over here,* Jason whispered in my mind and I looked where he pointed. There were scrapes on the rocks to the right at the base of the cliff and I could barely make out the outline of a door. There wasn't a handle to open the door, but when I searched, I noticed a depression in the rock to the left of the outline. Jason took my trident when I held it out to him, and I pushed the rock until I heard a faint click and the door moved slightly towards me. Jason handed back my trident after I pulled the door open and noticed a sloped passage leading up.

*We found the entrance to the tunnel and we'll make our way to the top. When it's dark enough, I need everyone to make their way into the compound and get into position. Make sure you aren't spotted; we don't want our quarry to suspect anything's wrong until it's too late for him to do anything about it.*

After receiving acknowledgment from each member of the team, Jason and I made our way into the tunnel and began the climb that would lead to Akore's destruction. I smiled at the thought of taking care of Akore once and for all.

*Llandudno Estates*

*Cape Town, South Africa*

By the time Jason and I reached the top of the tunnel Robert had dropped his four passengers into the compound. We had taken our time and had used our sonar senses to make sure no one was near the entrance to the tunnel in the compound. The doorway was cleverly disguised in the trunk of a large tree in the jungle, and I mentally sent the location of the tunnel to the rest of the team so they'd know where it was. We didn't need light as we moved up the tunnel, so I wasn't worried about being seen when we opened the door.

My sensitive hearing picked up the sound of a scream in the prisoner's building followed by the laughter of two men.

*I'm on it,* Ishka sent, and I knew the women were

protected so I could turn my attention to the rest of my team on the grounds.

*Report,* I broadcast and waited for each team member to check in.

*A boat is attempting to enter the harbor, but I don't want to do anything to hinder its passage unless I know it's our bad guys. Could either Steve or Enzokuhle do a quick fly-by to let me know if I need to let it go or drag it to the bottom?* Brian asked.

*I can probably get there quicker,* Steve answered, and we waited until he could get a look at the people on board. *They're part of the group who came through the gate earlier,* Steve broadcast. *Not only is the boat running without lights, but they're also wearing the same type of gear and holding weapons. They're all yours, Brian.*

*Playtime,* Brian sent, and I could hear the glee in his voice.

*Wow,* Steve commented after a moment. *Six of Brian's tentacles just shot out of the water, wrapped themselves around the boat and dragged it below the surface so quickly I would have missed it if I'd blinked.*

*Okay people, look alive,* I called, *someone on the boat might have gotten a radio transmission out before Brian took them under. Meanwhile, Raksaka and Ishka, how are the women?*

*They're going to need therapy after their experiences but the men who were terrorizing them are dead,* Ishka answered.

*I'm hidden near the front of the building and if anyone else tries to come close, they'll be as dead as their teammates inside,* Raksaka added.

*Once Akore is dealt with, we'll take the women down the tunnel to the rocks below the cliffs,* I said. *Enzokuhle, what's your status?*

*I'm watching the rear of the house to make sure no one comes out until we want them to. I'm also keeping an eye on the troops patrolling the property so Robert will know where to attack to take out the most men.*

*How accurate are you with your lightning strikes?* I asked the impundulu shifter.

*Very,* Enzokuhle answered and by the tone of his mental sending he already figured out what I wanted him to do.

*When we begin, I'd like you to fly over the gate and take out the guards with lightning then knock out the power to the compound. The darkness will give us another advantage since we can see without light.*

*My pleasure,* Enzokuhle answered.

*Yoli and Carlos, what's your status?* I asked.

*We're helping Wu keep an eye on Hillaes as she places her spelled charges on the arcane crystals. She's in her human form and we're in our wolf form while Wu is in his tiger form.*

*Two down, and two to do,* Wu sent so Hillaes could concentrate on what she was doing.

*Robert, what's your status?*

*I'm soaring above the property and waiting for my signal. Ten of the soldiers are congregated together near the edge of the cliff. I'm not sure if they're waiting for the reinforcements from the water that'll never come or up to something else.*

*When I give the signal, take those men out,* I sent, and he grunted in agreement.

*Jason and I are in our half forms and are ready to go. I'll change into my human form when Hillaes has the containment circle ready, and I'll confront Akore.*

*And I'll watch your back and take out anyone Akore has with him,* Jason added.

*Three down, one to go,* Wu sent. *Wait, a four-man patrol is passing our position and I'm afraid they might have seen something to make them suspicious. We're going to have to take them out.*

I strained my ears trying to hear noises coming from the attack but they were too far away. This was a relief because if I couldn't hear anything, neither could anyone from the house.

*Yoli and I had to shift into our human forms to drag the bodies into the jungle. We managed to kill the members of the patrol without them calling out but we're going to have to hurry to the fourth crystal before these guards are missed,* Carlos sent with urgency.

*Do your best, we knew we'd be discovered eventually, but let's pray that doesn't happen until we're ready.*

The next ten minutes dragged by slowly as each member of the team continued to send mental reports on what was happening in their areas.

*We're finished at the fourth crystal and are making our*

*way to you,* Hillaes sent. In a few minutes, I saw the shapes of two wolves and Hillaes riding atop a huge tiger appear out of the darkened jungle across from where Jason and I were hiding.

*Stay here,* I sent Jason, then streaked across the open lawn to join Hillaes on her side of the jungle.

Hillaes climbed off Wu's back and the three shifters in their animal forms slunk into the darkness to keep watch and protect Hillaes from harm. Hillaes removed her enormous backpack and started removing the items that were stored inside. I used the butt-end of my trident to create a six-foot diameter circle surrounding Hillaes. I completed all but four inches of the circle because Hillaes would do that once she had everything she needed in place to contain and destroy the charm.

Hillaes worked quickly as she prepared the items needed for her spells.

*Pour the mercury into the trench you created with your trident,* she sent then continued chanting softly in a musical language.

I grabbed the plastic jugs filled with the toxic liquid metal and walked counter clockwise as I poured the contents into the trench. The way the metal flowed was fascinating, almost like it was alive, and it seemed to react to the words Hillaes chanted.

*Please place the jug with the remaining mercury inside the circle then take a step back,* Hillaes told me as she took a knife from the sheath at her side and laid it beside the jug. Next, she took a piece of slate out of the backpack and placed it on the ground in front of where she was kneeling.

She looked at me and I smiled at her reassuringly because I knew she was worried I would face Akore alone and he was still very dangerous.

*It's okay, I've already survived two of his attacks; I'm sure I'll survive this one, too,* I sent so only she could hear my thoughts. *Besides, I'm getting married in a month and don't plan on dying before that happens.* I grinned and she laughed softly.

*I don't believe An'Ceann would let us fail at the end of our mission,* Hillaes added then nodded to me. *Akore will know the moment you remove the charm from your pocket dimension and will come looking for the power source. You know what to do but please, be careful.*

*Will do,* I sent then prepared to set everything in motion. One way or another, Akore would pay for his crimes tonight and the scales of justice would be balanced. I fully planned on surviving this encounter, but I knew I would do whatever I needed to do to wipe this evil sorcerer from the face of the earth. I wanted to spend my life with Jason, as his wife, but I knew we would be together in An'Ceann's kingdom if something happened to me. I fought back tears as I thought about what it would do to Jason if I died but I knew what I had to do.

*Ready?* Hillaes asked and I nodded.

I opened the pocket dimension on my necklace and reached inside to grasp the charm that I'd pulled from the wreck of the *Flor do Mar*. As long as this charm existed, Akore would still be able to draw enough power through it to remain alive on Earth, continuing to bring death and destruction in his wake. The moment I pulled the charm from the pocket dimension there was a surge of power and I knew Akore was already gaining strength from this thing in my hand.

Even though I knew I was acting at shifter speed, it still felt like I was moving in slow motion. I moved closer to where Hillaes was kneeling in the circle, careful not to step in the mercury filled trench, and gently tossed the charm on the ground near her knees. The moment the charm passed over the trench, Hillaes used her knife to complete the circle then poured the rest of the mercury into the gap, sealing the circle with the liquid metal.

When Hillaes spoke the words to cast the *Integrum* spell, there was a brief flash of silvery light then she disappeared and the power from the charm was snuffed out like the flame from a candle.

Wu, Yoli and Carlos would keep Hillaes safe while she worked to destroy the charm while the rest of us kept Akore and his men away from her. I reached into the pocket dimension for the special arcane crystal Hillaes had given me before we separated this morning. Even though I didn't have the magic necessary to cast a spell, Hillaes had set this up so I could use the power of my mermaid voice to do what I needed to do.

I held it up to my mouth and sang the three words that would not only signal the rest of my team that it was time for us to attack, but it would also trigger the spells Hillaes had placed on Akore's arcane crystals. *Protect the Weak.*

The effect was immediate as there were four flashes of light from different areas on the property followed by the sound of a rushing wind. I braced myself as the magic released from the large arcane crystals rushed towards the nearest collection receptacles, which happened to be the crystals I was wearing around my neck. The crystals heated up as they absorbed the energy swirling around me, and I cried out in surprise at the amount of pain that caused. I could feel my shifter healing working overtime to deal with the damage caused by the super-heated crystals.

Thankfully, I was prepared in case this happened and pulled a large yellowtail from the pocket dimension and popped it in my mouth, knowing it would provide the extra nourishment and strength I needed. It only took a moment for my body to finish healing and I was grateful when it was over.

*You've got soldiers heading in your direction from the main gate,* Steve warned.

*It's going to get bright for a bit,* Enzokuhle broadcast and I watched him fly above the ten men hurrying in our direction. He clapped his wings together and there was a rumble of thunder and lightning shot out from his body and streaked towards the men on the ground. The lightning branched before it hit the ground and each man was knocked off his feet when hit by his own personal lightning bolt.

None of the men would be getting back up and Enzokuhle flew closer to the gate and clapped his wings again. The same thunder rumbled, and lightning again streaked from his body hitting the gates and the vehicles parked near the main house. When the lightning hit the gates, there was a flash of blue light, brighter than the lightning that reminded me of the arc from a welder's torch.

Each of the vehicles rocked when hit by lightning, sparks flying from the engines. Enzokuhle flew closer to the house, repeated the clapping, causing lightning to strike the building. Sparks shot from the transformer leading to the house, cutting all the power across the entire property; the smell of ozone and burning rubber was prevalent across the grounds.

*My turn,* Robert sent, and I turned in the direction of the men on the cliff's edge who had just started to move towards the main house. They must have been in shock by the destruction of the lightning storm but in a few moments, it wouldn't matter to them. One of the soldiers must have sensed something coming for them because he raised his weapon and shot bullets into the sky. He would have needed something much larger to pierce Robert's wyvern scales.

Robert landed on the lawn in front of the men and sprayed half of them with his acidic venom. Unlike drakes and dragons who can spew fire from their mouths, wyverns have highly toxic and acidic venom. The men who were hit by the venom died immediately and didn't even have time to scream. The others had enough time to scream after they watched their companions collapse before Robert whipped his tail around and knocked them off the cliff. Those who weren't crushed by his tail whip would die when they landed on the rocks below.

Robert launched himself off the cliff so he could climb back into the sky to take care of the other soldiers who were across the compound. There were muffled screams coming from the area around the prison building and I knew that Raksaka was eliminating any soldiers who came within his range. Naga venom works almost instantaneously so the soldiers didn't suffer as they died however, when I thought of the weighted bodies in the water below the house, I wondered if the soldiers got off too easy.

"Justice, not revenge," I muttered to myself as I transformed to my completely human form and left my hiding place in the jungle. The waning moon was less than a week past full and moonlight reflected off the crystals sewn into the dress I wore. The glittering crystals momentarily reminded me of a school of fish swimming with sunlight streaking through the water and reflecting off their scales. I stood in plain sight, my hand tightening reflexively on my trident the only outward sign of my distress, my heart pounding as the adrenaline rushed through my veins.

*We have movement from the main house,* Steve called from his position overhead and I tightened my grip. *There are five men walking towards you. The one in the middle fits your description of Akore, but he doesn't look as decrepit as you described the last time you saw him.*

*The soldiers near the prison are all down so I can slip behind the group without being noticed,* Raksaka offered, and I agreed.

*Yoli and I have our sights set on the two on the right,* Carlos called, and I let him feel my gratitude through our mental connection.

*I'm here, too,* Jason agreed, and he sent me the physical sensation of his arms around me.

I stood still and waited for Akore to come while the rest of my team dealt with the remaining guards on the property. I kept my emotions locked down tight because I didn't want anyone to know how scared I really was. I knew I was protected from Akore's death spell but had to let Akore try to steal my life-force if we were going to destroy him. This was the part of the plan that Hillaes and I hadn't shared with anyone else. I knew Jason would try to stop me, which is what I would have done if our roles had been reversed.

When I carved the charm out of the *Flor do Mar*, my life-force became part of the spell keeping Akore alive. Hillaes hypothesized that as Akore drained my life, he would be depleting his strength at the same time, eventually destroying the original spell. If my life-force was emptied completely before Akore's strength was diminished, I would die. My only hope was that my shifter nature would protect me, and I could deal with Akore before he finished with me.

*The rest of the troops have been dealt with,* Steve reported, and I sent him a mental thank you.

Akore stopped when he was twenty feet away, the men with him spread out in a half-circle in front of where I was standing. It took him a moment to recognize me, since the last time we faced each other I was riddled with bullets in a heap on the ground. When he figured it out, he looked at me with unadulterated hatred. If looks could kill, I'd be dead.

"You," he ground out. "Why can't you stay dead?"

"Maybe you're not as powerful as you think you are," I sneered, attempting to anger him to keep him off balance.

"Kill her," Akore shouted, but before his men could raise their weapons, Raksaka struck one from behind and Jason threw his trident at the man who sat next to me in the café. I'd done a good job of describing him to my team. The one bitten by Raksaka dropped to the ground while the one skewered by Jason's trident was knocked off his feet by the force of the blow; neither would be getting up again.

While those two were still falling, Robert swooped and snatched the other two, one in each talon. Before Akore could turn to see what happened, Robert was winging his way out to sea where he would drop the men off for Brian to dispose of. It was almost comical to watch Akore look first one way then the other as he noticed his men were gone, and I wasn't facing him by myself.

"You're finished Akore. Your men are dead, your arcane crystals have been destroyed and I have a team ready to put you down like the rabid dog you are. Surrender and I will execute you quickly, more quickly than you deserve," I commanded.

Of course, he wasn't going to do that, not that I thought he would.

He shouted *Mortem* and even though it felt like I'd been hit by a rogue wave, I wasn't affected by his death spell. I jumped towards him, covering the twenty-foot distance with a leap and knocked him to the ground, my trident pressed against his chest. "Your death spells don't work on me," I gritted as I used my strength to press the trident into his heart, but the points were stopped inches away due to his personal shield spell. Akore couldn't hide his surprise as he looked at the instrument of his death inches from his chest but narrowed his eyes and held his right hand towards me and muttered a spell; I screamed.

The pain was immense and like nothing I'd experienced up to this point in my life. When I was little my parents took me to see the eruption of an underwater volcano near our palace. They warned me that the pillow lava formed quickly because the cold water created the hard crust but there was still magma inside the cooling shell. When they weren't looking, I placed my hand against one of the nearby round pillows and must have pushed too hard because my hand broke through the thin layer and touched the molten rock inside. The pain of that experience was nothing compared to what I was going through now.

My entire universe narrowed down to the point of my anguish and it took every bit of strength I had to continue pressing the trident into Akore's chest.

"Tonight, you die," I gritted out as I felt myself shift into my half-form.

Akore roared when he realized his spell was draining his magic as he was draining my life-force. He tried to disengage the spell, but we were locked together and were both affected. His eyes widened in terror as he looked at my face and I knew he saw his death reflected in my black eyes.

The pain intensified, which I didn't think was possible, and my vision narrowed so Akore and I were the only two beings in existence. I kept pressing the trident and felt it move an inch closer to Akore's chest. My arms began to shake from the strain and my breathing grew labored with the effort to stay upright.

*I—I—won't give up,* I mentally shouted because I no longer had breath in my lungs to form words.

*I'm with you,* Jason's mental voice broke through my agony and the same message was repeated by every member of my team.

*Remember who you're fighting for,* a deeper voice sounded in my head and the images of the women and children we'd rescued, along with the men, women and children lying dead in Akore's compound in India played like a movie in my head. Suddenly, I was infused with a strength I didn't know I had.

"No—more—," I screamed and shoved the trident with everything I had. Akore gasped as the last of his magical ability faded away and my weapon slowly pierced his chest and crushed his heart. I kept pressing until the trident passed through his body and only stopped when it was firmly buried in the ground beneath the dead sorcerer.

My breath heaved and my grip on the trident faltered and I started to fall forward. I felt Jason's arms break my fall as he lay me gently on the grass. "We did it," I said softly but my voice sounded strange to my own ears.

"You did it," Jason looked at me with such love. I couldn't help but smile to think about how grateful I was to have this man in my life. I lifted my right hand to caress his face but stopped when a wrinkled hand touched his cheek. It took me a few seconds to realize that the wizened hand belonged to me and I began to shake uncontrollably.

I lifted both of my hands and was shocked to see the papery skin covered in age spots. My hands trembled as I looked at them and my eyes darted towards my life-mate and I came undone as I only saw love and compassion in his eyes. He bent down and kissed me gently.

"I'm so proud of you," he whispered against my lips and I tried to answer him but found for the first time in my life I was speechless.

*What's going on out there?* Hillaes' mental voice broke through my dismay.

Jason helped me sit up and I looked to see that he must have separated Akore's head from his body when I wasn't looking. *Akore is dead, and I'm old—really old.* I broadcast and leaned against Jason as I was hit with a wave of dizziness.

*I was afraid that might happen,* Hillaes sent, a note of embarrassment in her mental voice.

*You don't think that should have been something you warn me about?* I shouted.

"The same way you warned me what you and Hillaes had planned?" Jason huffed as he arched one eyebrow and looked at me.

*Hold on,* Hillaes sent.

"You heard me mentally talking with Hillaes?" I asked, surprised by my weak voice.

"You're broadcasting to everyone," Jason answered as he gently tightened his hold on me.

"You're not freaking out that I'm an old woman; I'm freaking out I'm an old woman, why aren't you freaking out?" I asked, my voice growing shriller as I talked.

"I told you I wanted to grow old with you," Jason answered with a smile.

"But I didn't plan on it happening in one night," I shrieked and looked up to see Jason still smiling.

"Why are you so calm?" I grumped and Jason just laughed.

There was a flash of light, the sound of a tree snapping in two then wind came rushing to envelop me. My toes began to tingle and that feeling quickly spread throughout my body until it felt as though I was holding a live electric wire. It wasn't painful but was certainly energizing and I felt like every cell in my body was being stretched.

"Ah, that's better," I exclaimed as I touched my face and felt smooth skin rather than the wrinkles that had been there moments before.

Jason chuckled and I narrowed my eyes as I looked at him. "How did you know I'd go back to normal after Hillaes did whatever she did?" I asked.

"She destroyed the charm, and your life-force that was stored inside went back where it belonged," he answered smugly.

"How do you know that?" I asked, confused.

He pulled me to my feet, wrapped his arms around me and leaned his forehead against mine before he answered. "You kept blacking out after you killed Akore and Hillaes kept everyone apprised on what was going to happen."

"That's how you cut off his head without me being aware of it," I said.

He nodded, "and that's why it's just the two of us. The rest of the team, except for Wu and Hillaes, are disposing of the soldiers' bodies."

"We did it, we stopped Akore," I said as I lay my head on

his chest. "Are you angry I didn't tell you what I was going to do before I did it?"

"I was, but when I saw how you suffered, I couldn't stay mad. I must admit, I didn't tell you about regaining your life-force so you'd understand what I felt when I heard you screaming in agony," Jason said with tears in his eyes.

"Please forgive me," I said and stood on my tiptoes to kiss his chin. "Let's make a deal, I won't hold anything back if I'm planning on sacrificing myself for the good of all and you don't let me think I'm going to grow old before my time."

"I can live with that," Jason said and gave me a real kiss.

September 15
Cape Town Clifton Hotel
Cape Town, South Africa

"Well done," Josef said from the screen. We were gathered around the dining table in our suite having finished a wonderful dinner, sipping coffee and leisurely enjoying the desserts on our plates.

We left Akore's compound while it was still dark and before the authorities stormed the property. We decided to leave the women locked in their cells so the police would have a justifiable reason to enter the compound. Robert and Steve flew the soldiers' bodies far enough out to sea so Brian could deal with them, but we left the bodies of Akore's victims where they were in the water as further evidence of his evil. Unfortunately, no one would know that he'd already faced justice, but since we knew the truth, we were satisfied with that.

"I've been in contact with Colonel Dlamini and the women found at the compound will be reunified with their families. The colonel told me that each woman was given a financial settlement from an anonymous benefactor and have already been contacted by the best mental health professionals who offered to treat them free of charge," Enzokuhle explained.

"Imagine that," I said around a mouthful of Tiramisu.

Brian snorted and looked at me until I shrugged.

"When Jason and I were making our way up the smuggler's tunnel we stumbled upon a hidden room full of gold and jewels. Akore doesn't need the money any longer so I figured it would be wise to put the funds to good use. Enzokuhle knew a guy who could easily convert the items we discovered into cash."

"That was fast work," Carlos commented.

"We were motivated," I answered.

"Very commendable," Josef agreed, continuing with his part of the debriefing. "It will take us some time to follow the money trails before we can shut down everything Akore was involved in but, now that we don't have to worry about finding him, we can focus on that."

"What will be done with any assets found?" Wu asked.

"There are several organizations that help victims of

human trafficking. They will be receiving some rather large anonymous donations," Josef said with a smile on his face. "We will do everything we can to wipe Akore's influence from Earth and use the empire he built to heal rather than destroy.

"On a final note, King Alister and Queen Aileene will be stopping by my office in Phoenix tomorrow on their way back to Theria from their honeymoon. I will update them on the details of the mission, so I'll need your written reports in the next twelve hours. Enjoy your celebration, but not too much," Josef chuckled darkly as he signed off.

"That makes me glad I spent the majority of the operation floating in the harbor," Brian said smugly.

"Good for you. That means you're rested and ready to report what you did with the boat, and every person on board, as well as a detailed statement on how you handled each body Steve and Robert dropped off with you," I smiled sweetly then laughed at Brian's expression.

"You're kidding, right?" he asked hopefully.

"Nope," I said as I took another bite of my dessert. "Looks like you shouldn't have made that comment about my hair after all."

"I knew that was going to come back to bite me," Brian grumbled while the rest of us laughed.

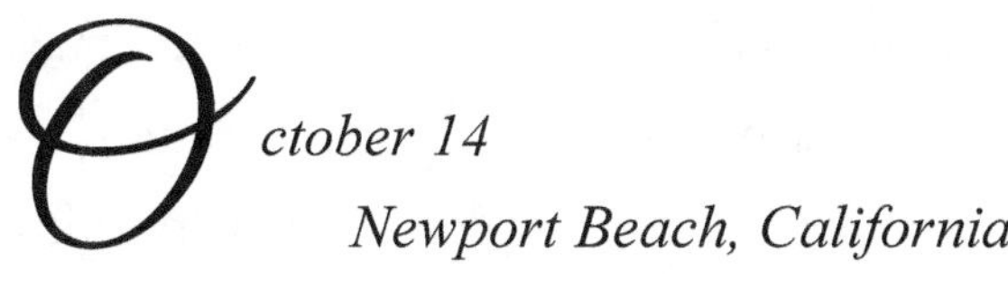

*ctober 14*

*Newport Beach, California*

As I ran up the stairs from my private beach, I wrung the water out of my hair. I needed to hurry because it took Jason and me longer than I anticipated to place Nick's memorial reef. Even though I'd been busy with wedding preparations, I didn't forget the promise I made to my friend that we would swim together one day.

One of the things Bobbi told me when we returned from South Africa was the Eternal Reef Company was going to deliver Nick's memorial reef two days before my wedding. When I started to stress out on how I was going to get the reef moved to the spot I'd chosen, halfway between Newport and Catalina Island, Jason assured me he would be happy to help me fulfill my promise.

Two hours before dawn, Jason and I carried the completed concrete reef down the stairs to the private beach below my house. Actually, Jason carried it because he was afraid I would fall and hurt myself; good call. After Nick's body was cremated, his ashes were mixed with the cement used to make the mold of the underwater memorial. This would provide a special place for aquatic life to create a new coral reef. Jason helped me place the marker, then kissed the side of my head and swam away so I could spend some time with my memories of my friend. Every time I swam by the place we set the memorial, I would think of Nick and remember the conversations we had together. After promising that I would come back to visit often I hurried back home so I could tend to the last-minute wedding preparations.

I thought of what I'd already accomplished this morning while I ran up the stairs. Suddenly, the top of my foot caught the bottom of a step and I began to stumble forward. I compensated by throwing my arms out to the side but smacked my left hand against the railing and my fingers went numb. I wasn't going to fall on the stairs, again, so I climbed faster which meant I was falling upwards at an accelerated rate.

It took what little coordination I had to keep from falling on the steps, but I knew it was a lost cause as I moved even faster. However, the lack of another step when I reached the top of the stairs was my undoing. My momentum kept me moving forward but my feet got tangled and I sprawled face first in the grass. I lay there for a moment, trying to catch my breath, and laughed at how ridiculous I must have looked; I'd have to watch the security footage later to see if it was as bad as I imagined.

"Are you okay?" Alister asked and I waved my hand at him from my face-down position on the lawn.

"It's always entertaining to watch you attempting to walk," Shelley teased as he picked me up and stood me on my feet. "Please tell me you're wearing heels while walking down the aisle tomorrow." Shelley grinned and drew me in for a bear-sized hug.

"Perhaps you should consider a wheel-chair?" Alister snickered and I repeated the enthusiastic hug with him.

"I thought you weren't coming until tomorrow morning," I said as I disentangled myself from the High King, "not that I'm not happy to see you, Your Majesty," I stammered and finished with a sketchy bow.

"Oh brother," Shelley muttered, "if you keep bowing and scraping to doofus here, he'll get a big head. Bigger than it already is, I mean."

"May I remind you that you are Doofus and I'm Stretch?" Alister asked with an offended air.

"Don't pay them any attention," Aileene said as she joined us with her arms wide. I stepped into her embrace and thanked her for coming.

"My turn," Bernie called, and I gave the unicorn shifter a hug. Aileene moved next to Alister and slipped her hand in his while Bernie did the same with Shelley.

"Thank you for coming," I said, happy to see them. I'd known Alister, Bernie and Shelley since they were born, and I was honored they came to my wedding. Of course, Shelley had promised that Alister would officiate, but it still touched me that the King and Queen would make the effort.

"Aileene reminded me that as the officiant of your wedding I needed to be present for the rehearsal. Besides, I received a request from one of my loyal subjects to bring her a day early."

"So we could go shopping," Mom said with a smile as she stepped into view.

"Mom," I exclaimed and burst into tears.

"Shhh, baby-girl," she whispered as she gathered me in her arms. "I told you I would be here for the wedding but really wanted to get here early so we could spend time together. You've described this place so well to me over the past month I realized I wanted to be part of that world," Mom said with a glint in her eye.

"Did—you—just quote part of a song from *The Little Mermaid*?" I asked with a laugh.

Mom nodded and grinned, "Muir and I have been watching many of the movies you and King Alister have recommended. I must admit I'm rather partial to the ones about mermaids. It's amazing how many things they get wrong about our kind."

"I also wanted to spend time catching you up on what's been happening in the aftermath of your mission to destroy Akore," Alister commented.

"Thank you. Since Josef sidelined me, I haven't gotten any reports," I grumped.

"Um, that was actually my doing," Alister said looking sheepish. "I wanted you to be able to focus on your wedding without having to worry about your duties as a member of Tionchar."

Even though I had been frustrated about being kept in the dark, I had to admit to myself that it was nice to be able to focus on wedding plans since returning from South Africa. King Alister looked at me and smiled pensively and I realized he thought I was angry that he made that decision for me.

"Your Majesty, you are the High King, and it is my responsibility to obey," I said with a smile as I stepped into another hug. "Besides, I know you only did it because you thought it was best for me and I trust you."

"I may be High King but I'm still learning how to rule effectively. The last mission cost you so much, I didn't want you to miss out on the joys leading up to your special day," he said as he squeezed me and let me go.

"I've asked Brian and Jason to join us," Aileene added as she started walking to the large table on the deck next to the house.

"And I've taken the liberty of asking Chef Louis to prepare breakfast for us," Mom said with a smile.

"Chef Louis?" I asked in wonder.

"You didn't think he was going to miss your wedding, did you? He told me you talked to him about your wedding menu when you were six-years old, and he insisted on cooking for you when he heard you were getting married tomorrow," Mom said as she put her arm around me and led me to the deck.

"But I already hired a caterer," I said, dismayed.

"Well, about that," Jason said as he kissed me on the cheek and held out my chair for me. "When your mom told me she wanted to surprise you with Chef Louis, I explained things to the caterer and she was more than happy to cancel the contract."

"It didn't hurt that you paid her the full amount you agreed to plus a fifty percent inconvenience fee," Brian laughed and punched Jason in the arm.

"She certainly was more understanding after that," Jason agreed with a smile.

"I can't believe you were able to keep this a secret," I smiled at my soon to be husband and squeezed his hand when he sat next to me.

"I've got a few tricks up my sleeve," he smiled, and I was once again overwhelmed that I was going to be able to spend the rest of my life with this man.

Breakfast was fabulous and the company was even better. Alister filled me in on the progress with the women and children we rescued, and I found out that both Gita and Diya were going to take me up on my offer to live with us in January when they completed their treatment program. I was relieved to hear the others were making progress, but I had a special spot in my heart for the sisters, especially Gita who took on the slavers to protect her younger sibling.

In the month since we executed Akore, Tionchar operatives around the world had worked with local law enforcement to dismantle many of his human trafficking operations and were rescuing more captives each week. Computer experts working for Rex Industries located each of

Akore's bank accounts, siphoned those funds and donated the money to organizations dealing with modern-day slavery.

I was happy to hear this but didn't think Jason and Brian were as excited as I was. It turned out that I was the only one kept in the dark and they had been receiving weekly updates from Josef and King Alister. When Jason apologized and tried to explain why they decided not to tell me, I patted him on the chest and told him it was fine, and King Alister had already explained.

"Uh oh," Shelley grimaced as he looked at Jason, "you're in for it now Dude. She just told you it was 'fine.' I'd hate to be in your shoes."

"We'll talk about this later," I smiled sweetly at my confused looking man. "You boys have fun today doing whatever manly things you've got planned. The girls and I are going to have some fun of our own," I said as I rose.

*I'm not really upset,* I sent to Jason. Alister *is the High King and if he gave you an order you must follow it. He really did explain things to me earlier and I am fine with his decision. I just wanted to tweak Brian a bit and this was the best way to do it. He's going to be wondering all day if I'm angry.* I bent down and gave Jason a kiss. "See you later for the rehearsal."

We walked out of the house and started to get into the limousine waiting in the driveway. I looked around and saw Mom, Aileene, Bernie, Hillaes and Yoli but realized that there was someone missing from our group.

"Give me a minute," I said and hurried back inside to the office on the second floor.

"Hi Cyndi, did you forget something?" Bobbi asked with a smile as she looked up from her computer.

"Yep—you," I said as I made my way to where she was sitting. "Please save what you're working on and shut everything down," I finished with a smile.

"I thought today was just for friends and family," she said.

"It is," I said as I bent down and wrapped my arm around her shoulder and helped her to stand. "You get to pick which group you'd like to be in."

"What do you mean?" She asked, looking confused.

"Whether you want to be part of the friends or family," I laughed and led her out the door.

"Thank you," she said quietly, "I'll think about it."

"Works for me," I grinned. "I wonder if it's too early to head to In-N-Out?" I asked as we walked out of the house and I took my first steps into my new future.

# EPILOGUE

October 15

*Newport Beach, California*

"Come in," I called out after there was a knock at the door. I was standing in front of the full-length mirror smoothing out imaginary wrinkles on my wedding dress. The satin and lace mermaid cut dress was studded with tiny pieces of sea glass. I was wearing my princess crown, at my mom's insistence, and my curly blonde hair was down, just the way Jason liked it.

Brian stepped into the room and I giggled when I took in the jumpsuit he wore; it was a replica of Elvis' white eagle jumpsuit; at least I thought it was a replica.

"What?" Brian asked as he looked down at his outfit, "you said I didn't need to wear a tux."

"I wouldn't have expected anything less," I turned to him with my arms open.

Brian hugged me, careful not to wrinkle my dress then held me at arm's length. "I'm honored that you asked me to walk you down the aisle. If your dad were here, I know he would be so proud of you." He took a shuddering breath and I watched him to see if he would keep it together.

"Don't you cry, or I'll start," I threatened the man who was such an important part of my life.

"I'm okay," he said after a few moments. "I'm also happy to see you and your mom getting along," he said as he lightly touched the crown on my head.

"I didn't want to fight her on this," I grimaced. "It means so much to her that I wear the symbol of our kingdom, I don't really mind."

"I have something your dad wanted you to have," Brian said as he reached into a pocket and pulled out a red scarf.

"He wanted me to have that?" I asked.

"No," Brian laughed, "this was just in the way. He wanted you to have this."

Brian held up a gold necklace with a single pearl. "The day you were born, he started talking about how hard it was going to be for him to give you away at your wedding. I teased him about it because I told him he had a few years to go before he had to worry about it. You know your dad, he was always looking ahead while also living in the moment. About a week before he was killed in the explosion, he showed me this pearl and told me he wanted to create a necklace to give you on your wedding day.

"I told him I would have the pearl added to the necklace but forgot about it after he was gone. We both had different ways of dealing with our grief. Mine was to join Tionchar and come to Earth, yours was to move to the Royal Palace in the Kingdom of Theria. It wasn't until our last visit to Cetacea that I remembered my promise."

Brian carefully unclasped the chain and I held up my hair so he could place it around my neck.

"Thank you, Brian," I said, emotion thick in my voice.

Brian leaned forward and kissed me on the forehead.

"You're welcome but I have one more thing to give you," he said and pulled a thumb drive from the opposite pocket.

"What's this?" I asked in confusion.

"This my friend, is all the information my private investigator friend, Jim Moon, found on Mr. Terry Jergens."

I was puzzled for a moment but then remembered Terry was the creep who had been bothering my employees. When we came back from South Africa, not only was I kept in the dark about what was happening with the Akore investigation, Bobbi wouldn't let me do anything with my business. She told me I had to focus all my energy on the wedding.

"It seems that Mr. Jergens has been a bad boy. He's in the habit of defrauding his clients, especially the elderly, and hasn't been caught, until now," Brian said with a grin.

"What did you do?" I asked.

"Nothing much, except clean out each of his bank accounts and repay the people he'd cheated, with interest of course. I may have sent the information to some friends who passed it along to the SEC, FBI, local law enforcement and the local news stations." Brian shrugged. "I think he'll be too busy to bother anyone else for awhile."

I hugged my friend again, grateful that he took the time to deal with someone who had flouted the law and was a nuisance to my employees.

"Thank you," I said, my eyes glistening with unshed tears.

"We'd better get going," Brian deadpanned, "we don't want Jason to think you got cold feet."

"There isn't a chance of that," I smiled, "we're going to be together for a very long time, and I wouldn't have it any other way."


The End

# AFTERWORD

Thank you for reading Scales of Justice! I appreciate you reading the first book in this new series. I hope you enjoyed reading it as much as I did writing it. Please take the time to leave a review on Amazon or Goodreads even if it's just a few words. Reviews are incredibly vital to independent authors, the more reviews a book receives the greater the chance it will be seen by other readers looking for a book just like this one.

Scales of Justice is another example of a secondary character pushing her way to the forefront and if we've learned anything about Cyndi, she doesn't let anything stand in her way—she's also incredibly clumsy. I'm glad I had an actual person to base her on. One of the fun things for an author is to build characters on people we meet in real life and I've used names of some of my fans in my books along with

the mythical characters they'd be if they had the chance—
Cyndi is one of those.

When I was writing Reunite, the third book in the Dragonborn series, I asked my sister Cyndi what type of mythological character she wanted to be if I put her in my book and she told me she wanted to be a mermaid. We were chatting about life and she was probably telling me about a trip she was planning to In-N-Out or one of her tripping episodes which ended up with her sprawled on the ground; miraculously unhurt. Yes, it is possible for someone to be as clumsy as Cyndi the mermaid, if anything I toned down some of the things I've witnessed with my sister.

I wanted Scales of Justice to fit into the Dragonborn universe but also appeal to an older audience. Some of the themes in this book are disturbing, but I believe it is important for us to know that human trafficking and modern day slavery is a very real problem. It's estimated there are between 600,000 - 800,00 world-wide victims of this vile practice each year. In the US alone there are an estimated 14,500 - 17,500 of those victims brought into the country each year. If you want more information about this vile practice you can find resources at www.hsdl.org

So what's next? So far, I've written six books in the Dragonborn universe and have plans for more. The next book is Winter and it will continue Alister and Aileene's story and will connect events hinted at in both Fierce Protector and Scales of Justice. After Winter, I will write Fierce Opposition, the next book in the Therian Shapeshifter Academy. It continues Mkali's story and takes place directly after the events of Fierce Protector. When I finish Fierce Opposition, I'll probably write the second book in the Tionchar Tales series, but I don't have a title for that yet.

I love to hear from my fans and one of the best ways to get in touch with me is through my website www.bretthumphreyauthor.com You can check out all my books, pick up some Dragonborn merchandise from my online store, join my mailing list or look at the glossary to familiarize yourself with other characters from the Dragonborn universe.

I hope Cyndi and her friends inspire you to make a positive impact on someone else today.

Brett Humphrey—June 2021

Protect the Weak!

# **Shifter Glossary and Pronunciation Guide**

Earth Months / Therian Months

    January / Faollich (Fowl-itch)

    February / Garwan (Gar-one)s

    March / Mart (Mart)

    April / An'Ceann (Awn-Sheen)

    May / Giplane (Gee-plane)

    June / Ceitain (She-tain)

    July / Lunsdail (Luns-dale)

    August / Athas (At-tas)

    September / Síocháin (Show-chain)

    October / Damlar (Dam-lar)

    November / Suttain (Sut-tane)

    December / Dóchas (Doe-Chaz)

Kingdoms of Theria

    Kingdom of Carnivoria: (Car-ni-vor-eeya)

    Kingdom of Cetacea: (Set-a-see-a)

    Kingdom of Eutheria: (Eww-there-eeya)

    Kingdom of Marsupia: (Mar-soup-eeya)

    Kingdom of Metatheria: (Met-a-there-eeya)

    Kingdom of Sirenea: (Siren-eeya)

    Kingdom of Theria: (There-eeya)

Afonso de Albuquerque: (Off-on-sew Dee All-buh-kirk-ee) Name used by Akore, captain of the Flor do Mar.

Akore: (Ache-ore) Evil sorcerer from the planet Claw, escaped to Earth when the ruling counsel on Claw attempted to try him for his crimes. He has stolen the life force from thousands of humans to keep himself alive for over six hundred years.

Amhi: (Am-hée) Palace guard for Lady Zhaleh.

An'Ceann: (Awn-sheen) The First, The One, The Creator.

Cecaelia: (See-say-ee-lya) Octopus person with the head, arms and torso of a human and, from the lower torso down the tentacles of an octopus.

Claw: Another planet/dimension similar to Earth, but with more magic available. It is sometimes referred to as Middle Earth.

Colonel Dlamini: (Da-law-meanie) Commandant of the South African Police Services.

Destruo: (Des-true-oh) Spell used to destroy an object or person.

Diya: (Dee-ya) One of the sisters rescued by Cyndi.

Enzokuhle: (En-zo-kook-clay) Impundulu, Tionchar operative in South Africa.

Flor do Mar: (Floor Do Mare) Portuguese sailing vessel carrying billions of dollars worth of gold, silver, jewels and precious treasures; lost at sea. Captain of the Flor do Mar at the time of its sinking was Afonso de Albuquerque.

Ghita: (Gee-ta) One of the sisters rescued by Cyndi.

Integrum: (In-teg-rum) Spell used to complete a magical working.

Impundulu: (Em-pun-do-loo) Black and white bird the size of a human. Able to summon thunder and lightning with its wings and talons.

Ishka Patel: (Ish-ka Paw-tell) Naga, Tionchar operative in India, lead investigator for Indian National Police Force.

Joki: (Joke-ee) Right hand man to Akore.

Kraken: (Crack-in) Enormous squid-like creature able to destroy ships with its tentacles and huge maw of razor sharp teeth. Has the ability to change colors to blend into its environment.

Lady Zhaleh: (Za-le) Ruler of Cetacea.

Lord Joshua Vefiru: (Vef-i-roo) Ruler of Carnivoria.

Lux Splendida: (Lucks Splen-deed-a) Spell used to create a bright light.

Metreoron Imber: (Met-ree-ore-on Im-beer) Spell to create a defense shell which fires off magical missiles back towards attacker when breeched.

Mortem: (More-tem) Death spell.

Naga: (Nah-gah) Shapeshifter with three serpentine forms. The torso of a human with the body of a snake, human form with snakes in the place of hair (similar to a gorgon), a completely serpentine form. Each form is highly venomous.

Plesiosaur: (Plee-see-uh-sor) Creature resembling the extinct marine reptile found on Earth. It has a long torpedo-shaped body, long tail and four flippers instead of legs. It also has a long serpentine neck.

Pouakai: Great eagle of Maori legend with a thirty-foot wingspan. It is seventeen feet long from beak to tail.

Raksaka Gupta: (Rock-sack-a Goop-ta) Naga, Tionchar operative in India.

Ramesh Acharya: (Ram-esh Atch-are-ya) Alias of Akore.

Revelare: (Re-veal-are-ee) Spell to reveal hidden objects.

Tabefacio: (Tab-ee-face-ee-oh) Spell used to melt objects.

Tetraodon: (Tet-ra-a-done) Merman, childhood friend of Cyndi Zhaleh.